D1808409

THE REIGN OF QUEENS

~A Kingdom of Diamond Antlers Novel~

Zachary James

~Praise For~
THE REIGN OF QUEENS

"From page one of book one, to chapter three of book two, your writing is 'different', don't want to say improved because it makes me feel like that means it was bad before…it wasn't. I find myself reading and forgetting I'm supposed to be editing," **Heather Falotico,** *prized English teacher and passionate editor.*

"Once again, Mr. James brings forth another incredible fantasy novel, riddled with more twists and erotic scenes to keep you locked in! *The Reign Of Queens* is a sequel that blows its predecessor out of the water! Queen Ariadae will stop at nothing to end the cruel reign of Evaflora. With new detailed locations, enthralling characters, and more passionate romances, it will keep the reader never wanting to put the novel down!" **Nicole DiRienzo,** *obsessive reader and novel enthusiast.*

"His brilliance and expertise in the writing field is truly captivating. The way Zachary James looks on life and portrays it into his books makes for a masterpiece that won't leave your mind"-**David McMunn**, *an awakened reader.*

~Praise For~
THE RISE OF TITANIUM

"Excellent example of where one's mind can wander, what the imagination is capable of, and how one man's creative ideas can take readers on a journey beyond their own imaginations. With its whimsical settings, dynamic characters, and twists and turns along the way, this book will keep you entertained and engaged. This is your chance to read the first book written by a future best-selling author," *Selected five star Amazon review.*

Edited by: Heather Falotico
Cover Design by: Eight Little Pages
Ages: 16 and up

First Edition
10 9 8 7 6 5 4 3 2 1

Danielle and James
You two have helped me more than anyone will
understand; this book is dedicated to you.

2 2

Pronunciation Guide

People
Ariadae Vox- *Are-e-ah-day Vox*
Zube Mindelow- *Zoo-be Min-dee-low*
Evaflora- *Eva-flooruh*
Lhys- *Lease*
Molaris- *Moe-lair-iss*
Fayla- *Fay-lah*
Lunan- *Loo-nin*
Archaeminza- *Are-kay-min-zah*

Fae
Fae- *Fay*
Succumbus- *Suck-um-bis*
Mindinae- *Min-dah-nay*
Tempestatis- *Tem-pest-tah-tis*
Telekinae- *Tell-e-kah-nay*

Forsaken
Nymph- *Nim-ph*
Dreag- *Dray-guh*
Troglodyte- *Trog-low-dite*
Wendigo- *When-de-go*
Umbra- *Uhm-bruh*

Places
Alpri- *Al-pree*
Vampyra- *Vamp-ear-ah*
Solaria- *Soul-are-ee-ah*
Marzia- *Mart-zee-yuh*

The Reign of Queens

Part One
WINTER SOLSTICE

CHAPTER ONE

~Ariadae~

I've been at the jaws of death. The darkness it resides in, welcomed me with an evil grin, but I am alive. Every day I am reminded of the blessing I received to still be here on this continent, although I'm not so sure this is a blessing anymore. I keep seeing the ghosts of Gaston and Novid- the sentinels I lost during the travel through Elkwood this past summer. I try not to be scared of their presence and it's sad to say that their spirits are a common sight, but I had seen them in Elkwood. They are always around the castle now and both make a point to frighten the living day lights out of me. It's like all the air leaves my body and I just become a husk.

His wheezing breath echoes from the corner of the room and I can see him watching me from the shadows. Novid has been worse than Gaston. I am not sure why, but he likes to appear more than the Gaston and I still have yet to see Seri. With Gaston and Novid around so often I have been waiting for my seamstress. I still miss her blue skin and golden hair. I feel that even in the underworld she is trying to protect me and be my friend. The only way I get the demons that were once my friends to go away is if I ignore them. *They're not there*, I tell myself and when I open my eyes they're gone. I do the latter and Novid's wheezing has vanished leaving me in the quiet bedroom.

      The door to my personal library creaks open; a seam of light from the lit hearth inside sends a beam of light cracking the dark of my bedroom in two. The shadows recoil in silent hiss from the rippling glow. When I roll over I feel the empty space beside me. Jax is up late again. He has been staying up night after night since my death four months ago. He claims that he is fine, but in all truth I think he is haunted of nightmares from that day. June twelfth is the day I died and November eighth, a week from today, is my birthday. My mortal birthday isn't going to be special, I am immortal. Every birthday from June twelfth on, won't matter. I no longer will age like Jeremiah, or the other mortals around the castle. I remember a time when I feared my demi-fae heritage thinking it would make me different. I'm even more different than before.

      I rise from my bed and wrap the bone-chilling silk blanket around my naked body. I grit my teeth against the cold. The sheet whispers along the floor as I open the library and lean against the doorframe. His onyx hair, now long and wavy, hangs down just past his hunched shoulders. A quill and inkwell sit on the desk beside stacked papers as he writes and fills out papers after papers. He has been rewriting and rejuvenating the laws of Equadoria. After I repealed the magic ban in my kingdom things have been different. The slums have grown happy, in a way, and the upper class citizens seem to fear the 'conjurors' as they call them. I want to abolish the divide between the mortal and immortal, so Jax and I have made it our duty to change Equadoria for the better.

He looks up at me, his ice blue eyes look like pulsing lights from the flickering fire on the opposite side of the room. He doesn't smile.

"Did one of them wake you," He asks quietly, as if when he speaks about my dead friends they will suddenly appear. I can't help, but wonder the same thing. I told him about everything that happened when I died and for the first two weeks after I awoke, I pointed out each time one of them appeared and what they were doing, if Jax was around that is. He suddenly started vanishing for hours at a time and I wouldn't see him until he was in bed later that night. He started to sleep in my chambers because he believes he is 'protecting' me, but I know it's more than that. We are more than just a queen and her guardian. We always have been something different.

"Yes," I respond, my words getting lost to the echo of the library. "Novid decided to wheeze his way out of my dreams and into the corner of the bedroom."

"Is he still there," He questions rising from the leather chair. He walks around the wooden desk and saunters to me, looking past my head into the dark beyond. I look up at him and pull his attention back on me.

"No," I whisper.

"Good. I would hate for him to be a bother to my queen."

"Why do you call me that," I ask sounding a bit negative. He places his hands on my hips and pulls me into his body. Any previous negativity leeches from my every pore and vanishes in the brisk night.

"Because you are."

"I am not," I correct him. "I did not knight you because you told me that your allegiance lies with your father." His father is the Winter Kingdom High Fae. Jax was a prince until he decided to lift all his duties and become a sentinel and military leader.

He nods in agreement and lifts me into his arms carrying me from the library back into the bedroom. A giggle passes my lips as he falls back onto the mattress and I straddle his hips the plush bed fluffing up around us.

"Be my queen," his voice shudders seductively and I can't help, but feel the urge to listen. "For tonight and every night you want me." I place my lips to his and start to kiss him.

"Just for tonight," I growl against his mouth. Hot heavy-panted breaths pour from him. Laughing I lay more into his hard body. His strong muscles become less tense and loosen to my touch. It feels like my own form of power. It's like I am his weakness, but in many ways, he is mine. Ever since our time together in Elkwood I've been undeniably attracted to him.

He begins to move beneath me when he says, "Let me just-." I press him into the mattress and look down at him, dominate him. His slightly longer canines gleam against the moonlight streaming through the window. Strands of my hair hang around my shoulders and I drop the blanket away, revealing my whole body to his ravenous eyes. My hair hangs past my breasts and although it wasn't as long as it was before my mother cut it off, my immortal body makes my hair grow much faster.

I always wanted him. I wanted his hands touching my breasts and his mouth against my neck the moment I learned who he truly was. It's as if a physical attraction to Jax was immediate after realizing the true skin beneath his fur. I may have liked Jeremiah, my child-hood best friend, before, but now that I have felt Jax inside me and his hands along my skin I know what I want- Jax.

"Let me," passes from my tongue into the night. He always pleasures me, but I still have yet to return the favor. He lays back and I remove his trousers revealing the thick length of him.

I grip him firmly and he moans loudly, the sound echoes off the walls. He throbs and pulsates in my grip and his whole-body squirms and writhes beneath my touch. Laughing I crawl up to him and grind my hips into his firm form. We become a painting, a dance, a work of art. Our bodies move as one and we transform into growling beasts wrestling through the sheets. Our primal and Fae instincts make us animalistic and hungry for the taste of each other. I smell the dirt beneath his nails that dig into the sheets and I can hear the throbbing beat of his blood pumping through his veins. I see the particles of dust flurrying through the air above us in the dark as I claw aimlessly at his back. Being immortal has transformed and turned my focus into a sharp blade, my senses are too strong to be healthy, and my powers are honed as if crafted by a fine-toothed comb. They can be a constant pressure, but Jax is my distraction from it all. He releases the pressure within me that is clawing to come out.

I scream as he dives into the apex of my thighs. Back and forth we rock making the springs in the mattress squeal in anguish. I press down on him as he pushes up into me making my pelvis flood with bliss. I moan provoking his growl in answer. A warm flutter builds in my stomach as I watch his back, the rippling muscles tense and thrusting. I claw through the pain and moan at the blooming flower of feeling within me. There's no stopping the explosion of butterflies beneath my skin and a blush that turns me pink. I want him, and I want to love him. I want to say that I love him but for some reason I can't. I have so many different feelings for Jax, but I'm not quite sure I truly love him with all of my heart. I am not going to lie; I do love the sex, although he is the only man I have ever been with intimately. I don't want him to be the *only* man I am intimate with either. I've never heard of someone's first relationship lasting forever.

We later reach our bending point and I am positive our screams shook the castle. The euphoria making white fire burn my brain and my body tremble. After we finish he falls asleep, like always. I was completely awake and he just rolled over. I stare unhappily at his heavily scarred back. *Asshole.* I wanted to talk to him and ask what he was working on, but why wake him to ask when I can look for myself.

Rolling out of bed I walk to a velvet chair in the corner of the chamber and pull the heavy dress-like robe from atop it, wrapping the silk around me. The fabric reminds me of Jax's fingers along my body. My wardrobe dramatically changed after I became queen and it's almost every day I have to go to the tailor's and get measured for a new dress he creates. His name is Rasgard. He and his handsome husband, Theon, create the most amazing gowns. Tomorrow I have a dress being made for the Winter Solstice ball.

I head into the library and close the door carefully, not to disturb sleeping Jax across the room. The library is dark and heavy with just the fire in the center of the room, now small and will soon be embers. I ignore the temptation of poking around the logs to flare up the flames and instead head straight to the desk where Jax had been sitting. His dark quill sits inside a rippling inkwell. I dig around the stacks of papers not sure what to look for and I notice something different amongst the stacks. A written letter, sprawled in handwriting I recognize. It isn't Jeremiah's, Jax's, or Zube's. *It's my mothers.*

Dear Ariadae Vox, Queen of Titanium Antlers,

Are you enjoying your new body and mind? I can't wait to see you and your horrible Kingdom fall to the ground. I know what you're thinking. Is my mother really writing to me? The answer is yes.

Ignoring the latter I am writing to you because I am gifting you with warnings to end your rebellion against me. No more of my people will die by your hand and I hope you know that the Forsaken have been begging to get their hands on your mortals. Now, you can write back to me and this can all stop. The murder and destruction of Equadoria will end if you just write a simple letter. A letter stating that I will own everything inside Equadoria. If not, well, I hope you have an army prepared because I will be sure to ruin everything you love, including that little mortal boy of yours, Jeremiah.

If you refuse to answer my request by Winter's Eve I will make sure to collapse Equadoria and every Mortal kingdom on Abella. I hope you understand.

> *Love,*
> *Evaflora Vox, Queen of Diamond Antlers*

I hope Jax only received this letter today because if he has opened and read this earlier without telling me then I will be more than angry. I will be livid. Who am I kidding? I *am* livid. I pull a blank piece of paper from one of the many desk drawers and begin to write my own letter to Jax.

Dear Jax Lycus Archaeminza,

I summon you to the throne room and make sure to bring the letter that my mother wrote to me. I hope you have a good reason for your lack of telling me of this devious threat.

> *Sincerely,*
> *Queen Ariadae Vox*

I drop the note onto the center of the desk and leave my mother's threat beside it. I head back into my chambers ignoring my flaring rage at the naked male sprawled on the mattress and saunter into the closet where I begin to dress myself. I need to distract my mind for a while so I decide to spend that time deciding on what to wear. I want to wear something simple, but when you're the queen nothing is simple. I also have a court meeting after I report to the throne room where I will decide the fate of four individuals who have done treasonous crimes. I barely remember their reports, but I recall reading that they had murdered six young children in search for some 'prophet'. In no way does searching for something for religious purpose make murdering citizens alright or disregarded. I don't even know how to punish them. From the sound of what they done I have the urge to rip out the bones from beneath their skin, but I know that's not what the court will vote on. Trying to grasp these courtly rules has been a lot harder now that I am queen.

I tighten the bone crushing power of a corset and slide on a heavy blue velvet gown. The neck line plunges downward which lets the world see the curve of my breasts. It may not be appropriate for court but it's truly a beautiful piece of clothing. I don't want to think or worry about today. I don't want to think any day and I just want everything to stop. I do not want to be an immortal and I don't want all my friends to die before I even look to be seventeen. This is what my life has become though. Never dying or aging because of immortality. Dressing nicely, sitting on a throne and watching generation after generation of my people come and go. It's not pleasant, but neither is death, so I guess this was the better option. Or did I make a mistake trying to come back when I died? Should I have not fought the legion of decaying Fae in the underworld?

I remember after I had come back from the dead, Jax said he used the leaves from the Tree of Light to wake me from the cold grasp, but a part of me thinks it wouldn't have worked unless I fought for life. What would it have been like if I hadn't fought back? Would I walk into the darkness and join my corpse friends or would I have wandered into the light? It doesn't matter what would've happened because now I'm here, and it's behind me.

A maid enters the closet pulling me from my thoughts. Her tightly bound black hair gleams as she bows before me. I hate that bowing is part of court etiquette. Although respectful it reminds me of the title I don't want, don't deserve. There was a time when I wanted to be queen, but that was before I was reborn as immortal, before my father was murdered by a curse that spoiled his mind.

"May I assist you in dressing, Milady," she asks. I nod in answer, but what hurts more is I can't even remember her name. She is close to my age, my *mortal* age. Maybe she is one of the older maiden's daughters.

She gets busy pulling out a pair of black leather boots and small accessories. Laying the jewelry down, I sit on a chair and allow her to put my boots on. Even when I was a princess maids would help me dress. Although I don't need them, it's nice to not be alone or surrounded solely by men for once.

"I don't mean to bother you, but I seem to have forgotten your name. Is it alright if you tell me? I will understand if you're upset with me," I whisper to her. She only giggles and pushes away the worry in my voice.

"Desirae."

"I am terribly sorry," I voice concerning as I grip her hands for her only to wave it off.

"Now let's get you all jeweled up," She laughs pulling me to me feet. I smile in return and let her do what she thinks will look best. She places a silver necklace onto my collarbone, the heavy jewels the color of night. The twinkling looks like the stars from the sky that looms above Equadoria. She takes a belt made of soft purple silk and wraps it around my waist and hips. Adding some earrings to my pointed ears and a bracelet accented with a large amount of rings, I am finally done.

I look like a regal force to be reckoned with, a menacing queen, and an immortal beauty.

"Perfect," Desirae squeals clapping her hands together in excitement. I push away the dark thoughts.

"Thank you," I say as I look into the mirror. The whole outfit looks absolutely stunning even with the sweeping neckline. "I look amazing."

"Of course," She bows again deeply. She urges me to the door and I head over to the vanity. Ignoring Jax's snores I sit and light the candles with a small flint and steel mechanism. "Should we do your hair in the wardrobe?" She is worried of waking Jax. I seem to forget that most people are frightened of him and most of the court has only seen him in his tiger form. Equadoria only knows that I have a white tiger that lies at the foot of my throne. Nobody knows who he truly is.

"No," I grunt glaring at his disheveled form through the mirror. "Don't mind him, he is insignificant." It's true, he doesn't matter right now, but later he will get an earful about the letter he conveniently forgot to share with me.

"Oh, Milady I don't want to disrespect you, but why would you see such a *powerful* male as insignificant?" She questions and my anger flares at her wording. Does she not notice that he is just as powerful as the Fae sitting in front of her? And who gave her the right to speak of *my* male's power? The glare I was making shifts from Jax to Desirae and I hear the beat of her heart, the pumping blood in her veins. The heavy odor of fear that pricks at my nose; it stings the air. "I am so sorry your majesty."

"I think it's best if you just do what you are ordered to and not speak," I growl trying not to lose control. It's been five months since I returned from Elkwood and became a Fae, but I still have trouble keeping a rein around my powers, strength, and especially my emotions. It's bad enough being queen of an entire kingdom, but also sixteen while having extreme menstrual cramps. Because of the pain, I haven't been able to train in fighting techniques with Jeremiah, but he is busy dealing with enough as one of my military leaders and also a lord in my council. He is a high member of my court.

So instead I train with Jax about once a week on my abilities, but I'm starting to think it's not enough. I barely keep a hold on having a flare, like I did in the Ravine of Wisps. I am too strong and I know it because even from all the way over here I can see the scratches raking down Jax's back from my nails. They are healing, but since Evaflora chopped down the Tree of Light the Fae have been affected. No longer do the immortal bounce back so quickly from cuts. I think *all* of the races of magical beings have been affected, but I'm not sure in which way. I know that the Fae have somehow become more powerful while also losing the ability to heal quickly. We certainly don't age like the mortals, but part of me wishes we did.

Desirae finishes braiding and curling my hair along with adding charcoal around my eyes and caking on a thick beige powder to my skin. She darkens my lips and applies a black powder to my eyelids. I look like a fierce queen. A *Fae* queen.

CHAPTER TWO

~*Ariadae*~

My stomach rumbles from the lack of breakfast. I was planning on eating, but the sentinels pulled the prisoners out early for trial. I'll just have to eat afterward.

I sit on my sleek silver throne. My family's bow and a quiver lies behind me and a dagger hugs the inside of my boot. Jax lays at my feet in his snow tiger form and almost every sentinel I have stands poised and ready for action around the room. I feel regal, and beautiful, but menacing at the same time. I don't need all of this protection, but I am told it is part of the precautions after my death. And ever since Elkwood, I keep my heirloom bow in the library in my bed chambers and a dagger nearby, although it's not the dragon bone dagger. That was lost in the colosseum in which the Tree of Light was destroyed, devastated by my mother and her henchman.

A white haired man, a hunched over woman, and two teenage boys sit on their knees beneath my dais. They must be a family of sorts.

"Through the law of Equadoria the tried individuals have a right to speak on behalf of their crimes," Zube's resonating voice breaks the silence in the room. I look around and we seem to have an audience. Aside from the sentinels; lords and their ladies have encircled the four criminals, but someone is missing. Scanning the crowd for Jeremiah, I notice that he's not present.

One of the two teenage boys stands and looks to me. His brown eyes have a heavy gloom and his mud stained face matches his radiating odor of filth. I ignore the urge to recoil from the scent and give him my undivided attention. Everyone, no matter what their criminal prosecution may be, deserves to be heard.

"Speak your name and then give your statement," I say. The boy frowns and looks disgusted at Zube and me, along with the other Fae in the throne room.

"Eric," he groans, rolling his eyes. I focus on the beat of his heart. People say that the Fae can tell if someone is lying and the truth is we can. If a human or Fae is lying, our powerful hearing will pick up on a change in heartbeat. It could be a flicker or a significant change in pace, but we will know. "I murdered six children with my brother and parents." The crowd gasps in shock and his family smiles. Their yellowed teeth are crooked and eerie.

Well I didn't expect this trial to be a confession, but that only makes my job easier. His words are gut churning. "What would make you want to commit such treasonous crimes?" I question.

"They were conjurors," He claims as if that makes his actions okay. "My family has killed more than just those six children. We have murdered close to seventeen families of conjurors." What is wrong with him? Why would they do such a thing? At this rate these sick people may not live through this trial if I have control of this kingdom. You don't make such an idiotic claim to a queen who is Fae.

"Well. Eric was it?" he nods, "Are you aware that your queen is a 'conjuror' as you call us."

"I am very aware, Milady," he voices, bowing deeply. "You and every other Fae in Equadoria and across Abella are swine. And I am also enlightened to know that my queen is a bedswerver." I rise onto my feet and glare into the boys eyes. Who raised this boy with such a vile tongue? Or was his mind poisoned by the toxicity of the slum's crime lords. His low beating heart rises to a heavy thrum. Oh how I am going to rip him to shreds for what he has done. He deserves every ounce of pain he caused to other people. "Your majesty, fucks men who are married and single alike. She is a whore!"

Jax roars at Eric and he recoils several steps and backs into a sentinel's rapier. The lords and ladies scream in fright at Jax's fangs and I can't help but be angry. The hate-fire inside of me grows to a raging flame. My body boils and my heart beats to the song of blood lust. Nobody else in his family has spoken, nor should they. I walk from the dais and approach the boy. My nose wiggles at the sting of fear and wretched scent of grime that soaks into his pores.

"Your accusations will only lead you, and your family, to what you rightfully deserve," I laugh and lick my long pointed canines for effect. "Death."

"NO," Zube shouts from the dais. "The trial has not finished. The Court must decide their true fate."

I look to Zube, clad in a golden tunic and black pants. His slick hair makes him look handsome and he appears nervous as I purr, "I *made* the Court, Zube."

"Milady, I apologize for my outburst," Eric whispers to me and my cackle echoes through the throne room. He knows the wrong he has done, but is now afraid of the consequences. The sound of my laugh makes my body quiver with awful memories from the Summer Kingdom.

"It is far too late to apologize. Now you claimed that you murdered those children because they were *Fae*, although in your written report that, you claimed to murder them in search for a prophet." Eric nods nervously and his body starts to shake as my Telekinae ability strokes the soft ridges of his spine allowing his brown eyes to focus on me. "Tell me if you find him."

I throw my palm towards the boy and press down with my fingers. His whole body wrenches backward and he screams as his brittle spine breaks, the cracking and shattering bone echoing through the room. He continues to cry since my blow didn't kill him. People shout and scream and I leave my body. I see what I'm doing and I can't stop, can't control it, no longer do I know who I am.

"YOU CU-," Eric's mother screams running to his body, but before she can finish I wave a hand in her direction tossing her across the room like a dirty rag. Dropping my grip on Eric's body allowing him to slump onto the ground, I look to his mother who is a crumpled mess in the corner and whisper with every drop of venom I can muster. "I will not allow *that* word to be spoken in my home." Her sobs echo through the room and my burning anger begins to cool. My mind returns and I begin to regain control as regret floods into my every pore. Jax looks from me to the woman as I walk back to the dais. "This Trial is over."

A tear slides down my cheek as I realize how much like my mother I had just become. I am not like her in anyway, but sometimes I need to be a tyrant. I am a new queen and I don't want my people to think they can walk all over me, which is exactly what Eric was trying to do. I hope the audience understands that.

With a wave of my hand, Eric is carried away unable to move and crying with the rest of his family. They are headed to the gallows.

Zube stoops low into my ear and whispers with pure anger, "You shouldn't have done that."

"You shouldn't have talked back to me in front of all those people, Zube," I spit trying to change the subject before the tears fall down my cheeks.

"I apologize, your grace."

"Don't call me that! You are my friend and I command you to speak to me like one unless you have forgotten my name?" He stands up and his face looks disgusted.

"I remember, it's Evaflora," he growls. A cry escapes my lips as a flush burns my cheeks. How dare he refer to me as my mother? There is no longer a stone in my chest like there was when I was a demi-fae, but now I feel something else. Guilt? Sadness? I am not sure, but it's best that I don't focus on it because it hurts. It pains me like the sword in my gut that my father had put there. The blade had cut through me, killed me, and now it just stings.

I walk from the throne room and push past the gaping crowd. I will not allow them to see their queen cry. Not today anyway.

"What were you thinking," Zube shouts, his voice echoes off the paneled walls of my bedchambers. I already feel sick to my stomach about who he called me, *what* he called me. I sit on the edge of my bed, face still wet with tears, and sulk as he scowls at me.

Jax prowls from the corner and a muscle in his jaw feathers breaking the tension in his glare.

"She wasn't," He mutters and I couldn't agree with him more. I wasn't truly thinking correctly. Being a queen is a lot harder than I would have imagined and the letter from my mother wasn't helping. "She was oblivious to the task before her and was clouded by judgement and selfishness."

Woah, when did we all decide it was pick on me day? I know I screwed up and became an evil bitch, but never did I want to start a mutiny. I stop being silent and decide to pull the attention away from me before there is an uprising. I say the first words since Zube and Jax came into my room. "If we want to talk about being selfish than lets discuss you keeping a threatening message from the High Fae of the Summer Kingdom from me," I growl at Jax.

Zube almost doubles over in shock and his green eyes bulge from his skull. "Evaflora threatened you?" He questions. Zube looks around the room as if someone else could hear what he said. I nod and look to Jax whose pointed ears become red. What a cub.

"I opened the letter moments before you walked into the library," He claims, but I don't believe him. I don't hear any flicker in his heartbeat, but he must be lying. Although that letter wasn't the only one sitting in the center of the desk, there were plenty of opened letters tossed about as if he searched through the pile for it. Jax finishes, "I wasn't being selfish."

"You never answered my summons." I look to the end table and notice a crumpled piece of parchment. I assume that's my letter to him from this morning. I may have had the same reaction if I were him.

"You are not my queen," Jax chuffs and binds his hair into a warrior's bun.

"That's not what you said in my bed last night."

Zube's face flushes a dark red and he begins to laugh. His loud cackles erupt through the room as he chokes out, "You guys have been having sex?" I roll my eyes because of course that is all he is taking from this conversation. "I knew it."

"Shut up, Zube," Jax shouts.

"Untighten your trunks, Jax." He looks at me and snarls. I answer in a growl and try to change the subject, "Are we going to tell the Court about the threat?"

"Of course not," Zube follows my subject change without realizing. The last thing the mortals need to know is that the Fae with whom we are at war, is threatening to take my kingdom and destroy my people.

"They deserve a right to know," Jax says glancing at me and Zube as he paces around the room. "If we tell them then maybe they will have an idea about what to do."

"What *can* we do, Jax?" I ask, failing to stop his pacing which makes me uneasy. "It isn't like we can just run back into Elkwood and kill her. She has an army of Forsaken bowing to her throne and what do I have?"

"You have more strength than you know, Ariadae."

Zube interjects, immediately changing the mood of the room and says, "What we do need is numbers. In the court meeting I will ask about the soldiers fighting in Solaria and see how many men we can bring back to fight against your mother and protect Equadoria."

"The entire Equadorian army is down there, Zube. They're all fighting because the threat of Solaria is too big right now, so I am not sure if I want to pull men away from that battle. Anybody we bring back will not be enough." A maid knocks on the door and Jax allows her to enter. It's not Desirae, but it is another familiar face. After bowing she looks to us and I hear the pounding of her heart. It's beating as fast as a butterfly's wings.

"The court is ready for you, your grace," her high pitched voice squeaks and she runs off as quickly as she came. I can't help, but wonder if she was in the throne room during my outburst and if I am the source of her nerves.

I look to Jax and Zube and say, "We will finish this conversation after the meeting."

They nod in agreement and we head down the hall, passing bustling servants in blue uniforms and guards alike. Trailed by Zube and Jax nobody meets my eyes nor theirs. It's like my own people are frightened of me. I don't want to be my mother or some tyrant ruler who abuses their disciples. Now I'm really regretting what I did in the Trial.

We take two other corridors and enter the large meeting chambers. Flanked by guards, the senators and lords of Equadoria sit around a large wooden table. The weight of the crown on my head becomes apparent when they all rise and deeply bow. Nodding my thanks, I head to the end of the table, while Jax and Zube take their places beside me.

"What shall we discuss first?" I question. One of the youngest nobles in my court- Samuel Francis I- perks to full attention and rises. Meeting the eyes of everyone around the table, I gesture to him so he may start his claim.

"I have received a dire revelation from one of our envoys in Solaria," He says as he pulls a piece of parchment from his satchel and begins to read off the paper. What urgent news could come from our spies in Solaria? Other than the fact that my army being stationed there, nothing from that kingdom should be spoken of or sent to Equadoria in case of trackers. I glance to Jax and Zube who look just as pale as me, before giving Sam my attention. "The Legion of Equadorian soldiers has been decimated by the Solarian warriors. Only a duodenary amount of the sentinels survived the annihilation," He stops reading from the letter. I had sent a legion of over six hundred foot soldiers to Solaria and only twelve survived. "I'm sorry, your majesty."

CHAPTER THREE

~Fayla~

His breath rises in small tendrils into the thick air of the bedroom. Climbing through the kitchen window and grabbing the knife was all too easy, but sliding the blade against Wayloran wife's throat was even easier. I don't expect Duke Rywell, my dead captor, to mind missing his sister-in-law and brother in the afterlife. After I electrocuted Rywell and stole a dress of the finest silk I walked off into the night and up several blocks to a nice inn. I didn't have any money, so I just stole a sack of coppers from a drunk and paid for my stay with stolen change. I've heard revenge is a powerful drug and all I can say is I am extremely high on it. Bloodlust fills my every pore and just the thought of murdering Wayloran is stimulating.

Once word spread of Rywell's death, I quickly ordered a carriage and road eastward to Alpri. I left my past in Junio behind me and now, after talking to many residents, I learned which home was Wayloran's. The large manor was painted dark grey with white trimming and the third floor happens to be the location of Wayloran's bedroom. I love the thrill of a new kill. It's euphoric in a way only a damaged person will understand.

Wayloran's bride would've been spared, but I heard the hitch in her breathing and the fast beat of her heart as she woke up when I entered the chamber. So I covered her mouth and watched the plea in her eyes as I took her life away. Blood lust is something that can't be described in simple words. It's a complicated emotion only few can muster and once you're hungry for the taste of blood, the pull in your body is too overpowering. That's why I'm here now. I followed the pull in my gut and I happily watch Wayloran sleep in the hot blood cascading down his wife's throat.

I saunter around the bed, so I can drag the blade along his sharp jawline. His features are soft in sleep, but I know beneath that handsome face sleeps a wicked monster with evil intentions. The coppery smell of blood fills the room and stifles the scent of mildew and the sweat on Wayloran's forehead and palms. The summer-like heat is seeping through the glass window, making the room suffocating. His hands are large with thick fingers. I remember how they felt on my waist and breasts. Memories of the way he violated me and touched me, ruining my humanity. No longer will he be able to lay a finger on another helpless girl. Never again will he be able to touch someone the way he touched me. Maybe I should start by removing his invasive fingers.

Thinking better of the thoughts, I place the tip of the blade against his throat. Some people say killing someone in their sleep is cowardly, but I find it more exciting! When people are sleeping they are vulnerable and easily over powered. Being a Fae also allows me to hear the slow beat of sleep rise into a fluttering panic and lastly fade away with their life. I wait for a second too long, drinking in the thought of Wayloran's blood spreading across the blanket and mixing with his wife's.

I hear footfalls down the hall, but ignore them. It could just be a passing servant. The door swings open and I turn the blade away from Wayloran's resting throat before dropping into a crouch facing the frail maid who steps into the chamber. She looks to me and the blade and lastly Wayloran's still, unmoving wife. The maid's heart pounds a million times a second and the room quickly fills with the sour smell of fear. The girl's amber eyes widen and she screams. Her cry gives me goosebumps and I look away from her and dive on top of Wayloran. His green eyes open and he looks to me. *Shit.* He thrashes and writhes beneath my weight and I aim the blade at his chest. Lifting my arm high, I notice the recognition he has of me take over his panicked features.

A heavy piece of furniture cracks against my back and the pain bounces down my spine and through my adrenaline filled veins. Wayloran rolls onto the floor. I pull myself together and off the cooling corpse in his bed. I have never received training for fighting, but the primal Fae instinct inside me knows exactly what to do as I whirl the dagger behind me. The maid's cry echoes through the manor and she falls to the floor with blood trickling from between her shoulder blades. Wayloran is causing me to take innocent lives. *What a shame.* I guess we both take innocence, but just for different reasons.

Gathering my skirts I get off the bed and stomp on the frail mortal beneath me as I enter the illuminated hallway. The chestnut paneled walls are decorated with beautiful portraits and paintings made by artists I do not know. The red carpet makes the hall have a warm feeling of home. Wayloran rounds the corner and bounds down the stairs and I can't help, but giggle. If he knew about the Fae than he would be aware that we are born with immortal strength, grace, and power. Our bodies are made to run five miles in minutes, but I want him to run. I want to follow my prey like the hungry predator that I am. Let's play some cat and mouse then.

Once I reach the bottom of the steps I hear the front door slam. Following his panting breathes and pounding steps, I run from the house and bound onto the cobblestone street. The manors pass in a blur and the cold night air rips through my hair, pulling long uneven strands from my moon white braid. Wayloran's scent fills my nose and I stop at the alleyway. It isn't long before I drag him from a vagrant's home of trash.

I pin his sleep-weak bones against the stone wall of a large mansion. Pressing my forearm into his chest, I let lightning travel from my core, through my veins and along my bones, so it can sparkle in my palm. "You're going to have to be quicker than that," I whisper and let my breath blow along his cowering face.

"Please, please, I didn't know-"I slam him against the wall. He winces as I cut off his apology.

"You knew *everything*. You knew I was barely old enough to be a woman, and you knew that I couldn't fight back when you took advantage of me. I was chained to a wall like an animal and you just relished in that."

He only grows sorrowful. "What could I do?" He pleads for a merciful outcome.

"You didn't have to pay Rywell and go through with what you did," I growl. The more he stares at me the more I want to kill him. The song in my ears is singing a promise of death.

"You weren't supposed to escape. You were the only thing my brother wanted. He just wanted a child..."

What the fuck? Reyluke just desired something to control and be on top of. I wouldn't have trusted that man with a woman made of muscle let alone a child.

"If he wanted a child he should've treated me like one, but all he did was use me as a personal whore!" I am starting to get sick of looking at his tanned features and I let my sparks fly. The blue chords dance along his body and crackle with blinding light. The few vagrants inside the alleyway scurry off into the darkness before something stabs into my stomach and I drop my hold on him. I quickly pull away and place my hand on the burning. An old rusty blade he must've grabbed from the ground protrudes from my abdomen. Wayloran's convulsing body slides to the ground and I slam my booted foot against his face making his skull crack against the wall and blood fly from his nose and mouth. Spitting on him I walk from the alleyway and stumble into the street leaving his body to rot alone.

If I remove the blade I can heal. I do so and wait for the warm feeling to fill my body, but it doesn't. I haven't gotten hurt since the Tree of Light was chopped down. Oh no. this can't be happening. The magic from the tree allowed the Immortal to heal fast, but now we are left mortal in the healing process. Any wounds will bleed until it's clotted and if not treated, we will get infection. The Immortal have now become mortal.

~Ariadae~

My army is gone. My men are gone. What was left of them? *Nothing*. My mother will always be a threat, but this sort of attack can't go justified as a win for Solaria. This ends now. I will go down there myself and solve the dispute between our kingdoms. I will stop the war that has been waged for centuries. The men who began the battle no longer walk this earth, so why must our kingdoms suffer? Why must we wage a war of dead men? I have only one option to stop this and to end everything. I will tell them about my mother. She not only plans to take my kingdom, but during the summer, when I was her prisoner for a month, she said to me that she will enslave every mortal kingdom and make them do her bidding… starting with mine. The only way for me, and the other mortals, to beat my mother and her army of abominations is to work together and fight her. What else could we do?

I don't say anything to the council as we finish the meeting. I barely heard a word anyone said after I received the information of the state of my army which is nonexistent. Zube is at this table for a reason. He holds all of the records and information of Equadoria and its politics, economy, army, etc. What felt like hours are only minutes before Zube calls off the rest of the meeting. I stagger and weave through the mumbling nobles and bound down the hall. Maids call to me and I brush them off and leave their voices behind me, like dust beneath a rug, like my army beneath Solaria's sword. So many families lost loved ones. People who were dearest to them and I feel their pain. I lost Novid, Gaston, Seri, even my father…if he was here he would know what to do. He would know who to talk to and what to say to the families of his soldiers. What can I do? Who will I talk to? What will I say?

Slamming my bedroom door I strip off my revealing dress and take out my braids. Through a waterfall of collapsing tears I saunter to the bathroom and place my crown on the sink and slide into the tub. Using my power, I turn the knob and let the water slowly fill the tub and steam up the stone chamber. A hole has opened in my chest and I can't fill it. Friends, brothers, sisters, fathers, mothers all of them dead. I don't care how…I don't want to know how. All I want is to tear the flesh from the Solarian king's body and hang him from the gallows before his entire kingdom. Equadoria is now left to nothing, but the guards and sentinels walking through the streets.

My sobs echo so loudly I barely hear the hesitant knock at the door. I don't answer and the knocker enters the room anyway. Ice blue eyes burrow into my naked body.

"You look horrible," Jax whispers and I chuckle through tears. It's an exasperated, dry sound. I can only imagine my tear stained cheeks, puffy green eyes and my dripping, matted down hair. "Do you want to talk about it?"

I violently shake my head. I want to think about nothing. I want so badly to forget what Samuel told me, but it won't leave my skull. It's locked in an imaginary cage and I seemed to have lost the key somewhere in the darkness.

"What do you want to talk about?" he asks and I only shrug. What else is there to talk about? "We can think of something...are you excited for your birthday?"

"Why should I be," I croak through a raspy voice. My throat is raw and my mouth filled with cotton. "I'm immortal now and I will never look a day older than sixteen, so it's not like it matters."

"Just because you're immortal doesn't mean you lose all mortal mentality." I roll my eyes at him as he sits on the floor next to the tub and rubs my shoulder. "I mean, sure, you have powers and you won't die from age, disease, or infection. You also heal incredibly fast, but those are just perks, Dae. Think about this as a gift. Not a curse."

"Sometimes I just think to myself...would any of this be happening if I didn't wake up? If I didn't survive my father stabbing me, I wouldn't have to be here and watch my kingdom crumble to the ground."

"If you didn't survive, you'd be leaving your kingdom to crumble on everyone who loves you. Me...Zube...Jeremiah, we'd be left to fix the kingdom and I don't think we could. I wouldn't even be coherent without you." His words lift my heart and make me smile. The soft concerned tone of his voice makes me only think that his words are true. Fae can lie, but right now Jax isn't.

I pull my knees to my chest and Jax rises. He kisses the top of my head and I grab his wrist. "Wait," I whisper. "Don't leave me." He nods and pulls off his shirt. Dropping his pants and trunks he steps into the tub and looks at me. I pull the cord from his bun and let his night black hair fall in shaggy waves. "It's so long."

"I know," he smirks and winks. I howl in laughter.

"I'm talking about your hair, you freak." He joins in on the laughter. He lifts his calloused hands and glides his rough fingers along the jagged white scar on my shoulder. When I was trying to escape the Summer Kingdom an archer shot an arrow and tore open my shoulder. Throughout our nightmare in Elkwood the wound kept opening, so we cauterized it. Burned the skin closed because the constant pursuit of enemies kept it from healing.

"Why hasn't this healed," he whispers. I look to the marred skin and look back to his concerned features.

"I didn't think it was supposed to heal."

"Of course it's supposed to heal, you're *immortal*." I am a curse. I am a never aging or dying body. My blood is worth the world, my bones are stronger than titanium, and my skin heals in what takes mortals weeks, but for me, its seconds. I have never tested what would happen if I got cut or hurt, but when I returned home from Elkwood I never wanted to go back in. I didn't want to risk getting cut, broken, or bruised. I no longer wanted to fight for my life, but now it's different. What life do I have to lose? I am going to live forever anyway.

My heart flutters and a chill rattles my body and I look to the bedroom.

"What is it? Jax questions grabbing my face and pulling my attention to him. That's when I smell it. The scent of salt from an ocean and the sweet aroma of lilies.

"My mother is here."

CHAPTER FOUR

~Ariadae~

Jax lifts himself from the tub and I look between the door and the shifting cords of muscle on his body as I do the same. I follow him and he is wearing his pants before I even finish securing the silk robe. Something shifts in the bedroom and I hear a door creak open. The sound of a soft beating heart begins to fade away becoming distant. I look to Jax instantly.

"She's going into the library." My voice is barely a whisper, but he nods like I said it normally. What would my mother be doing in Equadoria? Unless she is here with her army, I don't think she'd be stupid enough to come alone. Jax slowly opens the door and sneaks into the darkness of our chambers. Although I am shaking like a scared kitten, I will my feet forward and follow him. Approaching the golden beam of light that illuminates the room, Jax loses his patience and kicks in the door of the library. Last time I saw him he was a hulking bear with curling horns protruding from his skull. Now he is purely human looking, aside from the immortal beauty and the pointed ears. His violet eyes flicker between Jax and me. Darwin grimaces and holds a small sack of dark leather.

"I missed you, princess." Darwin drawls, his voicing echoing through the silent chamber. I missed his heart. I almost killed him in the Summer Kingdom, but I had missed.

"It's *queen*, now." I answer. He only laughs and waves away my words with a dismissive hand. Every muscle in each of those fingers would easily tear me to shreds. He is a very old and powerful Fae. Although I am powerful in many ways, I am much younger, a mere dust particle on his years. The question ripples from my throat, "What're you doing here?"

"Oh right. What are they calling you now a day? The Queen of Titanium Antlers was it?" he laughs and ignores my curiosity. "Well I must be on my way." I shudder at the thought of his teasing and playful nature of murdering people. He probably created the expression playing with your food because he loves doing the latter.

"Do you really believe your leaving?" Jax asks as he pulls a large sword from a small umbrella tin that was transformed into his personal armory. Jax stalks into the library and Darwin backs up slowly. Their game keeps continuing with every step. "Shut the doors." Jax orders and I quickly make work of the lock. I can't tell if what I did was the right or wrong thing. I just locked myself in a room with two immortal warriors that want nothing less than to tear each other apart.

Following the train of this thought I step towards the hearth where the heirloom bow hangs above the mantle.

"Don't move." Jax growls without even glancing in my direction. He prowls towards Darwin who only backs away between two large towering bookshelves.

"You tell your queen what to do?" Darwin laughs and his voice bounces around the room and echoes into my skull. Although Jax said not to move, I need to defend myself if Darwin tries to come after me. I'll have to move as silently as possible.

"She's just smart enough to listen to me," Jax purrs and metal swords whine against one another. I take two steps within the loud clash. I notice how Jax doesn't deny me being his queen, but in many ways I am. It's a smart tactic though, not letting the intruder acquire information. Jax adds, "Why are you here?"

Swords scrape and scream and someone is slammed against the bookshelf which teeters on its legs. If that shelf falls over, the hundreds of books on the shelves will litter all over the library and desk, but will also start a chain reaction of shelves falling. The thought of the crushing weight pushes me forward another six steps. Just two more and I can grab it. It's so close yet so far.

"Why is the queen of Equadoria listening to a Fae prince?" I groan at Darwin's question and he chokes out a strangled giggle. Jax must have his arm on his windpipe. Two more thuds and knuckles crack against bone and a strangled growl erupts in the library.

I shout, "Jax what's going on?"

Another thud resounds in my pointed ears and the bookshelf begins teetering again. This time the weight rocks the twenty foot wooden tower. A chill rattles my body and immediately my brain tells me it's going to fall. My Fae senses are always aware, that's how I knew Darwin was here before I even smelled him.

Reaching into the darkness of my core I lift and control the glowing braid of my power. Projecting my hand towards the bow helps me direct my ability. It's what Jax told me when he trained me to wield my Telekinae ability and not let it control me. As if on command the bow rolls from the mantle and flies into my grasp as the rocking shelf begins its dissent. An ear shattering explosion hammers into my skull as wood splintering crackles like thunder through the library. Books rain from the falling shelves and they collapse like fluttering birds. The hard covers hit me like hammers on my bones and I can't stop the scream that rips out of my throat. I lose the bow in the clutter and roll away as another shelf crashes right where I was standing.

Jax suddenly goes flying past me through the air and slams against the wall. His eyes are shut as he slumps to the ground and his sword clatters to the stone tile. Looking towards Darwin I watch as he runs towards the door. I need to get Jax up, but I also need to stop Darwin. I knowingly grab the pommel of a rapier and angle the blade at the hulking beast that has just yanked at the iron door handle. My voice is like honey on bread as I purr, "Where are you going?"

Darwin's shoulders bounce as if he laughs, but I know better. He would get me in a useless position and then laugh. Darwin looks back to me and grimaces in the candle light as he whispers, "Back to the Summer Kingdom." Before I can react he throws a book and it slaps my skull. Falling to the ground I hear the *thud, thud, thud,* of my heartbeat and lastly the iron lock snaps. He's going to get away. I have to act now!

I stagger to my feet and let the momentum of my body push towards the moving and shifting door. Everything is turning and spinning as it comes in and out of focus. How could a person throw a book that hard? Then again he isn't a person and has immortal strength.

Gripping the door frame I step into my bedroom and Darwin's large brute figure climbs into the window sill. I can't let him leave, I can't let him escape with the pouch that he had in his hand. Jax seemed seriously attached to it and was willing to fight to unconsciousness for whatever is inside.

He looks back and laughs at my ragged figure, but his loud cackle only boils my blood. Feeling the soft hum of my magic makes me smile as I project my hand towards him and direct my powers at the man who should've died from my arrow. But something goes wrong as a shattering pain laces through my arm and body. A bright flash blinds me temporarily as I see bright purple sparks and swirling smoke like fire twirl from my finger tips and slam into Darwin pushing him from the ninth story window to the cobblestone below. His scream fades and I hear the twin snaps of his legs breaking.

I look to my finger tips and gaze at the purple oblivion twirling and spinning with unknown power. Something is seriously wrong.

CHAPTER FIVE

~Fayla~

I sit in the alley as the blood leeches from my abdomen and pools in my lap and across the cobblestone. Agony rakes at my burning skin. I cry out in sudden pain at the stinging wound. I will be dead in a matter of hours, maybe minutes. I can't tell anymore

The sky is slowly lightening as the sun begins to peak the horizon signifying the start of a new day. I will get to see one last sunrise before I die, before I am forgotten by the world, before I become nothing, but a broken Fae with uncanny abilities. Dying this way is shameful, repulsive. Only vagrants die in alleys of wounds, disease, and anything else that I really don't care about. I am no vagrant; I know that as much as I know the power beneath my veins, which happens to be very well.

As if they heard my thoughts, a man saunters into the alley with a gait only a very old powerful immortal could achieve. His blurred figure is shadowed in a dark cloak. A silver sigil glints into my eyes. Squinting, I peel my face away from the man.

His voice is like a snake's hiss as he says, "What happened to you?" He smells. Fae typically have a scent that any immortal would know, but this man's aroma reeks of death; bitter, but also sweet. It's metallic, coppery in nature. I smell blood.

Blood gargles up my throat and out my mouth as I laugh through bloodied teeth, "Someone attacked me." This stranger doesn't need to know what I did in return. He won't know that I was the predator, not the prey. "Please help."

"I will help you, immortal," He whispers in a lover's tone. He squats to my level and breathes in my scent. His breath is cold against my skin. "I will offer you something even better than what you desire." Oh no. There is a 'but' coming in this statement of his and I don't want to know what I will have to offer in return. "I will make you stronger, faster, and more immortal than any Fae form can." I shudder at his tone, but as he continues talking my breath comes in rasps. I really do need help. I don't want my life to end this way.

"But?" I ask my voice barely above a whisper. He only laughs and waves a dismissive hand.

"You let me *bite* you…" I almost laugh at his response. Fae do bite one another in bed when sex becomes primal, ethereal, something I never got to feel. "Do you agree to the terms?" I nod since that is all I have left to do. My voice is gone, my life is slipping and I am bleeding out in an alleyway in front of a stranger who is offering godly gifts. How can I deny his offer?

He presses his hand into the stone wall next to my head and I lay my skull on his forearm. Brick crackles and splinters beneath his hands and the crumbling dust falls onto my shoulder. He leans his face forward and I get a glimpse at the dark crimson color of his irises. They are flecked with black as dark as night and his pupils dilate as he looks to my face. His breath reeks of blood and I suddenly notice his pale skin, ash hair, and plump lips. I hear a snap of fangs sliding from his gums and I gulp down my scream.

Fangs puncture my throat and his lips suckle around the stinging pinches of his teeth. Blood seeps from my throat and right when it touches his lips I scream. Light blares in my vision and a ringing squeals in my ears. Small needle like stabs race up and down along my skin and I thrash and writhe through the shocking pain. I don't know what's up, what's down, or even if I'm screaming. He promised power, healing, speed, and immortality better than my own. He never mentioned this. The pin pricks of fire dance along my pores and I thrash one more time before everything goes black.

I awake in a large bed of red silken sheets and a black wooden frame. The room is adorned with ruby red, onyx, and gold accents. Everything is decorated, carved, detailed in contrasting sharp angles. No longer does pain rake my body. I touch my stomach, no wound, no blood.

I slide from the bed and immediately feel light on my feet as I approach the silk crimson gown decorated with a large gold belt and slim embroidered sleeves. An opening reveals the cleavage location of the gown. Whoever created this place likes silk, and the colors black and red because that's all I see other than the small gold details around the room.

I change into the dress and quickly begin to braid my hair and I scream at the black color hanging from my head. I run my fingers through the long smooth waves and some black smudges splotch along my hands; it's dyed, and was dyed recently. I step towards the door and I'm across the room in seconds already turning the door knob. He said I would be fast, but how could I be this fast? This is almost impossible. It's like the jumps I can do through dimensions to new places. I think of where I want to go and I flash into a bright light and appear there. It coordinates with my lightning ability. I don't know how though. During a storm lightning comes from nowhere and vanishes before arriving somewhere new.

I step into the hall as the door across from mine opens wide. I see the same guy from the alley. I blink and suddenly his body slams against mine and he pins me against the wall of my room. The door is shut and we're alone. I think my heart is going to thud and I wait for its comforting beat, but it doesn't come.

"What did you do to me?" I venomously hiss. He looks down at me with amazement. His crimson eyes stop for a second too long over my breast, so I wrap my hand around his throat immediately choking him. He stumbles back and before I blink he throws me to the ground and sits on top of me.

"I gave you what I promised!" he quietly shouts. He looks to the door and sweat beads on his forehead. I have no idea how old he is or what he is, but I am not going to deny the fact that he is dashingly handsome. He smiles as if he read my thoughts and purrs with a lovers tongue, "Thank you."

"How did you do that?" I ask confused and amazed although I don't let either emotion change my resting features.

"I'm your maker; I hear everything you think and I even feel your blood beneath my skin." What? He's my maker? I am starting to think this is all a wicked dream until he looks back down to me. "You're my prodigy," he says. His eyes flick to the door and back to me. "You're *my* Vampyre."

"I'm your what?" I shout and he clasps a hand over my mouth. I bite hard letting my already elongated canines draw blood. Immediately the aroma slams into my nostrils like a punch to the chest. No longer does it reek of copper, but instead its sweet scent reminds me of tarts and small hard candies my wet nurse gave me when I was young. My elongated fangs slide further from my gums. The moving teeth cause chills to erupt on my skin and a small tremble to rattle my bones. My stomach groans in desire. He yanks his hand away from my mouth afraid of this uncontrollable hunger that has taken over me.

"Control it, someone is coming." He rises from on top of me and offers a hand. I wave away his gesture and stand on my own as I fluff out the dirt from the crimson gown; the color of blood, the color of this man's eyes. I hear the footsteps and instinctively flick my face to the door. My breaths come in heavy pants as my new hunger has become ravenous.

Put your damned fangs away, He whispers and when I look to him his lips haven't moved. How? *I can speak to you through telepathy. A gift given from our god's.* I roll my eyes and a blond haired man opens the door. I take in his sharp features, pale skin, and dark eyes; he's a

Vampyre. His eyes look to me and the open cleavage of my gown.

I growl in answer and his gaze flicks back to my eyes. His voice is like a rock scraping along a blade as he says, "The queen demand's to meet your prodigy." What? There is a queen of Vampyre's? Why not a king? Why do I care?

You care because we serve her. Queen Molaris has been a vampyre since the curse transformed our ancestor's from Fae to gods of night. What she demands is what we offer.

She seems like a bitch, I say in my head and his lips go thin along with the heavy glare he shoots my way. A look like that would make most men soil their pants. I am not like men; I don't subdue to orders anymore. Who cares what Molaris thinks?

Flicking my onyx waves over my shoulder I follow the blond man who escorts me from, what I only assume, is my new bed chambers and down the hall. We pass many rooms and closed doors, some with guards outside and others that appear as if the door might fall to pieces by a strong wind.

My maker, if that's what I can call him, follows me and the blond male up a flight of winding stairs. The dark wood is ornate and gleaming with a fresh polish. Once we ascend the steps, a pair of towering twin doors rise from the floor and touch the ceiling high above our heads. Bowing, the blond male opens the doors to the throne room. Stars twinkle and flurry around the room, like snowflakes frozen in time. The dais is made of stone and the tiled floor is cold against my bare feet. I look to the sentinels clad in dark, pointed armor. The soldiers appear like urchins beneath the heavy metal. A swath of midnight blue fabric is worn as a hanging sash across the men's waists.

Molaris is sprawled across her throne of gleaming night. The dark and sharp chair is ominous and wickedly appealing to the eye. Molaris is wearing a skin tight suit of black leather and silk. It looks like a body forming armor, like a second skin. Across her skull sits a crown of silver stars, the shining points gleam against her ivory hair that just reaches her shoulders. A long heavy cloak of midnight blue is draped across her throne like a decoration; she seems like a decoration.

"Acacius," Molaris called into the stars floating around her throne room. The small glowing lights, pulsating like heartbeats, illuminate the dark chamber. My maker falls deep into a heavy bow as he drops to one knee. I stand showing no emotion to the queen as she glares. Her white crystal eyes burning holes through me as I barely give her the time in my immortal life. "And who are you?"

Acacius seems to lean in as if to hear my response because my maker still doesn't know my name. I am his prodigy anyway. I want to speak the truth, but I don't. I left Fayla behind in that alleyway. She is dead to me. "Athena," I say without question or hesitation. No remorse lies behind my words. "Athena Barrow."

Molaris conjures a wicked smile and her blindingly iridescent eyes darken. "So, my prodigy has turned you." It's not a question, but a statement. She may not question, but I do.

"Well that appears so," I groan in boredom. I should be intrigued by all of this, but I also don't care what this queen thinks of me.

Watch yourself, Acacius hisses within my head and I ignore the urge to roll my eyes at him. This is going to get annoying quite quickly.

"Why did he bite you?"

"She was bleeding, your majesty," Acacius says blandly as he rises from his knee.

"So?" The queen questions confused.

"To death," I add. Molaris flicks her eyes back to me with a wild eagerness. It looks as if she is hungry and trying to decide which snack to eat first.

"Was I speaking to you, Vampling?" Her wild eyes again become dark and evil. She is probably thinking about the ways she can use me in her kingdom.

"What did you call me?" I laugh showing the first sign of amusement or emotion since I had awoken.

"I said *Vampling*; do I need to repeat myself again? Is this prodigy missing any form of a brain?" I let my eyes burrow holes into Molaris as she only stares back. Sometime in the future I see a battle that could bring down worlds. She may be a queen of Vampyres, but I highly doubt she has lightning that can melt bone and flesh.

"Watch it you dead, rotting, whore!" The words leave my mouth and as the word *whore* rises into the air Molaris is off her throne and hissing her drawn fangs in my face. Her hand gripped firmly around my throat. Long nails painted black are stabbing into my skin. I hiss right back.

"Do *not* touch my prodigy," Acacius growls at Molaris. I'm not quite sure how he even got there. Molaris is crushing my windpipe with her immortal strength and I don't feel the circulation of air. I don't need it. I guess Vampyre's don't suffocate. Through some Vampyre rules I assume Acacius' order works on her because she releases my throat and she backs away. Her eyes tell me all I need to know. *We will finish this later.* She spins on a dark heel and I watch her trailing cape pull swirling dust clouds from the floor. They intermingle with the floating stars creating a dark galaxy before my eyes.

"Dismissed," the queen purrs and Acacius pulls me by the elbow out of the throne room. He pulls me away from the immortal bitch who I want nothing more than to rip out her throat with my new fangs. But first I need a meal. I am getting quite hungry.

CHAPTER SIX

~Fayla~

"*Careful,*" *Acacius moans* from his bed. After he dragged me from the throne room and away from Molaris we came into his chambers. Upon our arrival he ordered two fresh humans. I am not going to lie, but I couldn't control myself when the young girls stepped into the room with nothing on their soft fragile skin. Instantly I was across the room and my teeth sank into a brunette's collar, right where her shoulder meets her neck.

I suck, and as her warm blood touches my lips my knees almost buckle at the delicacy. I remember blood always tasting like metal and smelling of copper, but now that I am a Vampyre it smells like pastries and tastes like warm liquid sugar. The euphoric meal makes me completely ravenous and savagely thirsty for more. The frail girl shudders and her fast beating heart slows to a sleeping beat. I look towards her face and her eyes flutter closed. My lips touch the small pockets of scars from past Vampyre's. Her heart stops. Acacius jumps from the bed pulling me off of her instantly. He screams in anger, "What did I tell you?"

"What?" I ask through heaving breaths. Trickles of crimson slide down my chin, but I don't make a move to wipe them away. Drinking has somehow made me tired and out of breath. I'm not sure how I'm out of breath because I don't need air.

Acacius lays the brunette down and I notice that her skin has paled to a frightening shade of white; it's lighter than my skin. He pats her soft face and listens to her chest. My ears don't pick up any heartbeat, but maybe he can hear something.

Fire burns in his eyes as he looks at me. "You. Killed. Her." His growl is angered and his words are clipped. I might be a bit naive, but I am not seeing the problem. She was just a cattle being drained countless times and from the bite I received from Acacius I'd be happy to die. I wouldn't have been sad to lose my life if I was in her position. Humans and Fae alike are not meant to be cattle, food, or property, but in my circumstances I have to drink blood, I assume.

I saunter from my maker and the dead girl and run my fingers along the large table stationed before the hearth. Flames crackle and spit small flurrying ashes into the musky room. His chamber is much bigger than my own, but I don't fancy the layout. My bedroom has a vanity, cloth mannequin, and a closet. His room is just bland and crammed. There's his oversized bed, the table, a lounge area- which consists of one arm chair before a coffee table- and an armoire with a bathroom right next to it.

"Do you not care?" Acacius whispers. I barely hear his voice above the crackling embers. I shake my head in answer and let his sigh fill the quiet room. He looks to me as he says, "What happened in that alley? Why were you truly bleeding to death?"

I sit on the armchair and stare at him as he rises to his towering height. His grey tunic is taut across his large firm chest. His white shirt is like a second skin as his corded muscles shift beneath the fabric. He rolls his sleeves in silent wait.

"Why does it matter?" I question. Pulling my eyes away I look to the flames, full of shadow and darkness, but light all the same. "I am dead anyway. We are both dead."

"You are not what I expected." His voice is quiet, calm, and unnervingly displeased. Anger flows through my veins like water in a river.

"And you think you are what I expected?" I shout in anger. He looks to me without shock or emotion. His furrowed brow is nothing more than a mocking stare. "You asked to bite me and I assumed it was *just* a bite. I didn't expect to become a damned Vampyre!"

Acacius stalks to the table and lifts a large dagger with an obsidian hilt from his belt. He slams the blade into the wood table and I notice the blade had gone two inches deep. Someone has a serious temper.

"I warned you-,"

"You *promised* me," I seethe. He never gave me warnings of the pain or the outcome of the bite. "You told me of god like powers and immortality better than my own. Not death."

"Sometimes gifts come with a price, so now answer my question."

"What question?" I roll my eyes and pick the dirt from beneath my nails. I need to relax before I rip him to shreds. Although I'm mad he is the only one telling me anything around here.

"Why were you bleeding to death in that alley?"

Silence follows his prodding. He doesn't need to know anything and I will never tell him. I want to leave that life behind. Fayla died when I was born. I am Athena Barrow, Vampyre prodigy, storm caller, and death bringer.

He laughs and in a demanding even voice he says, "As your maker I command you."

The words fall from my mouth in a heavy waterfall and the crashing water is too fast and hard to stop. I have no control over my mouth or voice as I say, "For thirteen years of my immortal life I was being raped, beaten, and violated by a man who stole me from my family and locked me in a cellar. He used shackles laced with mountain ash to keep me from killing him, but once the Tree of Light was chopped down the mountain ash no longer hurt my skin and I was able to leave the cellar. I took great joy in killing him. I quickly tracked down his brother, who also participated in my daily abuse, and made a fun scene of killing him and his wife as well. As I was about to kill him, he managed to stab me. Since the Tree of Light has been chopped down, I couldn't heal as before."

"Holy gods." Acacius groans through a shadowed stare and frightened features. He runs a hand through his ash hair making it tousled and messy for the first time. "I am sorry."

"What the hell was that?" I shout and run to his side where I grip his jaw between my bone crushing fingers. How did he make me tell him that? That's not fair!

"Makers can command their prodigies to do whatever they please," His voice becomes soft and distanced. "Molaris used those words on me more than a few occasions as well. I know what you went through."

"You have no idea what I've been through," I hiss and let my fangs slide further from my gums. He doesn't understand what I have endured in my lifetime. He has no right to even offer empathy for my past. I still see the white scars on my wrists where my shackles laid and I even sometimes feel the invasive hands touching my skin. It makes me sick and this anger makes me want to vomit on the floor.

He grabs my wrist and throws me back into the chair. He braces his hands on the arm rests and he leans into my face. Our noses are centimeters from touching. "I do, Athena, I really do know what you've been through. Growing up, a small Fae boy, I too was beaten. By my uncle who raised me. When Molaris found me, and turned me into a Vampyre, she loved commanding me into her bed chambers. This has been going on for the past six century's, Vampling. Please don't tell me what I have and have not endured."

Two sides of the same coin, I say within my skull and pray he hears it.

Indeed, he coldly whispers, the word not reaching my ears. A tear slides down my cheek from my burning eyes and my vison becomes a red gloom. Wiping away my tears I look at my palms. Crimson smears my skin and I realize; Vampyres cry blood.

CHAPTER SEVEN

~*Evaflora*~

The fire crackles from the hearth behind her as she leans over the map of Elkwood. Her onyx hair is unbound and blowing on a slight breeze from an unknown origin. For hours she's been brooding and waiting anxiously for the return of her second, Darwin. When he was sent to acquire the item it was a well flushed out plan that should've taken moments, unless that little twat got in the way. Evaflora wouldn't even consider that possibility. She couldn't imagine her kingdom without him being the blade to the sword she holds.

Ariadae can do whatever she wants, because no matter how hard she fights, her mother knows every way to make her crumble and break at the seams.

Equadoria will be Evaflora's. She'll do anything necessary to have it.

A small knock and Evaflora grunts the acceptance of entrance. A bustling maid scurries on swift feet into the chamber and bows deeply. "Speak," Evaflora growls.

The blue skinned faerie stares at the queen in horror as her soft voice announces, "The general will not return." Evaflora's blood boils and she barely stops herself from destroying the entire chamber. "He was captured by the Titanium Queen, I'm sorry, Your Majesty." Before the faerie could turn on a heel to leave Evaflora spilled her blood across the walls and carpet and floor. The High Lady roared loud enough for the damned gods to hear. Ariadae will see her end soon, but first, Evaflora wants her second in command back.

~Ariadae~

My purple oblivion of power vanishes before, what seems like, a legion of sentinels' barrel through the door and begin looking toward Jax and me with stone cold faces. "Where's the assailant?" A young voice asks from the back of the squadron.

I point to the window and order through gritted teeth, "He is in the rear courtyard, his legs are most likely broken, but if he is alive take him to the dungeons." I have never seen or used the dungeon myself, so why not start putting the area to use. Besides, I have a few questions to ask Darwin.

Jax moves toward me on unsure feet. I can't stop an unknown shaking that rattles my bones from my core. He pushes aside his unsure demeanor when I break into outrageous tears and cries as I slump to the floor. What is going on with me? I'm not healing like the Fae and now I have a second power. I don't think any Fae have had multiple powers besides High Fae. Am I a High Fae now? That would explain the extreme increase in control and strength. Jax and Zube said while we were training that my control was astonishing for being such a young Fae. They also didn't take into account that I was turned Fae and not born into this body.

"Whatever this is," Jax whispers into my ear while I squeeze my shaking body into him. "We'll learn how to control it and wield it. Don't be afraid, Dae."

Minutes pass and a sentinel enters the chamber. Jax looks at him and I just listen to what they say. "The attacker is seized, your majesty." Good.

Jax waves the boy away and I rise on unsteady feet. The room is spinning and my knees have become weak. I look down at my hands and notice that the sleeve of my robe is completely gone. The edge is black with jagged holes and tears in the singed fabric. This was one of my favorite robes, but that is the least of my problems. I will get a new one from Rasgard and Theon.

Damn! I was supposed to see them today for a gown fitting. Everything is just getting worse and worse.

I shake away a brief image of the blue skinned faerie from the Summer Kingdom who was my only friend there. Seri. She made the most magnificent gown for the Summer Solstice and it got her killed. It was entirely my fault. Just like Gaston and Novid's deaths.

"Get into bed, Ariadae." Jax says and leads me to the large silken mattress. Sleep calls to me and blurs the edges of my vision. "You had a long day." I peel off the robe and scurry under the covers quickly trying to escape the nipping night air. "Goodnight," Jax adds and kisses my forehead. I am whisked away into the depths of sleep before I even recall Jax removing his lips from my head.

~Jax~

She has too much on her plate and I can't scrape it off. I can see her wasting away each day and it tears me apart, piece by piece, and my hands are bound. What else can I do other than be a shoulder to cry on? I am trying in so many ways to help her, but I'm afraid it's just hurting her.

I saunter from my beautiful future fiancé and step into the ruined library. The small leather pouch Darwin tried to steal lies still on the cool stone right next to a ruined novel. How he knew where this was, I'm not sure. His need for what's inside is beyond me, but I'm glad that new power has revealed itself tonight.

Grabbing the pouch I slide into the chair of my desk and pull out the key that hangs around my neck like an amulet. I drop the pouch into the drawer and lock it safely away from the world. I guess I need to start locking everything again. I didn't expect one of Evaflora's guards to infiltrate the kingdom, let alone our bedroom. She is really on a path to destroy us.

I rise from the desk and make sure Ariadae is still sound asleep before I run to the back corner of the library. Good thing Evaflora isn't aware of this. I press a specially aged stone and it sinks inward triggering shifting hinges to open. When I discovered this place, I knew I couldn't let anyone else know. Not even Ariadae.

Walking into the dark tunnels, I descend the curving steps and pass ominous torches that crackle loudly through the silent descent. I reach the bottom of the stairs and peer into the sanctuary before me. No torches light up the chamber but the domed ceiling has perfectly arched inches above the glowing leaves of the Tree of Light. When I brought back Ariadae I had extra leaves and after seeing the effects of the Tree's magic I thought I'd try it out. I planted some of the glowing leaves into a dirt patch down here and I didn't expect in five months to already have a new fully grown Tree of Light, but the only thing I can't understand is why it doesn't work. I have tested its magic again and again through different trials and nothing works. *Yet* anyway.

~*Ariadae*~

    I rouse to the sounds of maids and servants cleaning the library. I feel guilty for the mess, but I couldn't help it. I'm actually shocked that Darwin and Jax didn't bring down the whole castle during their battle.

    I roll from my bed and stagger into the closet. Before any maids can come I put on a thin, plain day gown and a large cloak lined with fur. Darting through the chamber I try my hardest not to be noticed by the cleaning maids. I don't want to be approached by anyone or have anybody ask questions about what happened in the library. It would be the worst thing ever if the word about the intrusion spread around Equadoria. My reign as queen is already off to a rough start. My army was murdered and threats from my mother are arriving and a threat has slipped past the guards I do have. The last thing I need is for my own kingdom to panic that intruders are breaking into Equadoria. Well only Darwin has, I hope.

    Walking down the corridors I nod at passing guards and servants and I heed forward, ignoring their request to help me. I just want to go and get a new robe and my dress sized. After that I should have the day to myself. I need time to think things over. My current situation is awful and I fear it may only get worse unless I do something. Just what exactly I need to do is beyond me.

I take a left turn and the entry hall rises around me. I lift my hood and skip a few steps towards the door. A feeling of nostalgia takes over my pores as I prepare to go outside.

"Pardon me, Milady." A quiet voice says and I turn to face Desirae, the maid that weaseled her way beneath my skin yesterday morning before the trial. "The weather isn't well today for a walk. Would you like for me to call you a carriage?"

I give a condescending smile and answer, "No, I really would enjoy a walk for myself. The weather will be fine." It couldn't be that bad. Nothing could be worse than my night.

She bows and I saunter off to push open the large doors. With a loud grown, biting wind flows across my skin immediately cooling me to the core. Small wet speckles kiss my cheeks. The sky is dancing with slowly falling crystals. Iridescent stars flurry around me, a nearby child laughs with glee. It's snowing. It hasn't snowed in Equadoria since I received Snow, well Jax, who I thought was Snow, or who *is* Snow. I'm not sure how to analyze that.

I walk across the slick stones dusted with a light layer of white snow. My billowing crimson cloak throws up a trail of swirling powder and the bright red of the fabric is stark against the white gloom of the day. The courtyard is loud today. Bustling guards and sentinels brush past me in a hurry. What could be going on? If there was something going on I would know. They may just be going through watch rotations.

As if on command, the front gates to the courtyard swing open and two carriages, escorted by large steads, barrel in. I quickly jump out of the way of a particularly fast moving mare. The riders upon each of the horses wear the Equadorian sigil on their chest plate. Who could be arriving in such a haste?

The guards run to the carriages and the doors swing open releasing twelve men barely recognizable beneath the gore and grime on their skin and armor. They're what is left of my legion at the southern end of Abella. I run to a staggering man whose face is covered in large open wounds. He needs to get to a healer soon because he would be lucky if he survives the infection. He leans in to me and I call to a passing sentinel to take the heavy man to a healer. I turn to help another, but I slam into a firm, armor-plated body. I look up to chocolate eyes and a squeal passes my lips.

"Jeremiah!" I squeeze my childhood best friend and he hugs me back. "Are you alright? Where were you?" I look all over him for any wounds, but nothing appears to be out of order. He is still my perfectly unharmed Jeremiah.

He runs a hand through his brunette waves and just smirks lazily as if the chaos around us is nothing. "I was retrieving the survivors. I didn't trust anybody else doing so. If something went wrong I'd want to be there. And why do you ask? Did you miss me?" I poke his gut and the firm chainmail stops my finger from tickling him.

"No." A blush kisses my cheeks and I look away. "Well, yes I did."

"How did it go?" The image of Eric's back breaking flashes through my mind and I can't forget his mom flying across the room. A chill rattles my body.

"I'll tell you later."

He nods. "This weather is extraordinary isn't it?" He asks and gestures to the falling flakes. I reach out and catch one in the palm of my ungloved hand. The ice melts immediately once in contact with my skin.

"It's keeping the kingdom distracted for a while," I say under my breath.

"Distract them from what?" *Shit!* Jeremiah doesn't know about Darwin breaking into the castle last night. Well how could he know anything? He's been gone rescuing my people who need help the most.

A distant cloak tower booms the first chime of nine and I give Jeremiah a curt wave and head into the streets with a promise of conversing later on. He doesn't follow me and I am grateful for the alone time. The citizens playing in the snow don't even notice their queen quietly slipping past them. As I saunter pass begging vagrants I drop a few gold coins into their shaking hands and head forward towards the shopping circle within the center of the upper-class part of the city. Almost as if walking through a door, the people's clothes change from wool and hides, to fur and silk. Large bustling dresses kiss against the snow covered stones and men escort ladies across the open space. A streaming fountain rises above the hustling crowd, loud with excitement of the snowfall.

I excuse my way through the horde of humans and some, but very few, Fae. Giant glass windows revealing glittering gowns as white as the snow and also dresses as red as blood, greet my eyes. My stomach turns at the color. Ignoring the dresses I push into the shop called, *Lacus & Forma,* which is Couture & Beauty in the Fae language.

Warmth coils around my bones and my eyes look to the hearth burning brightly. The crackling flames are as loud as the small bell that rings above my head. Carpets and small pillow chairs circle around the large shop in little seating areas blocked off by chiffon curtains. The bright colors almost seem to glow from the fire. Strange paintings and vases full of flowers, that should be dead this time of year, are scattered across the room nonchalantly. It's been awhile since I last came here. Or at least it feels like a long time, but in all truth it's maybe been a week.

"Your Majesty." A soft voice quirks and I look to the male peeking from behind a curtain. His skin is covered in scales and large bat like ears protrude from his snake like face. His hands are big with long spindly fingers that are probably perfect for a needle and thread. I ignore the internal shout to run and remind myself I'm one of them. I am a Fae. I am not in Elkwood anymore…

"Hello, Theon." I say. I walk to him and we give one another twin kisses along our cheeks as a way of greeting. "I missed my appointment yesterday, so I thought I should come in early this morning."

"Oh don't sweat it, darling." He drawls in a flamboyant manner as he seems to dance around the shop. He has just such an open, happy freedom that I admire. His eye for clothing design is another trait I desire. "Rasgard knew you'd come in soon, so he is just preparing your gown in the back room." I follow Theon behind a curtain and he snaps his fingers making tea appear in small cups on a tray. He drops a sugar cube inside the amber liquid and drags a large cylindrical platform to stand on, next to the coffee table, but far enough away from the fire that we needn't worry. I grab a cup and take a seat on a small cushion. "So, Ariadae, how are you and your male counterpart?" I almost choke on my tea.

Through my coughing fit I barely choke out, "What do you want to know?"

"Well is he taking care of your needs? Being a gentleman? Helping you with your duties?"

"Yes, he helps me with ruling Equadoria and many of my political duties."

"How's the sex?" Heat immediately turns my cheeks pink and I try to hide them by sipping more tea. I've never been comfortable with sharing these details.

"It's fine…okay…I mean…Great! I'm sorry I am just bad with these sorts of things."

Theon just shakes his head at me and sorrow fills his eyes. "What's wrong, sweetie?"

"Nothing's wrong, Theon. Well I'm not sure."

"Spill!" he looks as if he is about to leap from his chair in anticipation. For a second I even think about changing the subject, but he is so approachable and I never really had someone around that I can discuss my issue with. Jeremiah wouldn't want the details, Zube would laugh at me, and I can't talk about Jax to Jax.

"Something is missing. Ever since I came back from the *dead* I mean," I cough on the word. "He hasn't been around much and anytime I just want to talk all he wants to do is have sex. And I love that he wants me and loves me, but I'm not sure if I love him. Well, no, I worded that wrong. I *do* love him, it's just how do I know if he is my... my-"

"Mate." A voice says from behind me and I nearly fly into the air and spill my tea everywhere. I turn around and look to a handsome male with skin of stone. His dark eyes greet mine and his mossy hair sways as he takes a seat next to Theon. "It's something you will know, Ariadae."

"Well how did you know Theon was your mate?"

Theon and Rasgard look to each other and smile. If only I felt that same kind of love for Jax. I want to love him and I want him to be my mate, but I don't know if he is. As much as I want to fully allow myself to be with him and lay into him I panic and I pull back. Something just doesn't feel perfect. And I know relationships aren't perfect, but your mate is the person made by the gods for you. What if I can't know my mate because I was reborn as a Fae?

"It's something in your gut that feels like a swift kick. It pulls the air from your lungs. The moment you connect eyes with your mate, the gods make sure you know. And if it doesn't happen instantly it will happen within hours of meeting them." Rasgard explains.

Theon jumps in. "Once you both know, there is this undeniable feeling that you will shatter worlds to keep them safe and for you two to be together." I certainly have never felt that way for Jax. Not while I was Fae anyway.

"I've been with Jax for months…"

"He isn't your mate, Milady. Unless it works differently since you were born of the Tree of Light." I nod in agreement and wipe away the tears from my eyes. I couldn't imagine my life without Jax and if he isn't my mate…then who is? "Let's get your dress fitted." Theon whispers grabbing my hand and pulling the red cloak from my shoulders.

The words keep clanging through my brain.

He isn't your mate.

He isn't your mate.

He isn't your mate.

Then who is?

CHAPTER EIGHT

~Fayla~

After my scolding from Acacius, I was sent to my chambers for bed. Of course I'm not tired, but since it will be daylight soon and I'm a Vampyre I will become weak if I don't rest. It's stupid and pointless, being a Vampyre. I spent years in a dark cellar never seeing the light of day and now I still can't. I just want to feel the suns warmth, or does it even have warmth anymore? Well, I wouldn't know unless I went outside! I'm sick of being property and controlled. The opportunity to be free came and I took advantage of it, so now I need to escape again, I have to break out.

On that thought, I rise from my bed and slide into the closet. Slipping on a sheer black dress adorned with crystals, I laugh as it makes me look like I've taken a swath of the night sky and put it on like an accessory. The clothing in the Vampyre kingdom is exquisite, I can't deny that, but I still don't like this place. I feel disconnected from everything. It's as if a strange voice in my head is whispering to me saying, "you don't belong here." I know it isn't Acacius because all he wants to do is sleep.

After throwing my unbound black waves over a shoulder I tiptoe into the hall of dark paneled wood and begin my walk around my new home. Maybe not all of the Vampyre's have to live in this damned castle. I would rather walk in the woods, or a desert, or maybe even through unyielding marshes because anywhere is better than this place. Queen Molaris is going to make my living here fucking horrible, but what can I do about that? I'm supposed to be loyal right? Well, why not make her keeping me here miserable for her?

A girl who was walking by, human by the smell, recoils at the sight of me. I look down at my dress and touch my face, but her blue eyes flick to mine. "Why are you up Milady?"

I just give her an adamant glare as I groan, "Well I just wanted to see my new home." She backs away even farther and that's when I noticed her ankles. Heavy leaden shackles against scarred and blistering skin, her wrist bare the same scars, but no shackles. I look to my own wrists on instinct and noticed the grotesque, ruined, and once blistered skin is now porcelain and smooth, but tiny white scars are barely visible against the paleness. My past is almost completely gone, but not forgotten. "You shouldn't be walking around should you?" my growl is guttural and terror fills my nostrils. It's a rancid, repulsive odor.

"I...I was...I was going t-to be t-t-turned...," The girl whispers. I just grin and my mind begins imaging the taste of her blood. I wonder if it tastes sweet and pure because of her unbitten skin. Her body would feel smooth against my lips. But the question is where to bite first. She tries to run.

Time slows as she begins to slowly turn and her hair moves like it's beneath water, but I am perfectly fine. I take two strides to her before grabbing her wrist and throat. I pin her against the wall and everything goes back to normal and I almost laugh as she screams. "Nobody will hear us," I purr into her ear.

"Please," she begins to beg. "I just want to go home. I want to see my family."

"I don't have a family."

She looks to the ceiling with a plea. "I'm sorry about whatever happened to them."

"I'm not. They missed out on the real torture I fully endured. I got to spend all my Fae-,"

Acacius grabs me and throws me to the floor. He holds the human behind him in a protective stance and I rise; my eyes saying everything I want to do to him and the girl. She silently cries behind him as he hushes her.

"You don't touch her," he threatens.

But I am hungry, I say in the silence of my skull.

I am too. We will talk about this later. Just follow my lead, he answers and my interest perks. Instead of fighting him like I usually would, I nod in understanding. He turns to the human and grips her shoulders, promptly acquiring her interest. "You trust me right?" He whispers. A gulp resounds in my ears from her bobbing throat and she nods. "Follow me than." And with that he grabs me and the girl by the wrist and sprints down the corridor towards the main stairwell that accesses the throne room. Although the human girl moves in slow motion, we run at an average pace. I guess that explains how fast the Vampyres are. Time slows for everyone else while we move with great speed.

In seconds we are in the entry hall and Acacius stops running. He drags the girl to the front of the castle and I scream out in terror when he throws open the doors and tosses the girl onto the cobblestone path. Bright golden rays glisten down upon his pale skin and I immediately feel the heat of them, although the sun isn't on my own skin. I feel the connection between us that he spoke of earlier. I wait for a second and he doesn't burst into flames or vanish into ashes. I always assumed

Vampyres died in the sunlight, but my assumptions were juvenile.

The girl looks to Acacius with watering eyes, "Thank you. I appreciate you so, so, so-,"

I hiss at her and she scurries away on uneasy feet. Her pounding steps resound into my ears and I stare at the dark evergreen pines bordering the castle and a very large lake to the right. To the left seems to just walk off into the horizon like the ground cuts straight into the clear sky. I gawk at the light and sun. The open blue expanse is full of large plush clouds.

"May I?" I ask to nobody in particular. I've wanted to be out in the sun for years and now... I might be able to. The inkling of urges is too much for me to listen to if he says no.

"Of course..." Acacius places a firm hand on my lower back guiding me through the doors and onto the cobblestone, smoothed by years of feet passing over them. When the sun touches my skin I gasp. It's like the feeling of being alive again. No longer do I feel covered in death's cold grip, now I am in life's warm coiling heat that enthralls my bones and skin. I instinctively squint from the bright light of fire in the sky and the burn from behind my eyes. "You can look around you know," He adds.

I leave Acacius' side and wander towards the place where the ground cuts right into the horizon. As I approach the edge I notice that it's a cliff that stands before me and at the bottom is a large amount of open water. Crashing waves slam against jagged rocks at the bottom and roiling foam swirls through the unyielding ocean of the deepest hues of blues. Tears spill down my cheeks at the sheer beauty of this place. The girl is long gone and no longer am I hungry for blood. I'm in awe. I'm in love with the sheer beauty the world has to offer and I realize how much I have been sheltered from and haven't seen.

I look to Acacius who smiles and saunters toward me with his hands in his slacks. "It's beautiful isn't it?" I look back to the looming ocean.

"How?"

"How what?"

"How is it possible that we can walk in the daylight?" I blurt out and he just shakes his head with a chuckle. I don't think I've seen him smile or laugh once, and I know for certain he hasn't seen me like this. There's a first for everything.

"I knew you were going to ask me about this once you wandered beyond the castle doors." I just wait for the explanation. Slow, never-ending minutes pass and he finally starts to answer my question. "I am. *We are* not only Vampyres, we are also partly Fae. Never has there been a hybrid since you and me, so we are the first of our kind. We are both life, death, day and night, light and dark, and even heads or tails."

"Why hasn't there ever been a Fae and Vampyre hybrid until now?"

"Well Vampyres came from the Fae." Shock rattles through my bones. "After the Mortal and Immortal wars, a treaty was created and this was written in the form of a book. *The Book of Ash.* And the contents of the book consisted of the laws, created by both man and faerie, that they need to abide by. The most important one was *'None, thy Male or Fae, shall breach beyond the bounds of mortal or immortal.'* These laws were written in both mortal and immortal blood forever binding them to the Tree of Light."

In all my years I don't recall ever hearing of this Book of Ash, but I'm also still confused how it is connected to the Vampyres.

He continues on. "But there is a breed of Fae called the Succumbus that can only stay youthful and immortal by drinking human blood. After the creation of the Book of Ash thousands and thousands of these Fae ran from Elkwood forest and into the mortal lands where they wreaked havoc upon Abella. About a century after all of the Succumbus established lives in the mortal lands, the Tree of Light got mad. Prometheus was upset with his creations. This is where everything gets interesting." I giggle a little bit and he barely notices as he continues to stare at the oceans churning waves. I take a seat and he joins me. "The Tree of Light had casted a spell. The aftershock of this magic was like an atomic wave of wind booming outward across all of Abella. Immediately the Succumbus Fae in the mortal land's skin began to boil beneath the sun and they started to catch fire. Not knowing what to do, they all ran, burning, to the Tree of Light, to Elkwood Forest. Some people even say the whole world shuttered from their pounding steps.

"As they broke the borders of Elkwood their skin stopped burning, but they all changed. Their skin tightened and their bodies morphed into wicked beasts and monsters that will forever haunt the dreams of children both human and Fae."

I jump in and ask, "So the Vampyres came from the Succumbus that entered Elkwood?"

"No," He laughs. "There were some who saw what was happening to the Fae when they entered, so about a quarter of a hundred Succumbus stayed behind and shielded themselves from the sun. They later transformed that night, when the first moon rose, and became what we know as the Vampyres."

"Well what happened to the Succumbus who turned into beasts?"

"They are known as the Forsaken now and are forever bound to Elkwood's borders."

His story only clears up some of my confusions. "If Vampyres originated from Fae why can't they go into the sunlight?"

"Well the curse created by the Tree of Light changed all of the Succumbus Fae, so their bodies can't withstand the sun's rays."

"Okay that makes more sense. Well than why wasn't there a Fae, Vampyre hybrid until now?"

"The Vampyres were afraid to touch the Fae until about four centuries ago when Molaris unknowingly turned a Fae into a Vampyre. And then I created you."

If Acacius has been a Vampyre/ Fae hybrid for three centuries than…, "How old is Molaris?"

"She was a Vampyre for seventeen centuries before she bit me, but I don't know how long she was a Fae for. I've always asked her and she has yet to answer my question."

Gods above, she must be the most powerful being since Prometheus.

"*You* are more powerful than her," Acacius whispers. "You, in strange ways, are the only one who challenges her and I don't know if it gives you some adrenaline rush, but just know she argues back because she is frightened."

"How could I ever be stronger than she? Molaris is over twenty centuries old, Acacius!" He sits onto his knees and grips my shoulders extremely hard. He even shakes me a little bit.

"You are like no other Fae I have ever seen. You have abilities that are stronger than anyone's on this earth. I feel it, deep within my veins, that you still have a beating heart. That's what she wants most from you."

I look down at my palms and bright cords of electricity sparkle across my hands and Acacius' eyes seem to glow with the blue sparks. He inhales deeply as his mouth falls open in utter surprise. He then smirks with a knowing smile before looking at me and saying, "You're the spark that ignites a fire, Athena. You can drag fear to its knees and watch it become ashes"

The rest of the week was thrilling because every day Acacius and I went outside. The sun kept my skin looking somewhat alive for a Vampyre. The nightly shower, which is a new luxury, has pulled all the dye from my hair revealing a soft gray with a silvery sheen. Although it's pretty, it isn't my snow white waves that I'm used to and I am starting to want the color back, want a life back, and Acacius is helping me do just that. Acacius showed me how to hunt outside in the wild and what animals to eat. He doesn't want me living off of the humans that wander the halls of my new home.

"Crimson Island," Acacius says as he briefs me on the history of the Vampyre society that has been living beside the Fae and humans for the past twenty centuries. Apparently, part of being a Vampyre, is having to know everything about the history between the four kingdoms. In the North is king Tyrion of Vampyra, a past lover of Molaris. Lastly, in the south, is King Aaron of the Dead Isles. Crimson Island is where I currently am and the western kingdom is Valkyrie, ruled by the cunningly brutal Scout. Molaris is the queen of the east and rumored to be the most wicked of all four.

Acacius went on and on about their histories and rulerships, but to none of it did I truly listen. Maybe I should've, but I live forever, why do I need to learn about them now? I have a lifetime to figure it all out.

"Why do I need to know this?" I spit into the open chamber of my bedroom. "Can't we go outside?"

"No, Athena." He bites back in a fearsome growl I wasn't expecting.

"Why not?"

"We can't risk anyone knowing about our kind," He growls. His scarlet eyes dance across the room quickly and land back on me, his stare making my skin crawl. "If Molaris learns of our Fae blood, she'll murder us before we can create more hybrids."

Rolling my eyes I pick at a chip in the wood table. "You said it yourself. I can defeat her. If she somehow found out, I'd kill her first."

As the words left my mouth the same Vampyre with white skin and ivory hair that I met on my first day busted through the door. Acacius rose into a fighting stance and I just looked back to him with a glare of adamant stone.

"Molaris has requested your presence," He purrs with a lovers tongue. Acacius begins to walk around the table and the man's eyes land on me. "She wishes for Athena's presence only."

Be careful, Acacius whispers into my skull like a persuading conscience. *I won't be there to protect you this time.*

I just look back at him as I exit the room I follow the tall sentinel back down the simple corridor and up the stairs into her throne room, where she lounges like a cat trying to find the sun that is sadly absent from the chamber.

The same floating stars fill the space of the otherwise empty room and Molaris sighs to herself. I take a mental note of the absence of her sentinels that once flanked her throne. I stare at her while she plays with her manicured nails. The looming silence makes me tiresome, so I decide to talk first.

"You wanted to see me?"

"Yes. Athena, I fear we have started off on the wrong fang." *Oh really?* "I would like to start over."

I pull at a loose thread on my leather tunic just to give my hands something to do even if it isn't worth my time. When I look back to her she has risen and is looking down her nose at me. "Is that so?" I feign a chipper mood.

Molaris answers with a curt nod. She is acting a bit out of character, so I ask, "Why did you really call me here?"

She laughs and the wicked sound bounces across the walls making me cringe. "I just have a few questions for you."

I wait.

"Like, where did Acacius find you?"

"The depths of an alleyway in Alpri," I still remember the mortal city that borders the eastern cliffs. After the bite that turned me I felt my past drag away from me. When I try to remember my childhood home and what the cellar had looked like, it's all fogged over and unclear. Almost as if I had dreamt everything.

Molaris hisses. My body goes taut. I lose the feeling in my bones and an uncontrollable twitch takes over my skin. The blood in my veins slows and changes directions. I feel veins explode and I can't even open my mouth to scream. What's going on with me? Why can't I move? Molaris laughs.

Her iridescent eyes graze down my body and she only smirks before I feel my blood pulse and pull my stiff body into a kneel before Molaris' dais. I scream as more veins pop, and bones crackle like logs in a hearth.

"You have never bowed in my presence," She sulks and just giggles. My eyes burrow holes into the floor. What is this power? I can't move a single limb or finger and as much as I will my toes to curl, they don't. I'm under her spell and command. "I'm sorry to be so violent with you, but your disrespect makes my temper flare." I tasted the lie the moment it passed her lips. "Look at me." She drawls.

I close my eyes.

"*Look. At. Me.*" She repeats. Molaris realizes I won't oblige to her request and stretches my taut spine backward until my eyes are glued to the ceiling. My eyes begin to burn and I, for the first time feel scared. Acacius said I could bring fear to its knees, but how? I'm kneeling before the most powerful Vampyre in the world and she is making me grovel before her. Acacius thought I was powerful, but now I realize he is wrong. He is so god damn wrong and I am nothing, but the pest beneath Molaris' shoe.

She looks down at me. Her blonde curls fall around our faces like an ivory curtain. Death is a beautiful, feral thing, and its name is Molaris. "I've heard that you haven't been sleeping during the day, *Athena*." She uses my name like a poison.

A crimson tear floods down my cheek in a silent cascade to the marble floor. Her power loosens from my bones and the excruciating pain ebbs and I almost cry out in relief.

"What've you been up to?" Her voice is like a whip cracking in a silent chamber. It echoes off the towering walls of the throne room and the stars seem to pulse with energy.

Acacius, please help me. She is going to kill me. I call out into the empty void of my mind and Molaris snarls, making an immaculate show of revealing her elongated fangs.

From the subtle release of her magic I stretch out my jaw. It aches tremendously as I whisper, "I don't answer to you." I have no lie or excuse to give her, so I won't tell her anything. Nobody can know of me and Acacius' faerie and Vampyre lineage.

Molaris' iridescent eyes seem to glow and radiate red from the rage deep within her as she is instantly growling against my neck, "Fine. I never wanted you in my court anyway."

My body shutters as her pointed fangs puncture skin and a knock resounds through the chamber. She pauses. I lose the breath I was holding.

The doors creak open and the escort that brought me to Molaris pokes his head into the chamber. His eyes don't even widen at the image of Molaris' fangs grazing my throat. I attempt to twist out of her grip, but than her power, that softened to let me speak, tightens and my blood pulls through me at her will. She drags my body across the marble floor and out of the throne room. I don't even feel my bones bouncing down the steps that descend to the doors that Acacius and I had left the castle from.

When I clatter to the floor the pain vanishes and I feel utterly violated. Molaris had controlled my blood and stopped me from fighting back. My bones groan as I lift myself from the floor on shaking arms. My bones feel weak. My blood is cold.

Acacius is at my side in an instant, helping me to my feet. His crimson eyes are worried and looking to me for answers. I think of what happened in the throne room and he sees my memories, analyzes them. His features contort to pure hatred and a glare shifts to the Vampyre queen now standing at the top of the stairs.

"How dare *you* harm my prodigy," Acacius growls. I shake from the chill that slides down my spine like a droplet of sweat. And I hope Molaris feels the same fear, but her face gives no information.

Molaris laughs. "We were only playing," Her eyes slide to me. "Is that right, Athena?"

I shake my head. Molaris hisses and is gripping my throat in an instant. Acacius puts his arm between us and throws Molaris across the room. She smacks against the wall with a satisfying crack. Molaris' guard, I assume, leaps onto Acacius and begins clawing at his face. Acacius fights back just as hard. I didn't expect the battle between Molaris and I to happen so soon, but I'm prepared, I am ready. I will not go down without swinging.

Guttural, animalistic screams escape the Vampyres as they roll, and wrestle throughout the room. I'm in awe and completely forget the most powerful Vampyre in the world is at my back.

I spin. Her hand locks to my throat and Molaris' iridescent eyes gleam with the scent of blood in the room. I don't know who's bleeding, but the odor filled my nostrils seconds prior.

"You should've never come here." Molaris whispers and I know she won't let me get away this time. I want to call out to Acacius, but my ears tell me that he is still in a heavy skirmish behind me. I need to help myself. Molaris smiles, her fangs glinting in the lamplight. "I'm going to kill you."

Suddenly I feel the current beneath my bones. Not Molaris twisting my blood, but my lightning. My powers can melt bone and flesh. Destroy humans and Fae alike. Never have I used them on a Vampyre, but Acacius says I am the spark that ignites fires. Let's make this island burn.

Seconds before I make a storm reign hell on Molaris I stop at a sound. A snare drum clatters outside the door and trumpets shout in a wondrous beat. The Vampyre who is fighting Acacius came into the throne room and stopped Molaris from killing me, but it wasn't on purpose. He didn't have time to warn her of the marching soldiers I hear outside.

My stare glides from the door back to Molaris and she releases my throat and adjusts her skirts. I wipe the wrinkles from my tunic and Acacius stops his brawl to stand beside me. We all stare at the large wooden doors and when the instruments stop no knock fills the castle. The doors just burst wide open.

Blue eyes, similar to mine greet us and instantly the Vampyre looks to me. Her dress is black and across the trim is a golden dragon that spirals up her skirt. I am suddenly aware that the Vampyre is the queen of the west, Scout is grinning at me.

"I thought it would be mannerly if ladies came first," Scout giggles and no humor is behind her cunning, foxlike features. Her brunette curls are in a knot atop her head behind a diadem of sparkling black wishbones of varying sizes.

Flanking her is a male with straight, dirty blonde hair and soft amber eyes. His smile, unlike Scout's, is genuine. I'm glad Acacius taught me everything about each of the Vampyre kingdoms because I know this male is Aaron, the Vampyre king of the southern island.

And as the expression goes, save the best for last, the Vampyre king of the north, Tyrion saunters into the castle. He has an entire legion at his side and I see the musicians amongst the warriors. Tyrion is freakishly tall, muscled, and to my surprise, handsome. He has short dark hair, mysterious brown eyes, and thickly veined skin showing off his intense exercise and training.

Molaris shifts uncomfortably and I remember that Tyrion was one of her lovers once. I can use that to my advantage if needed.

"Hello," Tyrion purrs and I realize his gaze is sliding over my curves. I try not to allow my skin to crawl, but I fail. "Who are you?"

Acacius steps in front of me snarling. Molaris looks to Acacius and pushes him aside. "Do not snarl at our guests! And the girl? She's nothing." Molaris doesn't let Tyrion see me. "She is Acacius' prodigy." I peek over Molaris' shoulder and Tyrion grins.

"I'm thankful for this humble welcome, Molaris. I hope you don't mind I brought a guest of my own." Tyrion gestures behind him and out of the crowd of sentinels slips a man from the legion and his bright yellow tunic makes me think of the sun during day and I become very aware of his sculpted muscles bulging from the fabric. "Lunan Berdu Walsh, High Lord of the Day

Kingdom." Lunan's Fae scent fills the chamber and Molaris becomes even paler than her dead body typically is. Her own lust fights Lunan's Fae odor and I think that Lunan might have been a lover of Molaris' as well.

"Why is he here?" She whispers and Scout looks between them suddenly putting together some puzzle that I can't see. She runs to Molaris and drags her up the stairs. I look to Acacius who just shrugs and the two Vampyre kings confide in warm conversation. Now that I am no longer looking over Molaris' shoulder I get a good look at Lunan and notice a thick scar from his hairline down through his eye brow, his eye somehow undamaged, and down his cheek to finally stop at his jawbone. His high cheekbones are reflecting the lamplight and I look at his eyes. They're as gold as the yellow of his tunic. He looks at me and my gut twists. My ears fill with a dull ringing and something cracks loudly in my chest. It's sound similar to a whip. All the air leaves the room and my knees become weak. Lunan's eyes widen and I realize he feels the same thing as me. My cold, dead, unyielding heart beats for the first time. I shudder at the fast beat now thrumming in my chest.

A voice in the back of my head, not Acacius', whispers.

He's your mate.

CHAPTER NINE

~*Ariadae*~

After the dress fitting, Rasgard sent me back to the castle with a new robe and I was happy to walk back into my room with the library finished and cleaned. I will send gifts to every servant who fixed up the damage later. I was disappointed to find Jax missing again, but I assume he decided to talk to the guards or maybe even Darwin. I have things to ask the intruder anyway, so I change out of the simple dress and into one of Jax's loose white shirts and a pair of tight pants and leather boots.

I head into the hall and ask the sentinels stationed outside my door to escort me to the dungeon. Although reluctantly, they oblige and lead me past the throne room and into a servant's passage. The dusty air is hard to swallow and the tight space makes me panic slightly.

After being chased through the tunnels of Evaflora's secret labyrinth these small corridors make me uncomfortable. I know I'm safe, but I can't shake the feeling of getting trapped.

After going down the spiral stairs and passing four doors, we reached the bottom where a door was slightly ajar. A beam of light shattered the darkness of the stairwell and the sentinels escorted me into a large stone chamber. The room was a dome and circular. The chamber has many doors and behind one on the far wall I hear loud, agonizing groans. My stomach turns at the thought of him behind the wood. When I shot him with the mountain ash arrow back in the Summer Kingdom I knew I missed his heart, but I had hoped he had died. I didn't expect him to come waltzing into my kingdom.

"Through there, Milady." A sentinel points to the door with the moans, confirming my assumption.

I make quick work of braiding my hair and walk toward the large wooden door. My shaking hand grabs the cold iron handle and the other sentinel asks, "Would you like us to come with you?"

Yes. "No thank you," I need to do this alone. The guard nods and unlocks the door and opens it for me. I thank him as I notice Darwin's rumpled form slouched in a chair in the center of the dark stone chamber. His legs and ankles are bent and twisted at sickening angles.

I hold back a gag that rises in my throat from the scent of feces and rotting vomit inside the dungeon.

I step in and a guard closes the door locking, me in with the man who once teased Jax and me in an herbal shop. He tried to kill us then, and he tried to kill us last night. He has a track record of murdering people that albeit is beyond the two times he tried to kill Jax and I.

"If you need help just shout." A muffled voice says from behind the door. I look down to Darwin. His wrists are shackled and his dark hair is ruffled and his shirtless back is covered in scars, cuts, and bruises.

"Hello Ariadae." The sound of his voice sends me back into the horrors of Elkwood. Darwin is one of them. I can still vividly see the day inside of the herbal shop in the Summer Kingdom when he taunted me with the threat of death. He heard the hitch of my panicked breathing and he was supposed to die with that arrow to the chest, but instead he came back. He followed me from Elkwood into my own home and he can't terrify me here, not anymore.

"Hello Darwin," I say trying to keep my shaking voice from sounding weak. I can't stop looking at his mangled lower half. "How are your legs?"

"What do you want?" He spits and flicks his face to me. His hard features are strange and I don't know why. The last time I saw him, besides last night, he was a bear with horns, now. Darwin is a man with the pointed ears revealing his Fae blood. If he wasn't a brutal killer he could be considered handsome.

"I just wanted to talk."

"About what?" Darwin seethes. "Your mother?" I jump back at his assumption. I'm not scared for being in a cell with my mother's personal guard, but I flood with fear at the idea that he knows more than I want him to. He even knew I wanted to talk about my mother.

"Yes." My voice is shockingly strong, adamant like stone. "I want to know why she wants to enslave my people and all the mortals of Abella. I want to know why she so badly wants to destroy my kingdom and why she is so angry." I'm panting from my boiling blood. "Can you answer that?" I add with distaste.

Darwin just chuckles to himself as he silently shakes his head, looking at his lap.

"What?" I growl through grinding teeth. He continues to laugh and it just makes me even angrier. My already boiling blood burns at a fiery hot and I begin to sweat from my every pore.

"I remember in June when you asked me to deliver Evaflora a message. You asked me to tell her that you mortals weren't weak and you will kill her and her kind." My heart begins to beat fast in my chest and bile rises into my throat. I was broken and angry and scared. I remember that day like yesterday. It was the day that I discovered my mother murdered Seri, my only friend in the Summer Kingdom.

"What I don't think you understand is that you *are* her kind," he adds. "You, Ariadae Vox, Queen of a human throne are just as much a Fae as Evaflora is, or Jax is, or even I am for that matter. I told her your message and it was childish on your part because now, Evaflora is challenging you. She is pushing to see how far you will go to abide by the promise you made. This all started because of you."

My whole body is shaking with rage. I can't say he is wrong because he isn't, but I can't admit that he is completely right either. My mother turned me into this, made me do this. I am the victim, not the enemy. "I am not like you." I hiss.

"The sad part is that you very much are. No matter how long you deny it, your mortals will hate you on their throne. The Fae will hate you because you should be a mortal and now you don't even have anymore control over yourself than you do your own kingdom."

I shake my head. I try to push away the memories of the boy's back breaking and his mother flying across the room during the trial. No matter how much I fight it the images don't vanish. And now, I realize that today, when I went to get my dress fitted that I didn't easily slip past people in the kingdom because they didn't notice me. It was because they were avoiding me, like a plague.

"Stop," My voice is barely a whisper.

"Your mother wants to take every human from beneath your feet and make them do what they should be doing, serving *our* kind." Darwin's voice is growing into a crescendo and I start to not only feel the pain of his words settling in my gut, but I feel the pain of my new power curling within my veins. "Humans are beneath us on the totem pole, Ariadae. Compared to you, Evaflora, me, they are nothing. Your mother wants to use them for something."

"I said *stop.*" I growl in warning. My power starts to become restless and writhe angrily in my palms. He's right I don't have control of myself or my kingdom.

"Let us take them, break them, and let the weak become what they truly are. *Nothing.*"

"*STOP!*" I scream and the room explodes in bright purple smoke and flames. Dancing and twirling my power spirals from my clenched fists, my palms bleeding from my fingernails, and Darwin screams as his pants, the chair, his shackles, his hair, and even his skin burn away. When I realize what is happening it all vanishes on a phantom wind and Darwin is a steaming body on the ground. His flesh is burnt, but he's breathing and coughing up blood. What have I done? I lost my grip, the only control I had if I had any at all.

The sentinels slam through the door and stop in utter shock. I look between Darwin, the sentinels, and my bleeding palms. What've I done? I wanted to stop this war between me and my mother. I didn't want to make it worse. If Darwin dies than she'll kill everyone, destroy Equadoria and move onto the other mortal kingdoms beneath the Elkwood borders. I need to get away.

I turn on my heel and the sentinels run to Darwin. I stumble to a random door and throw it open. A corridor is before me, I don't care where I'm going I just need to escape that smell of fire, smoke, burned flesh, and magic. The mixture of those things creates a vomit inducing odor that makes my head spin.

The long hallway is illuminated by a bright glowing light coming out of a doorway at the end. My stomach twists into an even tighter knot at the recognition of the illumination. The coloration distracts me from what I just did. It has a white glow that almost seems to pulse and I beg to the gods. It can't be. I spent my entire time in Elkwood trying to find it and when I did, my mother destroyed it. I saw that same white illumination in the afterlife. Its bright white waters lifted me from death back to life.

When I step into the large dome chamber the glowing leaves of the Tree of Light reflect off my tear stained face. The thick twisted roots break the cobblestone floor and burrow deep into the ground. My pounding heart starts to skip beats and I turn my attention to the grunting form lifting heavy buckets of water from a small pool across from me. His long dark curls bounce as the cords of his muscled back lift the pales. Jax's eyes meet mine and his buckets splash onto the ground, water spilling everywhere. He becomes just as shocked as me.

"Dae," he whispers, reaching to me. And even though he is very far away, I recoil. He lied to me. This explains where he goes for several hours a day. Why I haven't been able to spend a lot of time with him for us to focus on our relationship. All he does at night is crawl into bed next to me and want sex.

"Why?" I want to puke even more than I did before. The sickening thought of him lying makes me question everything. Wonder how much he is keeping from me. I knew we weren't meant for each other.

"I wanted to tell you-"

"But you didn't," I choke through unyielding tears. "After everything that's been going on you kept this from me? You lied to me! You told me you were working on laws and military planning for my kingdom! But this is all you did! How could you?"

He runs to me and I dodge his open hands. The fingers that touched me at night and the hands that belong to the man who told me he loved me, the hands of a liar, a god-damned fucking liar. I don't even have time to be happy that the Tree of Light has been remade, or curious if its magic works like before, instead my mind races back to *those fingers.*

His voice croaks, "I was going to tell you soon, but after last night and the trial and the court meeting I couldn't find time."

"Just take me back to our-," I stop myself. "*My* room."

"Okay." Jax points to a doorway behind me and I stomp up the spiral staircase hugging my shaking body. He lied about having a Tree of Light in my castle. He is no better than Darwin, but what makes them different is that I left Darwin burned and barely alive in a cell. Jax, I can't even think about touching right now.

I reach a brick wall and Jax reaches across me. I press my body against the wall. I don't even want him near me. His presence is already becoming too much for me to handle. He pulls a torch holder and it acts as a lever making the stones separate and slide open revealing a large bookshelf. *My library.*

"It was beneath my own library." Not a question, but a statement. I can feel his body cringe without even touching him.

"Yes." He whispers and I see him as a dog with his tail between his legs. *Bastard.*

"Don't sleep in *my* room tonight." I sob through my tears. I break and quickly run through the library, past the desk, into my room and land on my bed. My loud wails echo through the large chamber. The man I trusted, the man that slept in my bed, lied to me.

Evaflora's devious smile glistened in the cell. Water was trickling down the damp, moss covered walls and a shadow was hunched before her, his back facing me. I approach the deflated form shackled to the chair. Evaflora adjusts the metal rings that give her fingers metallic claws. She quickly grips the captive's shoulder and a deep groan escapes the male as his muscled back goes taut. Blood flows from her talons, deep in his scarred skin, and the rivers of crimson cascade down the groves and taut cords of muscle.

Evaflora doesn't speak as she takes a dagger and glides the pointed edge against his defined jaw. The male's hair is gone and when I take another step forward I almost vomit as my toes stick to the wet, blood soaked locks of dark silk on the floor. Evaflora cut off his hair, to the skin.

I hold back a gag and Evaflora's smile grows feral as she takes a quill pen and slides the point into the cut she made. He hisses and she pulls out a piece of parchment, starting to scribble she goes back for more blood, using the male as an inkwell. My stomach twists and I throw up onto the stones and my own bare feet. Wiping the tears from my eyes I look up at Evaflora who is no longer smiling and she becomes aware of my presence. Her sky blue eyes crystalized in the darkness of the cell and she hands me the parchment. Gripping the folded paper in shaking hands I open it and written in the male's blood is:

Winter Solstice

<><><><><><>

When I awake from the nightmare I release the innards of my stomach onto the floor. A cold sweat soaks my skin and I stumble into the bathtub, even with the boiling water in the tub I can't subdue the violent tremble that rattles my skin and bones.

I typically have nightmares about what happened when I died, but not since the summer have I dreamt about Evaflora. For a while I was thankful for not having the dreams about her, but something felt different about this one. It was more real than any other dream I ever had. Who was she torturing? Why would the paper say 'Winter Solstice'? Maybe it's just my brain overreacting to the upcoming Winter Solstice ball next week. That's probably all and it is nothing more.

The water in the tub became cold too fast and Desirae came in to help me into the closet. She found a woven sweater and a pair of tight black pants. I made quick work of dressing and I sat at my vanity as she brushed my damp hair. She doesn't say anything about the red surrounding my eyes or the blotched tear-stains on my cheeks. After I snapped at her the other morning I have been meaning to apologize, but I've been a little busy. Images of Darwin's burnt body flash in my mind and I shake the memory away like a wet dog.

I talk first, ruining the silent communication we had going on. "I'm sorry for the way I snapped at you the other morning. I wasn't having the best of days."

She doesn't meet my gaze in the mirror. "It's alright Milady, but I should be the one to apologize. I shouldn't have said such thing about your male."

What she doesn't know is that he isn't mine. He's a liar and he isn't even my mate. I calm my boiling fire before I snap at her again. Desirae's conversations have the best intentions I just take them too hard. "Ariadae," I whisper. Her delicate eyes meet mine in the reflection. She quirks her eyebrow in silent question at my name. "Call me, Ariadae."

"Well, Ariadae," She grins and her face seems to glow with happiness. "Upon Captain Jeremiah's return he has requested his queen's court for dinner in the dining hall." I haven't seen my childhood friend in weeks except for the brief moment yesterday. I have so much to tell him.

"What time does the meal start?"

"In about an hour," Desirae mumbles as she becomes distracted by the wet waves of my fiery red hair. "How would you like me to do your hair, milady?" she realizes her mistake and giggles, "Ariadae."

I join in her laughter this time and answer, "I'll leave it down today. Thank you for your help."

She waves away my thanks. "It was a pleasure. Anytime you need me just call."

After she leaves the chamber I sit in silence staring at my gaunt features. I've become awfully skinny since the start of my reign as queen. A day doesn't go by when I don't think about what happened to my father. He thought he loved a kind woman who faked her death and ended up murdering him. She put the curse on his crown that made him evil, which made him try to kill me. When I learned that Evaflora was my mother I just… my world as I knew it just shattered. I'm left with nothing to put back together.

I thought I could break the curse on my father by taking a leaf from the Tree of Light, but Evaflora chopped it down destroying all curses, and allowing the blood thirsty monsters to leave Elkwood forest. Thank the gods I haven't heard about any entering my kingdom, but it won't be too long until they start coming after the Equadorian people. I need to be here to protect them, but I can't do it by myself. My army is dead. I need soldiers to fight back.

The clock chimes six and I throw my drying hair over a shoulder and leave the chamber, silent and without Jax, the liar. No guards escort me to the dining hall and I'm thankful for the alone time before I enter the room.

When I arrive everyone is already deep in conversation and my court is happy to see me. I give polite smiles and silent waves to familiar faces and approach the backs of my friends, guardians, and teammates that traveled through Elkwood Forest with me.

Zube's golden hair reflects the chandeliers. Jax doesn't look at me as I grip Jeremiah in a tight, tight hug. Being the Captain of the Guard, he has become even bulkier since the return to Equadoria and the gleeful glow to his chocolate eyes has yet to vanish.

"I've missed you." I whisper to him. Jax's eyes stab into the back of my head. Zube looks between me and him, blatantly confused. I would've thought Jax told him everything and slept in his chamber last night, but I guess I assumed wrongly.

"We *all* have," Zube cuts in attempting to lighten the mood. "How was Solaria?"

Jeremiah's eyes fill with a dark gloom and his shoulders turn inward as if he is trying to hide. "We had to sneak into the kingdom and track down the dozen soldiers still alive. Each one was in a different place around the kingdom," His voice dropping low. "They were all underground in secret tunnels being tortured with different techniques and tools; each one worse than the last." My stomach drops at the thought. What Jeremiah had seen being done to those men must be haunting him. They're his friends, mentors, acquaintances. I could only imagine his pain instead of thinking of my own.

I decide to change the subject, "Well you're home now. The soldiers are safe here." I look at everyone in the chamber, but Jax. "Is anyone else hungry?"

Everyone becomes suddenly aware of the polished table covered with ornate silverware and delicate plates and glasses. Servants come in with large carts covered in salads, meats, starches, and fruits. I dine on the fresh roast, some greens, and a couple of sliced fruits. It is all delicious. The entire table was silent besides the sounds of forks touching plates and the occasional sip from a glass of wine.

I sit at the end of the table, Jax and Jeremiah sit on either side of me and Zube sits to Jax's left. Samuel Francis, the man who told me about my entire army being decimated, is beside Jeremiah. He looks at me and whispers, "We have received another letter, Milady."

Jeremiah goes for seconds and eats like a savage. I hold back a laugh as I ask, "Is it from Solaria? If so, now is not the time, Samuel."

Zube glares at Samuel as if telling him not to ruin the dinner. Samuel nervously glances between Zube and me. "It's from Pangea," His voice stutters on the name of our neighboring continent on the opposite side of the globe. There are two major continents on Corten; they are Abella and Pangea, but islands of varying sizes fill up the oceans. "They request our aid in fighting against a dark druid on their lands. They fear the druid may come for Abella once it's finished conquering there."

Zube slams his hand on the table and the whole court looks to the commotion. "Now is not the time," he growls. "You are ruining this happy occasion."

"Zube its fine," I whisper. I look to Samuel. His bright eyes don't meet my gaze as a blush blossoms on his freckled cheeks. "The truth is that we don't have anything to offer for Pangea. As much as I would like to give assistance to them we have our own issues to worry about."

"Like what your majesty?" The question comes from the other end of the table. The court knows we had problems within Elkwood, but they don't know about the letters from my mother and the war she is declaring on us.

"My mother," I start.

"Is dead," An older man cuts in. He was a member of my father's court.

"*Is very much alive.* While in Elkwood we had problems with her and she was the one who placed the curse upon my father. After his death, and the events that happened in Elkwood, she has been sending letters."

"What kind of letters," Jeremiah asks and I decide to stand, the entire table's attention is on me anyway. Jax and Zube shake their heads, telling me no, but they need to know that the threat is growing bigger every day.

"The letters are threats to enslave the mortals of Equadoria. She has requested I hand over Equadoria and all its power or we'll suffer the consequences." Whispers between the lords begin to flood the chamber and their voices rise with fright and anger.

"Ariadae," Jax groans. I ignore him.

"I am not handing over Equadoria. I am not going to let her enslave our people. We have nothing to fear."

"Not yet anyways," The same old man grunts and Jax's warning growl silences any conversation lingering in the room. Everybody looks to the Fae warrior poised to pounce on the Lord. Zube gets between Jax and the man and pushes Jax back into his chair and whispers into his ear.

Jeremiah rises from the table and runs from the dining hall, so I charge after him. I leave Zube and Jax to talk to the court and find Jeremiah walking towards his wing of the castle. I call to him, but he ignores me. He breaks into a sprint and I keep up with him gaining speed. I'm far in front of him when I look back to notice he's gone. I ran too fast, I completely missed him. He's my best friend, so I need his support more than anyone's. I can't let him get angry with me.

"Jeremiah?" I call down the empty corridor. Where could he have gone? Suddenly I remember where I am. Before I went into Elkwood I used to walk down this corridor every day. I sprint through a door and the dark room is illuminated by the moon shafting through the giant floor-to-ceiling windows on the far wall. The double patio doors are wide open and the wind floods in. Howls echo off the vaulted ceiling.

On silent feet I stalk through the maze of weapon racks. No longer do I need to train with weapons because now I am a weapon. My powers will stop any threat to me or my kingdom. Again, images of Darwin's burnt body flood my mind and I wonder if he has been healed by this time.

Jeremiah isn't in the training hall, so I move through the glass doors onto the patio and immediately notice the moon beaming down on his muscled back, which is covered in scars. If he was in battle I could imagine the blood sliding down his back like a waterfall. Déjà vu stabs through me like a sword, but I can't pinpoint why I have the familiar feeling.

Jeremiah swings a sword through the air and its twirling quicksilver blade flashes the moon-white reflection on the steel. His skin has darkened since his travel to the hot and sun heavy kingdom of Solaria.

"What's wrong?" My question hangs in the air between us and all that fills the silence is his heavy panting breaths.

"Nothing," He bites and I hear the flutter of his heart.

"Liar."

"If you're so good at knowing when I'm lying than why do you ask for the truth? Don't you already know?" He is beyond upset. I didn't expect the dinner tonight to end like this, with a fight. I was maybe expecting a fight between Jax and me, but not an argument with Jeremiah.

"I'm not Zube, Jeremiah," I say trying to keep the bitterness of my words to a minimum and fail horribly. "I can't read your mind."

He just drops the sword to the ground and the clattering sound of steel on stone makes me jump, but when he looks at me, eyes full of tears, cheeks stained with them, a cry escapes my throat.

"I thought after we left Elkwood all of our problems would be gone, left in that damned forest. I didn't want them to follow us out of there." He cries and I can only answer with a shuttering breath. I understand everything he is saying. Nobody expected this outcome when we first planned on going into the forest. Things were easy then. I was innocent then.

"I-I," I start to talk through shuttering breaths. "I thought it was g-going to be e-easy. I n-never imagined this, I'm s-so s-s-sorry." Jeremiah just grips me into a hug and a wail escapes me and him. In this moment when I try to think back to the day we left to go into the forest it feels so long ago. It's almost like it was a dream. What has my life become? What have I done?

CHAPTER TEN

~Ariadae~

Rasgard and Theon woke me up this morning and I rolled over to an empty bed, again. I'm still upset with Jax and haven't spoken to him unless I had to during court, but otherwise he hasn't bothered me. I can't lie and say that I don't miss having someone in my bed beside me, protecting me. It gets lonely. Through the seventeen years of my life Jax has slept beside me; whether he was a man or a snow white tiger, he was always there. Now I'm utterly alone.

Today is the day of the Winter Solstice ball that I am supposedly hosting. I begged the court all week to not continue planning the celebration because if we can barely handle a dinner together than what could we expect at a party? They all decided to have the event anyway to help the Fae citizens feel welcomed by Equadoria. Sometimes I forget my father banished magic sending the Fae into hiding, but after they made their point I agreed with the court.

The dress I was fitted into last week looked nothing like the one I'm putting on now. The corset is too loose on me, even with all the tightening and I apologize to the males. They ignore my apology with concerned stares. They've always cared for me. After getting into a tighter corset I am given an under gown and then finally the gown itself. The gorgeous chiffon is gold and it's so pale it even looks white. Across the hem and rising up the trail of the skirt are snowflakes embroidered to look like frost.

"This dress is gorgeous," I say breathlessly in awe. Not even in the Summer Kingdom had I worn something so stunning. It even challenges Seri's Summer Solstice gown that transformed at midnight. I doubt this gown has any faerie magic, but it's beautiful enough to go without it. "I love it."

Theon grins wickedly, his needle thin teeth shine in the light of my bedroom. Rasgard's stone skin actually flushes and I give them each a big hug and I'm careful of the sleeveless bodice covered in small white diamonds and crystals like snowflakes.

"May I do your hair?" Theon leaps with excitement and I don't deny him his happiness. We sit at the vanity and he curls my red hair into a beautiful loose bun at the base of my skull. "I notice the fading smell of a male. Is everything alright?"

I pick at my manicured nails, painted like iridescent pearls, pretending that I didn't notice the slowly vanishing scent of Jax that once clung to my every pore. "Yes, I mean no," I sigh through my nostrils. "Jax has been growing a Tree of Light beneath the castle and didn't tell me about it."

Rasgard's head whips to me and he stares at my reflection in the mirror. Theon's snake-like face becomes sickly pale. "How? I didn't even sense its power," Rasgard whispers.

"When Jax brought me back to life he used leaves from the Tree of Light and I assume he had some left over because he planted them."

"How did we not notice its presence?" Theon questions looking to his mate for an answer, but Rasgard only shrugs, they both look at me.

"I didn't feel its power either, so I assume it doesn't have the same powers as the original Tree of Light once did. It's different somehow." I just shake my head and become suddenly worried I may have ruined Theon's work, but he just smiles with a grin that doesn't meet his eyes.

After the conversation Theon hums to himself as Rasgard works on doing my makeup. He lines my eyes with kohl and brushes glitter onto my lids with a beautiful gradient of midnight blue and white. He glosses my lips very quickly and whispers, "You are very beautiful, Ariadae." My cheeks heat at the compliment.

"Thank you. Will you be staying for the ball?"

He shakes his head and I become sad.

"Why not?" I ask.

"Theon and I have nothing to wear, Your Majesty."

"Oh, but it doesn't begin for thirty minutes! I bet my maidens could find something in Jax's tunic collection for you two!" Rasgard only grips my hands and gives them a slight squeeze. He doesn't want to come. I was just excited because they are my friends and helped me not feel completely alone, even if it was just for an hour or two.

Theon finishes packing up their supplies in seconds and they give me deep twin bows and I answer them with even bigger hugs than before. I wish they could join the festivities of the ball. If they came it would also be two more people I can talk to instead of Jax.

Before I can process that I am alone, two sentinels enter my chambers and escort me down the long corridors towards the entry hall. They both seem to glow when I loop my arms in theirs and I smile. I feel like the princess I used to be. For once in my immortal life, I am happy and grateful to be enjoying a party. No matter how extravagant it is! And I think everyone in the court also needs this Winter Solstice, if not for the Fae, then for the mortal's tradition. We could all use the distraction.

The ballroom is already packed full of courtiers, lords, ladies, and even Fae citizens in their finest fashion. Every party goer is swathed in shades of blue and white accented by glitter or fur and the ballroom itself is a twin of the training hall, just without all the weapons. The golden marble of the room is decorated in glowing lanterns that are shaped as snowflakes and long strands of white fabric hang from the ceiling. Fae acrobats swing from some of the fabrics and put on a show of twirling through the silk, suspended above the crowd. Other performances are happening around the dance floor and mortal servants dish out the food on the buffet table while still enjoying the party. A band plays next to the giant floor-to-ceiling windows and I spot Jeremiah's brown hair next to the dais on which they perform.

I make my way through the throng of people and make sure to smile and make quick small talk. I don't want Jeremiah running off before I get to talk to him. After the night on the patio last week we kept going to the training hall and just doing what we used to do, train. My body, surprisingly, aches more than I expected, but he taught me how to wield a sword, the basics anyway.

I just finish thanking Samuel for coming to the Winter Solstice when Jeremiah sneaks up behind me and grips my sides making me squeal. Everyone looks at me and sees who scared me and starts to giggle. A blush heats the apple of my cheeks and Jeremiah's chocolate eyes sparkle beneath the snowflake chandeliers. No longer do tears prick his eyes or shadows fill our thoughts. We are enjoying ourselves for the first time in a long while.

"Hello," I chuckle.

"Good evening, Milady." Jeremiah whispers and places a kiss on my hand. I wail with laughter. Oh how much more obnoxious can court etiquette be? He chuckles and then hushes me. "You're ruining the moment," he says and the music shifts to a waltz. "May I have this dance?"

I decide to play along. Why not attempt to have even more fun tonight! "Of course, Lord Baldwin! How could I ever deny you and your stunningly good features?" I ignore the awkwardness of Jeremiah's last name on my tongue. We laugh as he spins me onto the dance floor where we waltz, in sync, to the music around us. We continue to dance to the sound of the violins, the people around us wisping away on a phantom wind and suddenly it's only me, staring into his glistening chocolate eyes. "I'm glad your back," My voice is barely a whisper. "I've missed you far too much."

He smiles and I'm amazed at how he heard me. "I'm glad to be back." Warmth fills my heart and for once I forget the horrors of Elkwood Forest and feel safe, collected, happy. Ever since I came back to life I haven't felt this way with Jax and the way my court is running things. Once this party is over I'll be making a serious change. But for now I will enjoy the presence of Jeremiah being with me.

I feel as if my spine grows spider legs and begins to tickle the skin on my back. My Fae senses buck, and kick like an angry stallion. When I stop dancing and look around the room nothing is happening. I don't know where to look as panic settles in my bones and then I hear the shattering of glass and screams of terror overpower the music.

A legion of Forsaken comes through the glass windows that might as well be nothing, but giant holes in the side of my castle. Wendigoes, the tall white creature that Zube's mother transformed into, crawl up the walls and pounce onto courtiers. Wood Nymphs stick to the shadows and begin to eat the teeth of screaming mortals who don't escape. Troglodytes shoot arrows into the wave of sprinting people and Arbors crush Fae beneath their giant tree-like feet.

Jeremiah hands me a blade that I didn't know he had and I barely have time to compose myself before an onslaught of Wood Nymphs come crawling towards me.

Their black eyes take up most of their head, so I swing low slicing into the screaming creatures. They eat human teeth, so just the thought makes me want to paint the floor in their guts. How did such a joyous event become a nightmare?

Black blood stains the marble floor and my sentinels begin shouting orders to the citizens. A ringing starts in my ears when I look over to Jeremiah driving his blade deep into a Troglodyte's chest. He doesn't notice the white Wendigo about to pounce on him, so using my Telekinae ability I tear the snarling beast's jaw from its skull. He gives a nod of thanks before an arrow whistles between our faces.

Two Troglodytes approach us with bows drawn and arrows poised on our throats. The chandeliers twinkle above as more Forsaken leap from the glass spectacle. I don't even think as I lash out with my power, as sharp as a blade, and snap the cord holding the giant spiked chandelier. It lands on top of the blue scaled lizard men. I almost laugh at the feat. Never have I had so much control and confidence in my ability. Being a newborn Fae definitely has its perks.

Stepping on to broken shards of glass I dash across the ballroom to an Arbor, who's holding a young Fae by the ankle. The catlike Faerie hisses at the giant tree monster and it roars back. The wind from the Arbor's earsplitting scream makes strands of fiery hair blow around my face. I don't want any more death. I want this war over. With all the strength in my immortal body I leap into the air and swipe down, using my body weight behind my blow, the blade cracks through the Arbor's thick root arm. The Faerie skitters away on uneasy paws as the Arbor locks its attention onto me. Only once had I faced this beast, when I was tracked down by my mother at the Tree of Light. I don't remember destroying any of the four beasts present, but a thought runs through my mind like a book that's fallen off a shelf and landed on the perfect page.

I mentally dive into the dark rippling ocean of my mind, bubbles rise around my conscience and I search for the braided cord of my power. I hear the muffled sounds of men shouting and flesh being torn from bone. The Arbor winds up its other arm for a swing and I quickly dodge it. Continuing my search I find the ocean floor and two chests sit adamantly against the bottom. One chest is open and I see the braided cord of my Telekinae abilities rise to the surface, illuminating the dark churning current of my mind. I dodge two more of the Arbor's attempt to kill me. I don't feel connected to my body as I swim to the locked chest and tear the golden lock open and release the swirling purple flames that turn the dark into a violet dream. I follow the power up and break the surface with it.

I once again feel connected to my body and the pain of the Void powers spiraling from my fingertips is bearable. The hungry power whispers within my skull and the sound of the rasping voice saying, *"I am the void"* sends goosebumps dancing across my skin. The purple smoke crackles against the Arbor as the beast roars and burns away into a pile of ashes. Violet smoke coils from the pile into the air. *"You cannot tame me,"* The voice croaks and the distraction costs me as a Dreag, its snarling mouth angled to bite my neck, slams me to the floor. My sword slips out of my grasp and I try to blindly find it, but to no avail. The dark skin of the Dreag feels like canvas and the beast's maw recoils, gathering its strength for a bite and I project my invisible weapon. The monster flies through the air and I feel its bones shattering against the wall.

More Forsaken flood into the ballroom and I push past the wall of sentinels towards the dais where the now dead band players once filled me with happiness. This needs to stop. Evaflora has attacked us while our guards were down. That immortal bitch will find her end. I scream as pain crackles through my veins and large purple smoke like flames erupt from my palms splayed to the legion of Forsaken. With dying wails they burn away on the flames that pulse from my draining pool of power. My energy is fading and I become light-headed.

A solid hand pulls me from my whirlwind of murderous power and I fall into Jax's arms. I push off of him and land on the bodies of my helpless courtiers. I look to the windows and no more Forsaken leak through the hole in the side of my castle and I look amongst the bodies trying to see if anyone was a friend. My heart begins to pound and I glance among the people still alive, I find Zube, Jax, and... I don't see his chocolate eyes, his taunting smile, and his brown curls. No, no, no, no, no! It can't be!

"WHERE IS HE?" My scream echoes through the chamber and all the sentinels look at me. When I look toward Jax his blue eyes lift above me. A cry escapes me as I look up to the body hanging from the ribbons of white silk now stained red. It isn't Jeremiah, but my relief is short lived. My bones rattle beneath my skin and rage boils in my blood as sadness grips my heart. In Troglodyte fashion, Samuel hangs from the ribbons on the ceiling. His blood drips to the floor and I realize that my nightmare last week was more than just a dream. It was the future.

Samuel's hand, dangling down toward me as if reaching for his fellow friends, dead on the floor, has a piece of paper nailed to his palm. I almost vomit from the words sprawled across it in blood. It reads:
WINTER SOLSTICE

CHAPTER ELEVEN

~Ariadae~

Jeremiah is missing, taken by one of those snarling beasts, and only half of the court survived the attack. And although some of those men were extremely loyal and powerful Lords I don't find the heart within me to broach the idea of mourning. Too much death has already shattered my mortal heart and either way, I am no longer a human. I am a Fae.

Rage or confusion, I'm not sure which has me stumbling down the servant's passage to the dungeons. Evaflora may have used the attack to distract me while she took back Darwin. A part of me doesn't think that Evaflora would actually come into my home to retrieve him. She doesn't like her hands to get dirty even though they are stained in centuries of blood.

When I reach the bottom of the slim stairwell I push open the door into the dome chamber and my eyes lock onto the two guards, the ones who escorted me down here last week, the ones who are now shredded to ribbons. Darwin's cell door is gone and I notice the wood splinters scattered outward across the room. He broke out from *within*.

An older woman cries out in the chamber and I run to the maid, her brown threadbare gown and apron drenched in blood from the open wound in her gut. Her insides sit on her lap and I don't gag. Now is not the time for that. Tears stain her wrinkled face and I cup her cheeks in my bloodied hands and wipe away the water as it comes out from her eyes. Scarlet liquid covers her face. I hush her stuttering whimpers and help her calm her breathing. There is no way she is going to survive.

"What happened?" I ask my voice calm and kind. I don't want to pry for answers in a time like this, but I need to know. I have to find out what happened to my prisoner, Evaflora's right hand.

"I-I was bringing t-the prisoner's food," she points to the tray of food, broken in half. My vision blurs and I become aware of my brain spinning. It doesn't feel like my blood is pumping. My body becomes heavy, but my skull becomes light. "The door e-exploded and a beast with h-horns a-attack-ked u-us."

My eyes burn and I hug the woman before my blurred vision slants sideways and my skull smacks against the floor.

My dreams aren't dreams at all. They are nightmares full of blood, Evaflora, Darwin, and worst of all, Jeremiah. I hear his screams in the darkness that coils around me like a second skin. My mind can't imagine the horrors Evaflora will do to him. I should've stopped the Winter Solstice ball before it even started.

A girl's cries pull me from slumber. Through drenched, squinted eyes I see Desirae shaking and sobbing. "She was my mother! How could you let this happen?" She yells in my bedroom. The maid whose innards were in her lap was Desirae's mother.

I want to say sorry, but when I open my mouth a strangled noise escapes my lips. My mouth is desert dry and my throat feels like shards of glass are stabbing into my flesh. Desirae silences her sobs at the sound of my painful gasp and Jax runs to my bedside.

"Ariadae," he coos. A piece of me is still angry, but with the loss of Jeremiah still a fresh wound I push away my anger towards Jax and welcome him with heavy tears. "I'm so thankful you're all right. You drained your power." His voice fades away into the depths of my room and the unyielding, adamant darkness comes flooding back and steals me from consciousness.

I expect the dreams of Evaflora cutting open Jeremiah to arrive, but they never do. A soft mist billows around my ankles and turns the darkness into blinding light. A clouded vision surrounds me, rippling like water, I see the merchants that once travelled all of Abella to see Equadoria fill the streets. Citizens, no Fae from what I can see, bustle between the wagons and carts full of weapons, ivory carvings, and silk in a rainbow of colors. Everyone stays clear of the cobblestone streets.

Right as I ponder what I'm dreaming of, I see her. I see *me*. Only much, much younger than seventeen. My red curls bounce as I dance between the skirts and legs of walking people and twirl onto the road. I am happily unaware… a carriage drawn by two white steads comes racing down the cobblestones completely oblivious of their princess at the center of their trajectory.

I know what happens, but it doesn't stop the cringe and scream that escapes me and the citizens surrounding the scene. Jeremiah, slightly taller than me, yanks me from the street and into his arms. He uses his tiny threadbare cloak as a shield from the dust and rocks that fly from beneath the wheels of the carriage.

The dust tossed into the air consumes the apparition of my memory and transforms into the mist that paints a new memory around me. Days spent swimming in the fountains or times Jeremiah and I snuck out of the castle to escape studying. I watch my favorite memories of growing up with Jeremiah and it all leads up to the moment where we kissed by the fire, our first night in Elkwood.

His chocolate eyes reflect the crackling embers and I stare into his irises. A fading blanket of night is above us.

"Ariadae," he whispers. I lean forward and he grips my face. "Ariadae." He repeats and I pull away. "ARIADAE!"

I scream and the sound of my sore throat echoes through my bedroom. Jax grips my shoulders and Zube leans against the library doorframe. "What is it?" I rasp.

Jax opens his mouth as if to answer, but Zube's voice fills my ears. "You've been asleep for a week and four days."

No wonder I feel like a filthy vagrant. I don't care though. My throat still hurts and I notice I'm no longer dreary. "Holy shit," I mumble to myself. I look to Jax as he hands me a glass of water and a folded piece of parchment. A wax seal keeps the letter inside a secret to the world. I look to the crimson symbol. It is a sun, surrounded by twirling vines, the Summer Kingdom sigil.

"It arrived a day after the ball." Jax's voice is barely audible. "I didn't want to open it for you."

I gulp down the glass of water and place it onto the nightstand. Jax and Zube hover over me as I touch the yellowed paper and crack the wax in two. The letter reads:

Dear Ariadae Vox, Queen of Titanium Antlers,

I want to thank you for releasing Darwin and giving me a very special gift. I will play with him for a very, very long time.

Best wishes my little princess.

High Lady Evaflora, Queen of Diamond Antlers.

My stomach does flips as my beating heart regurgitates into my throat. A cold sweat breaks along my pores as I climb out of the bed wearing nothing, but my lacey undergarments.

"What is it?" Zube asks suddenly concerned. Jax rises and I drop the letter to the stones.

This can't be happening. It all makes sense. Why I had those dreams last night and before the ball. I should've known she would take Jeremiah! I sprint past Zube who grabs the letter from the ground and into the library.

"Ariadae," Jax calls after me as he stares at me confused. I tear apart the desk trying to find it. I lift up the first letter my mother wrote to me. As bold as darkened ink in a book, Jeremiah is specifically named. "What's wrong?"

"She was planning this all along. She knew damn well we would take Darwin into custody and planned the attack as a distraction for him to escape with Jeremiah!"

Zube, sickly pale, stares at the letter I dropped to the floor.

"How do you know?" Jax questions and I hold up the first warning she sent.

"Evaflora warned us that she was going to attack! She *named* Jeremiah!" I begin shouting as tears roll in thick streams down my cheeks.

Zube hands the new letter to Jax and whispers, "And this is written in his blood."

CHAPTER TWELVE

~Ariadae~

"We don't need an army," Zube seethes. He is fighting my argument like always.

"How do you expect us to fight back with only six dozen soldiers?" Jax jumps in. If Jeremiah were here than we wouldn't need to have this conversation and I'd already be on pursuit to acquiring my soldiers.

"Ariadae," Zube matches my glare. "You destroyed an entire legion of Evaflora's monsters! We don't need to have an army since you have those powers." I cross my arms over my chest.

My bedroom becomes suddenly tighter and I begin to feel the air be taken away. "Zube, I don't know how to use my power well enough! I drained myself and slept for a week and a half! We don't have that kind of time!" My voice bounces around the room like booming thunder. My words slicing into all of us like a blade. We all know I'm right, even if Zube doesn't want to admit it.

Jax notices the shout in my voice and cringes a bit. Zube joins him. I throw my arms out in silent question.

"Where would you get an army, anyway?" Zube's question has already run through my mind a thousand times since I learned my soldiers were obliterated.

"I didn't want to bring the problem of Evaflora to them, but I have to," My voice is almost a whisper. I'm finally becoming the queen I never wanted to be. "Evaflora wants to enslave the humans on Abella and Equadoria is not the only mortal kingdom. There are fourteen others and at some point Evaflora is going after them if she hasn't already."

"So, what are you saying?" Jax shifts his weight back and forth, signifying his discomfort. A chill shakes me from the core.

"We need to ask them for help-"

Zube cuts me off and mumbles, "You're not saying that you-,"

"Yes, she is," Jax cuts back into the debate. He can't read my mind like Zube, but he knows where I'm going with this. "We have to go back into Elkwood Forest."

After Zube, Jax, and I talked yesterday morning we have been preparing for entering the forest. The thought of going back in has caused an uncontrollable shaking to curse my body, and no matter how much I tell myself it's going to be different this time, the shaking won't stop.

Zube is going to be staying in Equadoria to make sure all is well. He isn't cursed like my father was, so I won't have to worry about my people. I know it's selfish, but I'm worried about myself. I had too many near death experiences and after the events of Elkwood and the curse my mother placed on my father I *did* die. What will this second trek through Elkwood entail?

I shake the gruesome memories that are replaying in my head from my mind and change out of my day gown and into a silk nightgown. The smooth pale blue fabric is chilled in the exposure of night. I head over to the hearth in the corner and poke the dimly glowing embers until they are crackling flames. The warmth wraps around me like a fur blanket and I take a seat on an ottoman before the red and orange flames. The slithering fingers of the fire claw up the chimney and waft smoke up the dark tunnel.

The bedroom door clicks open and a part of me thinks of Darwin breaking into the castle, but I know it's not him. Before I turn around the corded muscles of Jax's biceps coil around my chest and his face slides into the crook of my neck. I forgive his lies, but I will never forget them. His actions speak louder than any words.

"I'm sorry," He whispers. I shush him before he can bring up the subject again. Any conversation on that topic will only make me upset again.

"I don't want to talk about it tonight."

"What do you want to talk about?" He quirks and a grin twists my features. The shadows of the flames making me look devilish.

I lay against his hard body as he places his thighs on either side of mine, sitting with me on the ottoman. I don't want to think about going into Elkwood tomorrow, but I can't get the idea of that damned forest out of my mind.

"Do you think the mortals will believe us about Evaflora wanting to enslave them?" I feel Jax go taut at my question.

He doesn't wait very long to answer. "Why wouldn't they? They know that the immortals are still in Elkwood, right?"

"I honestly don't know." The humans and Fae haven't fought in centuries. Ever since the creation of the Book of Ash eighteen centuries ago, there hasn't been a documented or memorable war between the mortal and immortal. "What if we don't get an army?"

Jax spins me around so I can face him as I sit on his lap. His blue eyes glow in the firelight and I stare into them, looking for what he is going to say, what he is thinking, what he wants. I hear his heart begin to gallop.

"We will get an army, Ariadae," His voice is a seductive whisper in the darkness in my- *our* bedroom. "I was thinking before we attempt to acquire aid from the mortal kingdoms, we could go to an immortal one."

It's my turn for my heart to gallop. "The Fae have never fought alongside the humans. What Kingdom would even help us?"

I stare into Jax's eyes and think of the snow, the winter, a cold bitter day. He is a Fae and I was once a human, we fought side by side, and if he is from the Winter Kingdom than maybe his people think the same way as him!

"The Winter Kingdom," I say before he can tell me and he only nods. I place a kiss onto his lips and he doesn't hesitate to reciprocate. Our tongues begin to spar one another and our breaths come in hot, heavy pants. My pounding heart makes my blood pump wildly as I claw at Jax who just moans against my mouth. His thick lips taste like peppermint and his scruff scrapes against my cheek. He begins to rise and lifts me in the process. We don't break the kiss as he lays me down on the bed and slides my nightgown up, up, up until it's at my waist, exposing everything he wants to see. I realize how much he missed me these past two weeks by the strength in his kisses that now glide along my collarbone and the firm tent of his pants.

Words that I haven't thought about in a month slam in my skull like a hammer pounding a nail. *He isn't your mate.* I break the kiss and he looks down on me with a furrowed brow. His beautiful face set in intense confusion. *He isn't your mate.*

"I can't," My voice is barely a whisper. At some point, he lost his shirt, so he makes quick work of putting it back on.

"I understand." There is no anger or hatred behind his words. My heart still gallops and my mouth remembers the taste of his lips, but my heart is saying yes and my mind is saying no. He gives me a curt nod before he strides for the door.

"Wait!" I call after him and crawl to the end of the bed to grab his wrist. He looks back to me, eyes swelling with tears. "I don't want to be alone tonight." A single bloated tear escapes his eye lid and cascades down his cheek and onto my hand. He lifts it to his mouth and places a kiss on the salty droplet.

"All right," He smiles as he crawls onto the bed. I shift under the covers and he slides in behind me and locks his arms firmly around me. I stare at the crackling flames as he drifts into an unyielding sleep and I fall into an intransigent wakefulness.

I watch the fire descend to charcoal ashes and the darkness of my room slowly fades to a warm pink and orange. The sun came too soon and my eyes still have yet to droop at the call of sleep. I waited for hours and my brain doesn't desire unconsciousness, but instead wants to get to the Winter Kingdom before I'm carved up by a Dreag.

The Winter Kingdom is located at the peak of Archaic Mountain, which is the tallest mountain in the Archaic Mountain Range that divides Elkwood from the rest of the continent. Jax and I would be crossing over the mountain to get to the rest of the kingdoms, so why not pay a visit to his father, the High Lord of the Winter Kingdom.

Jax never moved throughout the night, but his steady breaths and slow beating heart tell me he is in the depths of sleep, so doing my best not to stir him, I unlock the cage of his arms from around me and silently leave the bed chambers.

The corridors and wings of the castle are silent as I tip-toe down hallway after hallway until I find my way to the Training Hall. The twin of the ballroom is quiet, but instead of the floor-to-ceiling windows being destroyed as they are in the ballroom, they are perfectly intact. I walk to a sword rack and pull a rapier from its scabbard. I open the patio doors. The shocking cold pulls the air from my lungs and I gasp. I take the air in greedy gulps that burn my throat and chest. My nightgown feels as if nothing is stopping the cold from nipping at my bones.

I swing the blade and listen to the sound of the steel slicing through the crisp air. I feel the ghost of Jeremiah correcting my technique. *'The angle of your wrist is off'* or maybe *'you're not holding the hilt correctly.'* I won't let Evaflora kill him. *If she hasn't already.*

A rasping intake of breath has me spinning on my heels, sword angled, at nothing. The patio doors idle wide open and from the looks of it nobody is around. My beating heart begins to calm.

A hand grabs a fistful of my hair, exposing my neck. I swing the sword over my shoulder, but a mangled, broken hand with exposed bone and missing flesh grips the blade happily. The wheezing fills my powerful hearing until it's all I hear. My first thought is a Forsaken has come from Elkwood and into my castle grounds again, but then I remember Darwin's burnt corpse. The hand isn't covered in healing burns though.

"Forgotten me, have you?" Novid, one of the sentinels who helped me in Elkwood, rasps and I'm sad to admit I have.

"My mind has been a bit busy lately," my quivering voice shakes wildly like the frightened girl I am. Last time Novid visited me was in my bedroom before my birthday. Gaston never appeared since before that. They have never touched me before, and yet he is dead. This is too real to just be a ghost from my mind.

"Your friend is alive." Until when I want to ask, but also wonder how he knows. "For now," Novid adds. I try to press down on the sword, but his grip is adamant. Why is a memory hurting me? Stopping me physically? I remind myself of what's going on. *He isn't real. He's not there. He is nothing.* The words Jax has me recite don't work. My heart skips in an unsteady beat.

"You're not real."

"Are you sure about that?"

No. "Yes," I mumble more to myself than Novid. A chill shakes my bones as a breeze passes along my skin. Fog doesn't coil from Novid's rasping breathes like it does mine.

"Meet the girl who sparkles like lightning and the male who blazes like a thousand suns."

"What?" I question. His ragged breathing vanishes and the fist that was tangled in my hair is gone. I spin around and he's gone with the passing wind as if he wasn't there at all.

"Are you all right?" A soft voice quakes from the patio doors and my scream shatters the silence of the morning. Desirae immediately regrets her question and runs to me. Her eyes are worried and her brow is furrowed. "What have you done?" She coos and gestures to my hands.

I suddenly feel the burn and realize my fist is locked around the blade of my rapier with an iron grip. Blood drips down the silver sword and it coats my hand. The small layer of snow that accumulated on the ground is covered in crimson droplets that surround my bare feet, almost blue from the cold. I shudder and Desirae guides me into the warm castle. The nearest guard blankets me with his cloak and I violently shake as Desirae holds a torn strip of fabric from her apron over my leaking palm.

I try to think over everything that just happened and realize I am crazy as she urges me onward. We quickly reach the infirmary because it isn't far from the Training Hall, for obvious reasons. I sit at the old wooden table and Desirae clatters around the room, obviously anxious because of the situation. She walked outside and witnessed her queen cutting open her hand in a nightgown. What has gotten into me?

"I'm sorry," I whisper breathlessly. "I don't know what was going on out there."

"Don't apologize, Your Majesty," her voice is humble and sweet like honey. I smile at the childish and nonthreatening sound of it. "Even the gods can't stop themselves from being a little crazy sometimes."

"Yes," I think of all the times Prometheus and his pantheon of gods saved me. I remember all of their faces, burned in my memory like an oil painting that will last forever. They are the reason I'm alive and they are the reason there is magic in this world. "We *all* are a little crazy."

She giggles to herself and finds some gauze and cloth in the many cabinets in the clean, white marble room. She takes a seat in front of me and quickly cleans and wraps my sliced palm. I look at her face, childish and unthreatening, welcoming even. She looks just like her mother.

The image of her mother sitting in the dungeon with her innards in my lap brands my mind. I shake away the memory and whisper, "I know what it's like to lose someone." My chest caves at the thought of my father. I barely stop the sob from heaving out of my throat.

"You don't need to offer me your condolences," Desirae mumbles. Tears swell in her eyes and my own vision starts to blur. I understand her pain. "You've suffered much more than I."

"No one gets to decide how much you've suffered. And I may look strong because I try to be," Desirae nods, unable to speak without crying. "I do it for my people, but to be honest," the sob I was holding back erupts from me and my cheeks become instantly wet. Desirae begins crying and grips my hands. I take a deep breath. "I am terrified. I am scared to go back into Elkwood today and I am nothing, but a lie. I lie because I have to, not because I want to." She hands me a small cloth and I wipe my face, as she wipes hers.

We sit there in silence for a while. I don't mind it, but at the same time I don't want time to think about what's going to happen today.

Desirae smiles, our eyes both red from crying, "Would you like some tea?"

"I would enjoy that very much!"

Noon came too soon and after a quick meal with Jax and Zube I'm standing with the two of them at the front doors of my castle. Zube's face is so pale I become actually worried for the man; I would never admit it though.

Jax just stares at the two of us, his fur clothing matches mine and is mixed with leather undertones. We want to be safe from the Forsaken and the weather. My own outfit is made from different hides, leather and my fur lined gloves and cloak top off the whole look of a huntress. I am no longer the queen I am known to be. Zube drapes a fox cowl over my shoulders and Jax's.

"You don't have to go," Zube mumbles. "I sent letters to the mortal kingdoms."

Jax rolls his eyes for me. "And you think those will really arrive?"

"No, but it's worth a try. I'd rather letters got lost to Elkwood than either of you."

I grab Zube's arm and glare at him. He is scared to be here by himself or maybe he really does fear for me and Jax traveling alone through Elkwood and across Abella. Whatever his problem is, it needs to be gone before Jax and I leave.

I try to speak my mind as simply as possible. "I am fucking terrified of going back into Elkwood forest, but if this wasn't important than I wouldn't be doing it. I appreciate you sending the letters, but I'm trying to gather an army, not some new shoes. I need to go," my eyes fall on Jax. "*We* need to go."

Zube nods and looks to the floor like an ashamed child. "I just remember what happened to us when we first went in. What happens if you don't come out this time? We could lose this war and your mother will destroy everything."

"It's different this time," Jax cuts in and smirks. *I hope so.* "We will come back."

"We'll be fine," I add. "I promise. Just make sure everything runs smoothly here and don't let worry cloud your judgement. "

He nods, so Jax and I give him our departing hugs before Jax shifts into the white tiger I used to know him to be. Zube quickly helps me lay some supplies onto Jax's hips and shoulder blades. I mount him and I depart from Zube with a brush of our hands as he hands me six quivers and a bow. I pray to Prometheus this isn't the last time I see Zube.

Jax sprints into the cold before I can change my mind about leaving Zube behind. During the Winter Solstice ball when the Forsaken attacked the castle some stragglers ran through Equadoria. I notice the damage they caused throughout the kingdom as we ride down its cobblestone streets. Doors are torn from their hinges and sides of houses are covered in claw marks and dried blood. My stomach does cartwheels as I see more and more of the devastation. We dart past a particularly small girl with thick, fresh slices down her face. It mars her beautiful features, but in my eyes, she is still gorgeous. Our scars tell stories that make us who we are. I'm glad all of mine haven't vanished.

The closer we get to the edge of Equadoria the worse the damages gets. Some houses are nothing but rubble, and the slums look like a war zone. Arrows from Troglodytes stick out of rotting bodies and the wooden walls and doors of the small houses. With the lack of guards, I didn't have enough men to protect the borders. And this amount of devastation could not appear from just the night of the Winter Solstice ball. This has to be months of attacks. What have I been doing? I should've focused on this place first! The slums are right on the border of Elkwood Forest, so how could I have been so naïve to believe that there wasn't attacks? I've been so wrapped up in everything with Jeremiah, and the lies in my court, that I haven't thought about the people who need me most. The citizens who can't protect themselves look to me for help and I didn't look back. I turned my head in disbelief of what was happening. Once I get an army and the threat of my mother is gone this will all be over.

The citizens wandering aimlessly about are shaking in the cold. They glare at me and Jax as we ride past. I know they aren't staring at Jax as much as they are angry at me. I want to say sorry, but my father always said actions speak louder than words, so I will show them I haven't forgotten. I will fix everything in the end, but this, going into Elkwood, is the first step of many to build a better, safer world.

I pull up my hood in an attempt to avoid their glares, but even the wind making my eyes blur doesn't stop me from noticing the heavy stares. I've failed as a queen.

Before I can leap from Jax and forget my mission, Jax heeds onward until he slows to a stalking gait towards Equadoria's gate. The towering stone walls haven't stopped the Forsaken from entering, but they will be a defense against my mother and her army from destroying everything immediately.

"Open the gates!" I call to the watchmen in the towers high above. I'm surprised my voice carried through the howling wind, but the groan of the gate opening tells me they know what I asked whether they heard or not. "Thank you!" I shout as Jax slowly leaves the protection of the kingdom behind. His walk may be normal, but for me, every step closer to Elkwood forest is in slow motion. My beating heart gallops like a sprinting horse as he ascends the hill. The towering Elkwood trees, bare of any leaves, loom above our head, blocking out the grey sky.

CHAPTER THIRTEEN

~Ariadae~

The silence of Elkwood is just how I remember it, suffocating. Besides that, all familiarity is gone. Elkwood was full of lush plants and life all green in the mid spring, but now snow covers the ground making Jax's paws silent. All life seems void from existence.

My eyes are always scanning around us, and Jax's mane bristles at every groan of heavy tree boughs moving in the wind above our heads. As much as we hate to admit it, we are both terrified, especially here, in the forest of nightmares.

He stops for a moment of breath after trekking through mounds of white for two hours. I slide down from his back hoping to ease some of the weight on his spine. With a blinding light, he shifts back into his common form, Fae-form. His tousled black curls instantly become covered in a layer of snow that is lightly falling around us. His pointed ears are blushed pink, like the tip of his nose. The frigid cold reaches my bones, he must feel the same. The supplies that were on his tiger hips are now on his human-like back, the straps wrapping around his chest blending in with his bandoleer covered in knives. We're ready for anything.

"It's too quiet," I whisper, afraid my voice might summon a monster I'll recognize all too well.

Jax's ice blue eyes seem to glow in the growing darkness of Elkwood. I feel as if I'm walking through a nightmare, and his eyes are the only source of light in the surrounding shadows. "It's always quiet."

We head south and continue on foot. With the heavy thick snow, minutes feel like hours, and a soft ache slithers up my back. I want to ask Jax to shift back to the strong, fast moving beast, but I know that'll only tire him even more and if he's too tired to fight... I don't want to be left alone, or have him run off like last time. I can still hear his strangled howl when the Wood Nymph had dragged its claws down his back. I didn't know he was a Fae back then.

"How do we know when we reach the Archaic Mountain Range?" my question lingers for too long and I almost think Jax didn't hear me. When I am about to verbalize my thought again he finally responds.

"When we start going up," he mutters. What is with him? Everything seemed fine right before we left, so a moody Jax is not what I plan on dealing with at the moment. "It's obvious enough."

My nonexistent patience snaps. It's not like I pretend to have much of one anyway. "Why are you being such an insufferable ass? I've done nothing to you," my voice is louder than I thought. We both scan the surrounding brambles for any oncoming threats, but nothing arrives.

He heaves a sigh and glares at me. "I'm just nervous, alright?" He says angrily. I'm nervous too, but I'm not being a dick about it. "I don't want it to be like last time. I don't want you to be taken away!" Of all the places we were going to argue, I didn't think it would be *here.*

"You said to Zube that it isn't going to be like last time. And besides, I'm not just some weak little girl anymore," I growl. My primal Fae instincts have been going through the roof since the start of the monthly demon that claws out my insides. Jax isn't helping with my aching pains.

"But you are," Jax rebuttals. I lift my eyebrows in complete surprise. His face softens as he immediately regrets the words, "I didn't mean-"

"Don't," I whisper with a killer's calm. I don't want to hear his lengthy exasperated apology for voicing his thoughts, so if that's what he thinks of me, then I'll change his mind. He stops trying to speak and closes his mouth. *Smart man.* "I know what you meant."

Before he can respond a twig snaps in the bush behind Jax, he spins around snarling and I draw my bow faster than I thought I could. The feeling of the weapon in my hands is surprisingly foreign, but I let my muscle memory take over and try not to think about what I'm doing. My pounding heart resounds in my skull and I feel the blood pumping through my veins. Jax's cloak billows in the wind which also tosses the snow in swirling mists across my vision. Jax's guttural snarl is greeted by a deep, heavy growl rippling from the brambles, which are surprisingly dark in the afternoon light.

Time slows and every hair on my body stands on end. *Shoot*, my Fae instincts seem to purr and the arrow whistles into the bush. An ear-splitting howl shakes the trees above and large ravens take flight when the ginormous wolf leaps from the brush. Jax shifts into his white tiger form and the two beasts, equal in size, tumble to the ground where they wrestle through the snow. The wolf's fur is obsidian and I see the flash of its eyes, glowing green. I try to fire an arrow, but every time I go to release the string they flip and the arrowhead is trained on Jax. I don't know how to help without hurting him. Suddenly I realize something very important. Wolves never attack alone; they are pack hunters.

The snow behind me churns and I scurry to the right as another monstrous wolf, a twin of the first, erupts from the brush. This wolf's eyes meet mine; fear constricts my chest as I notice the beast is *crouching*. Monstrous is only an understatement of their true unfathomable height.

It bears yellow teeth and I smell the carrion on its breath. I draw another arrow and it pounces. I fall to my knees as the leaping wolf flies over me, my arrow strikes home in it's under belly. It doesn't even seem fazed as I aim at the monster again. Before I can fire the arrow the wolf is on top of me. Too fast. These wolves are moving too fast to be actual animals. It pins me to the ground within the snow. The fur of the beast is suffocating me as it growls in my face and opens its maw to strike. With the invisible hands of my telekinesis, I feel the wolf's bones beneath its flesh. Using an iron grip, I hold the ribcage and break the bones one by one, pressing inward. The splintered morrow shreds the beast's lungs and innards. It immediately whimpers and cries. The fur slides into its skin and the flesh flips into scales. The wolf has become a large lizard that struggles to scurry off into the brush. Before it can leave, I retrieve my bow and fire two arrows through its body, pinning the monster to the ground.

The silence of the forest muffles the beating of my heart which floods my skull with sound. In a panic, I glance back at Jax. Consumed with my own battle, I had completely forgot about him. He is no longer the white tiger and the wolf he was fighting is now a polar bear. Its white fur is covered in crimson blood and its stomach is torn open. Its fur and skin has sunken in as if…as if Jax broke every one of its bones. I guess the ideal way of killing these beasts is internally.

"What were they?" my question simple after the chaotic events that just occurred.

"Demised," Jax answers me and I quirk my eyebrow in question. "There are four clans of Forsaken; Dreag, Troglodyte, Arbor, and Nymph. Beneath those clans, in a form of hierarchy, are Factions. The Demised are beasts that can shift into any animal form."

Great, right when I thought I had an understanding of what I was going to be facing in Elkwood, a different breed of monster attacks. "Are there any others?"

"Yes," he mumbles as he wipes the blood from his mouth and hands onto the snow. "There is a second faction called the Umbra." A chill slides down my back as it seems my Fae instincts already know what they are. "They are the shadows and darkness that conjure your worst fears and use them against you until we are driven into insanity. The Akuji's henchmen when he raids your dreams." I remember the Akuji during my first trek through Elkwood when it gave me the scar on my shoulder, but the Umbra, I do not remember encountering it unless…I look down at my hand, still wrapped with the bandages from Desirae. "What is it?" Jax verbally wonders.

I want to tell him about the incident with Novid before we went into Elkwood, but then I remember our argument moments before the Demised attacked. "Nothing, let's go." I pull the arrows I fired from the Demised and refill my quiver, but when we begin walking again I can't stop looking at my hand. I can still see the cut across my palm. I saw Novid holding my sword, and pulling my hair, but when Desirae came outside he was gone, vanished, and *I* was gripping the blade. I knew it wasn't just a normal haunting from Novid, but now I ponder if it was an Umbra. How long have they been coming and haunting me in my own home? Was the Umbra the being that woke me up from sleep the night I found the first letter from my mother? A part of me whispers *yes*.

Over the course of the day the grey sky had melted into a palette of bleeding reds and purples that blended together beautifully along the canvas above. Night is coming. With every anxious breath and aching beat of my leg muscles, that keep pushing me through the deep snow, is another minute closer to the impenetrable dark that shadows the Forsaken so well. The curse that transformed all of the Succumbus Fae into the Forsaken had kept the monsters within Elkwood's borders, never allowed to leave the forest's edge because, as Fae, they broke the written rule of the Book of Ash. The stated law is that the Fae and humans must not cross the Elkwood borders into opposing land, but they didn't listen and they were punished by the gods for it. The Tree of Light, when it was chopped down by my mother, cleaved all of the curses at the root, allowing the Forsaken to now be able to leave Elkwood. I know they attacked my kingdom, but I pray they haven't headed south into the unsuspecting Mortal Kingdoms.

Snow clings to the different furs and hides that keep me warm. I haven't felt the cold bite of winter anywhere except my exposed face for a bit of time. The hood of my night-black cloak barely deflects the unyielding gusts of wind that throw Jax and me off our balance. I glance over to him. The wind throws a mist of snow into the air, making him look like a shadow beast, an Umbra in the only form I can imagine it. As the sky becomes a midnight blue, I grow aware that I can see every single star that twinkles in the swath of fabric above. Winter nights are the clearest skies I have ever seen. The sight is stunning. A shudder slithers to my core as I realize that night doesn't only bring beautiful skies, but also blood thirsty creatures.

"How much farther do we have to go?" I shout my question against the roaring of the wind. The howling is deafening.

Jax's immaculate hearing picks up my voice and he holds out his arm before his face as if that is going to stop the flurries from digging into his eyes and nipping at his skin. "We are almost at the base of the mountain!" his words sound muffled, but I pick up everything he says, I think.

"How do you know?" I don't know the last time he went to his birth home, but even for someone who knows Elkwood like the back of their hand, they would be lost in this blinding snow. I walk closer to him, so I can stop screaming so loud. He becomes clearer the closer I get and I quickly scan the surrounding brambles. There aren't many bushes to hide the wicked monsters.

"Look," he points up and my eyes trail his finger toward the trees that dance in the gusts of wind. No longer are they the Elkwood trees that I remember, tall and thick, the roots seeping into the ground and spider webbing the dirt. Now, they are bleeding into tall pines that are narrower and erupt in dark needles that blend above our heads. "Pine trees cover the entire mountain range and bleed into the Mortal Kingdoms bordering the opposite side." I nod in understanding and begin to notice the uphill lift in the snow. When I look forward, many yards ahead, I see the wall of snow that is the slanting mountain side. We're almost there.

The strong wind seems to instantly shift directions, and the soft flurries become heavy flakes that accumulate quickly on the already deep snow. A gale has reached the mountain just as we have and I feel the heat of Jax next to me, but when I look over I barely see him through this surprise blizzard. The cold blossoms like chilled seeds along the skin beneath my clothes and I shout to Jax, "We need to make camp! This is enough for the night!" I pray we survive it because it seems that there is nowhere to hide or take shelter.

Jax found a cave quite quickly, chasing my previous fears. We laid out all of our supplies in a nice pyramid towards the back of the tunnel to keep it safe and somewhat dry. At the mouth of the cave the snow is horizontal and Jax sits on a rock close enough to reach his hand out and grasp the flakes speeding past like a rushing river of white.

I unroll the fur lined sleeping sacks and I watch my breaths coil into the air within the darkness of this frigid cave. Icicles hang from the ceiling, so I make sure to put the beds in clear spots, so that if we end up lighting a fire, nature's spear wont skewer us in our sleep. If we get any sleep at all.

Jax just sharpens each of the blades on his bandoleer and I change the bandages on my hand. The cut isn't bleeding anymore and looks to be pretty clean, despite the blood that had covered them after the Demised attacked us. Jax's lips have darkened and his hands are stained with the metallic scent. I smell it from the opposite end of the cave and try not to gag at the thought. A cord of tension is taut between us in this silence and I have no idea how to clip it, so instead I ignore it. "We need to start a fire if we want to stay warm."

The whine of the stone striking Jax's blade makes my skin crawl. He doesn't answer me and although it wasn't a question, I expected a response. Maybe I should stop having expectations of people.

"Unless you plan on us freezing to death in your sleep," I add with a drop of venom in my words. He heaves a sigh that echoes through the dark grotto like a thunderous clap.

"Fine," he huffs and I can't help, but feel a bit smug. "I'll get some fire wood, but don't leave the cave. If I don't come back, go to the Winter Kingdom. They'll know what to do." I don't let the thought of his words sink in. I may be upset and we may happen to be arguing, I guess, but he'll come back. I know it.

He sheathes his newly sharpened blades and gives me a thin-lipped smile as he steps into the blizzard beyond. As a way to not notice his absence, I bide my time counting our supplies. We've got four outfits each, one for every type of environment. Four bows with six quivers, along with the six that Zube gave me. There are two satchels flooding with seasonings, spices, and medical necessities. During the trip in the summer, I remember we reverted to plants and herbs for medical supplies because the Troglodytes raided our camp and killed our horses.

After getting bored with organizing the supplies, twice, I gather some rocks around the grotto and make a nice circle at its center. Using my hands, I dig a small divot into the dirt and create a little pit where the fire will be. I even go as far as rolling up extra blankets to use as seats around the fire pit. My creation is complete. Well, almost complete. Jax just needs to return with the fire wood. So I wait.

And wait.

And wait.

And wait.

He doesn't come back. At first, I panic and pace around the cave because I don't know what to do as my mind thinks of a thousand things at once. He told me not to leave the cave, but he also said that if he doesn't come back that I should head to the Winter Kingdom. I know it shouldn't take almost an hour to find fire wood, but then again there is a gale outside and we're in Elkwood Forest.

I look towards the blizzard and see that the falling snowflakes are still horizontal, telling me that I have a strong chance of not making it there or even finding my way through the forest. The darkest shadows of night are beyond the cave mouth, but so is Jax. I won't-*can't* leave him to the dangers of Elkwood alone, not like last time when he got hurt. No matter how angry I am at him, he is still my friend. Someone I love.

I strap a quiver over my shoulder and snatch up my bow from the pile of supplies. I nock an arrow and stalk towards the unyielding storm. A thousand howls from outside resound in my ears and I wasn't prepared for how dark it is. The white snow seems to glow beneath the moonlit night, but the darkness of shadows is darker, blacker than before. My senses are on fire and my head is screaming *no, turn back*! But my heart pushes me forward, into the depths of Elkwood Forest. Jax couldn't have gone too far.

I haven't walked far from the cave mouth, but when I look back its gone, and I sob when I realize, *so are my footprints*. My way back to the cave has vanished and I run back from where I came. More trees, more pines, more snow. I am completely turned around. I run south and realize I'm heading down the mountain. My path should be up, so I quickly turn back around and start treading upward. I pray to the gods that I find Jax along my way.

I feel like I have wandered for hours, alone in the dark, when I stumble upon a pile of thick sticks. He was here. *Jax is here.* "Jax!" I shout instinctively. The quicker I find him the faster I will be able to head to the Winter Kingdom. I can't leave him behind! A screaming gust of wind answers my call. He might not be able to hear me, so I shout louder than before. "Jax!"

"Jax!" a voice echoes from beside me and I scream instantly terrified. I regret leaving the cave. I regret leaving Equadoria. I regret *everything*. But I can't go back now, not after I've come so far. The young girl with the clawed face flashes through my mind and I know that my kingdom needs me, the humans of Abella need me.

The echoing voice comes from a pine. The thin trunk could barely hide a person behind it, and my hands begin to shake out of fear instead of the cold. I feel with my telekinesis around the bark and the ghost of my hands touches a small fleshy arm. I recoil and the pain sparkles through my veins on que. No longer does the dark haunt me. The Void spirals and swirls around my splayed palm illuminating the snow barren forest a violet purple. My cloak snaps like a flag in the wind and I stare at the trunk, waiting, beckoning for the beast to show itself. It does just as I wish.

Small fingers slide up the bark of the dry pine and a child peeks from behind it. I don't rid my power as I take in the details of the delicate child's solemn face. The young boy's hair is midnight black and his porcelain skin is cracked, black veins spider web from his neck and bleed into his face. His eyes, maybe once blue or gold, are now a glowing red. A storm cloud of crimson roils in his whole eye, no pupil or iris visible. "Hello Queen of Titanium Antlers," he purrs and I barely hesitate as the purple flames fly from my palm, obliterating the tree and the apparition of the boy. My Fae instincts tell me exactly what that demon boy is and it's no monster to hesitate attacking. I peer around the violet forest for any more Umbras.

The Void is still in my grasp and I feel the sparkling pain of it sliding through my veins and beneath my skin. It's a living, breathing thing that pulses within me. I look everywhere in the purple wilds surrounding me. All I see are dashing shadows, glowing red eyes, and the snowflakes, still hailing from the blizzard. My pounding heart hammers against my ribcage like a drum, so hard it's almost painful. My body doesn't stop shaking and the hair on my skin is standing on end. The Fae senses at my core are screaming and roiling with confusion and fear at the disorienting snow.

A wicked laugh cackles into the air and my heart stops its heavy thrum. My eyes flick to my right and I see the woman I hate the most. My mother has arrived.

I scramble away and begin running down the mountain. My feet can't move fast enough as tears cascade down my cheeks. I stumble into a barrel-roll tumbling through the snow. I break through branches of trees, thorn bushes shattering beneath my body. The small needles are impaled into my flesh through the fur outfit and leather armor.

My descent stops and I get my feet under me as I wipe the tears from my face, my hand catching on thorns in my cheeks and blood stains the fur on my gauntlets. I look up at Evaflora, my enemy, the villain to my hero story, and worst of all, my mother. She smiles down at me. When I fell down the mountain, my powers slipped from my grasp, so I quickly illuminate the dark, a violet torch in the night, and take in the full image of my mother. Her dress is made of dark leather, scaled like a dragon's skin. Darkness mixes with her obsidian hair, unbound, as it flicks through the wind like tentacles. I know it isn't my mother because tendrils of night don't seep from her body on the passing wind. The boy, my mother, they're the Umbra. I had speculated earlier, but I am sure now.

Green flames erupt to life at the creature's fist and the colors of its fire and my Void battle in the darkness that ripples like ocean waves around us. Before the Umbra can kill me, I toss a ball of roiling purple at it and it dodges the blow with ease and vanishes into the dark above.

"No, no, no," I mutter to myself. The blizzard doesn't hide my voice or the snapping branches of the beast sprinting towards me out of the darkness. I can't see the details of what it is, but I notice the obsidian silhouette in the shadows approaching from my left. I break into a sprint heading further down the mountain dodging tree after tree, dancing between the trunks that seem to lean in my way. A guttural howl, familiar to my ears, resounds from behind me, the source of the pounding steps quick on my heels. I cast an orb of purple smoke-like flames at a tree and orange fire immediately blasts in the face of the beast behind me. It hisses at the flames and I don't waste time looking back.

I no longer hear an attacker in pursuit of me, but I don't stop running. The slanted ground soon becomes level and I'm trudging through the heavy snow, panting, every breath is burning my lungs from the core. I tried to find Jax and instead found the damn Umbra.

I try to make sense of my surroundings, but everything looks the same. Pine trees shoot up towards the sky and snow, thick and heavy, clumps around my calves. I am lost in the forest of monsters, nightmares, horrors. The Forsaken will likely eat me up before I can even find the Winter Kingdom. I want to start walking towards the birth place of Jax, but I think better of it. I just ran down the mountain from the Umbra and whatever beasts are also on Archaic Mountain. I don't want to walk straight back to them, not yet anyway.

On that thought, I start walking away from the mountain. I'd much rather arrive at Equadoria than be stuck in Elkwood. Fear flows through my veins, pumping quickly thanks to my fast beating heart. The rush of adrenaline when fighting the Umbra made me forget the bitter cold which is now creeping back through my damp clothing. The pelts and furs lining my leather-plaited armor are likely ruined. All of the supplies I would need are in the damn cave, lost from me, as I am lost from Jax, as Jeremiah is taken from us.

When my legs get too tired and my body aches from pushing forward, I finally collapse in the snow. The Void is locked away inside me and no longer painfully pulsating beneath my skin. I stare up at the sky and almost laugh at the pink now shattering the palette of night. The moon is still an adamant silver disk in the sky, but the sun will come out soon. The blizzard has either stopped or isn't reaching the base of the mountain. The pines still tower above me and I take my breaths in slow, greedy, gulps. *One. Two. Three.*

A snarl shakes the bones inside me from the trees nearby. A sob shatters through my weak, tired, aching body and I rise on shaking legs. The sky now becoming light allows more visibility in the forest of nightmares and I see the Dreag's grey, sandpaper skin crouched close to the snow next to a tree. I unstring my bow and fire an arrow at the beast. It misses and the Forsaken leaps from the brush. Three more arrows take flight in seconds from my quiver and I dodge the descent of the falling corpse. Its black blood leaks into the snow making the body sink further into the blanket of white mounds. I stare down at the Dreag and poke it with my fur boot; it doesn't twitch, satisfying my unease. I take a deep breath in the following silence that is music to my ears.

"Why don't you love me?" his familiar voice coos from behind. I scream in joy and spin to face my best friend, my lover, and not my mate. His words suddenly slap me in the face and I look at him for any signs of cuts or damage. Black blood covers him from head to toe and a small cut is stark on his cheek bone.

"I *do* love you," I whisper, my voice carrying throughout the forest clearing. I don't know why he is bringing this to me right now, but I'm just happy he's safe. The small, slowly falling flurries waltz around us. Relief fills my pores, but so does regret. "I'm sorry." I step towards him and a tear slides from his eye, trailing through the blood on his face before collapsing into the snow. I approach him on staggering feet and another voice, also familiar to my ears, echoes from behind me.

"Don't trust him," a second Jax steps from behind a tree and my relief vanishes instantly. I glance between the two of them and I hate to admit that there are no defining characteristics separating one from the other. In my eyes, they are both Jax. But I know one is not. I nock an arrow and draw the bow on instinct. "He's an Umbra." I am quite aware of that. But I almost cry as my shaking arms barely keep the arrow on the string.

The first Jax to appear lifts his hands at the sight of my arrow trained on him. "Ariadae, you know it's me, I'm the real Jax." How do I choose? Who do I choose? This is my worst nightmare. "You don't think we're mates and now you don't believe I'm real. What more could this cursed world bring my way?"

The second Jax jumps in. "Ariadae! Kill him! You know it's me! *I'm* Jax." I feel like I'm flipping a coin. My bow groans and my muscles continue to shake from holding the string. My grip is slowly slipping and I bite my lip as I try to come up with a decision.

"I-I," I can't keep the shaking from my voice. "I don't know." What if I kill the wrong one? What if the second Jax is making me choose because he knows if I kill the real one than he can take me to Evaflora? Or is the Umbra not part of her army because they follow the Akuji? I'll think on that later, but right now I try to find a way to survive my worst fear, my worst nightmare. My aim is starting to sway and tremble, more than before.

"Kill him," the first Jax seethes. "He is going to murder you."

"Ariadae," the second Jax begs and I hold back a frustrated sob. "It's me. I'm Jax."

Right as the arrow slips from my grasp and the string snaps, I hear the echo of the bowstring from off the mountain. Another arrow, not my own, from my right, whistles through Jax one and Jax two. The two males explode in a cloud of dark smoke like the apparition of the boy. An indecipherable sound erupts from my throat and I look to the source of the arrow. The most beautiful male I have ever seen stands next to a tall pine and I gather in his features. Long, shoulder length, dirty blond waves frame his angular face, covered in dark stubble and his eyes seem to pulse with light. They are a sea-green blue and my heart melts. With the recent shifting of the Umbra I draw my bow at the hunter in defense.

"Jax made it to the Winter Kingdom last night," the deep male's voice glides along my bones like smooth silk and I seem to shudder, in a good way. I shake the euphoric thoughts from my brain and remind myself this beautiful faerie is a stranger. Maybe even an Umbra. "Half of the Frost Guard has been trenching their way through the Archaic Mountain Range for most of the night. I am assuming you are, Ariadae Vox."

"Yes," I say, sounding like the queen I am. "And who are you?"

"Kane Drenth Archaeminza, Jax's brother."

"Heir to the Winter Kingdom throne," I finish for him and he smirks with a lopsided grin that makes him too handsome for his own good. Oh how this male could get me in trouble.

"Let's get you back to safety."

Part Two
LORD OF FROST

CHAPTER FOURTEEN

~Fayla~

The Vampyre kings and queen are staying for a month at the castle. I have a month to be with him, Lunan, my mate. I don't understand how it can be. Even though I'm half Vampyre and half Fae I can still have a mate. What makes the whole scenario even stranger is that mates are, so beyond rare, they practically don't exist. Until now, I've never met mated Fae or even heard of someone having a mate, but I know what it is, I knew what that feeling between us was.

After the unplanned arrival of the Vampyre royalty last night, Acacius sensed something was wrong and sent me to my bed chambers. I didn't get to see our guests be paraded through the castle on a grand tour, but the picture of his beautiful, but marred face is burnt into my brain like an image stained to a wooden plaque.

When I saw Lunan I felt something deep in my gut, heard my body tell me what he was. Before the voice whispered in my skull I felt it, my heart beat, for the first time in months since my transformation into a Vampyre.

I pull my legs tighter to my body as the water around me in the tub ripples; it has been cold for quite some time. I ignore the chill that now touches my warm body. The feeling of my heart beating and blood pumping is so foreign to me that I almost laugh at the tingling sensation beneath my skin. I was alive for twenty years before I became a Vampyre and in less than six months, practically minutes on my immortal lifetime, I've forgotten the feeling.

For once in my Vampyre life I actually slept during the day. Now that the other Vampyre royals are at the castle, I know Acacius won't go outside and there are more eyes watching us. We can't risk being caught by Molaris, nor her frenemies. I take careful precautions in the passing days. This evening I awoke to an insistent knock at my door. I opened it in a heat of anger and was greeted, not by a person, but a rather large box on the ground at my feet. I have yet to open the gift, *or trap,* that is now sitting on my bed.

I quickly glide the obsidian rock of dye through my silver hair making it black and quickly plait the wet strands. When I step from the stone tub, the water an inky black from the color, frigid air kisses my skin. A thousand droplets twinkle on my slightly tanned body. The sun had certainly made its mark on my skin and I understand why Molaris was so persistent to question me last night before the arrival. She knows that I haven't been sleeping during the day. That, in addition my tanned skin is basically waving a flag in her face, announcing I am not a pure Vampyre. I need to start being smarter with my decisions, especially now that my mate is somewhere here in this castle probably just as close to my enemy as me. And although I have no idea where he is staying, if I close my eyes and follow the feeling in my gut I know I'll find him in a lavish chamber of red and black. It feels as if a tether is connecting me to him, keeping us together, even when we're apart.

I leave the bathroom behind me as I head to the ominous box, sinking into the plush blanket on my bed. Whatever's inside must be a bit heavy if it is being absorbed by the comforter. The silver box is wrapped in a gold silk ribbon, tied neatly at its top. A small folded paper is tucked beneath the knot of the bow. I pull the card from the box and open it. The paper reads, in flawless handwriting:

It would mean a lot if you wore this to the feast tonight. I picked it out myself and only the most beautiful Faerie in all the land could pull off such an elaborate piece of artwork. It will be ravishing on only you, Milady.

No name is printed at the bottom of the parchment and I tear the paper into minuscule pieces. I don't need a name to see who it is. I can smell the warmth and sun on the shreds. He doesn't know I'm a Vampyre. He thinks I'm a Faerie in a Vampyre court. I don't need anyone cleaning through my room to find the ripped paper and put the pieces together like a puzzle, so I toss the shreds into the hearth. I stalk back to the box and tear away the ribbon that flutters to the ground before lifting the lid, revealing the masterpiece within. The gown is folded tightly into the square space and when I yank the golden dress from its package many, many, many lace and tulle skirts pool onto the floor. The gown is a warm gold, like a sunset yellow, and the bodice is like a large heart. The strapless top is made of fine, smooth lace. Crystals and gems of every shade of yellow are sewn to it like a mirror.

It takes far longer than I wish to put the artistry on and when I stare at the mirror in my room, surprised by how well I fill out the dress. The fire makes me look like a radiating star. I am a burning sun in the dark night of Crimson Island and I quickly apply some makeup onto my face. I put kohl on my eyes, a pale pink tint onto my lips, and lastly some dark color to fill out my cheeks. My dry, onyx hair is crimped from the braid. I toss the length over my head, hiding my usual middle part and causing a dramatic, yet elegant lift to my otherwise lifeless waves. I set the new part with a glittering golden comb and rise from my vanity where I keep my makeup.

The red and black chamber of my room is awkward against the bright coloring of my dress.

A curt knock jumps me from my thoughts and I run to answer the door. It could be him, I think to myself. But to my disappointment Acacius waits behind the wood. "Don't you look," he chews on the right words to say. "Quite ravishing?" He doesn't look bad himself as I notice the velvet black tunic, accented and trimmed in gold.

"Thanks," I say sounding more bland than gleeful. He quirks his eyebrows in silent question. I make a twin of his look.

What's wrong? He asks within my mind and I roll my eyes before walking down the hall towards the familiar entry hall. The disappointment must be written all over my face, so I shake away my features and place a permanent smile onto my lips. He runs after me and takes my arm in his before we arrive at the stairs that lead up to the throne room. We ascend the flight, my trailing skirts gliding up the steps, and reach the platform above, but make a left turn to uncharted territory. Many servants bustle through the dark corridors, illuminated by a few lamps on the walls. The dark light doesn't stop my eyes from glancing at the crescent moon scars on the servant's necks. Almost all of them have visible signs of being fed on. I wonder if, besides the girl Acacius saved, if any human in this castle hasn't been fed on. Each scar on a human body is a reminder of what I am and what Lunan thinks I'm not. What if he hates me for being a hybrid? My stomach threatens to spill on the floor.

Acacius doesn't notice my discomfort and keeps leading me onward down the never-ending corridor. The walls become barer and thicker, cobwebs fill the alcoves and cover the statues. I know we are somewhere that Molaris never uses. The doors at the end of the hall gape open like a yawning mouth and Acacius enters the room with a wide grin. I try to match his smile, but my eyes defy me. The two kings and queens glare at us and don't even care about the adamant anger on their faces. They are outright bored with this dinner and it hasn't even started.

Lunan is seated next to Tyrion and I get the best seat of the house, across from the Vampyre king and between Scout, to my right, and Acacius, to my left. Molaris is seated at the head of the table and Aaron is beside her and Tyrion is next to him. Strange looking Vampyre's, fill the other two-thirds of the dark wooden table that dwarfs the dining chamber. A glittering chandelier hovers above the feast spread out before us. I ignore the livers and organs, my stomach turning at the thought of the people being carved up to feed the monsters sitting around me. No longer do I care to feed on human's blood. My discomfort must reek because I notice Scout's nostrils flare. Her sea-green eyes seem to be welcoming, but her demonic smile and face say otherwise. I hate to admit it, but she is regal in the black gown, accented in scarlet red.

Molaris is holding the title of queen very tightly tonight with a crown of twisting black thorns that circles her skull, like a demon's halo, atop her head. Her once short, but now long ivory hair is braided over a shoulder and her dress, tightfitting to show off her alluring curves, is made of scarlet lace. I swear its blood red in the light of the dining hall. She keeps a horrifying grin plastered to her face as she scans the guests around the table, one by one, taking it all in person by person, Vampyre by Vampyre. Her iridescent irises hold onto me for a minute too long as they glide over my dress and then shift to Scout.

Aaron is the first to speak. "You have a truthfully beautiful home, Molaris."

Tyrion quickly jumps in, pulling the attention back to him. "Not as wonderful as my castle in Vampyra." I can only imagine what the Vampyre Kingdom must look like because from what Acacius taught me is that Molaris is the only Vampyre to not have a kingdom with living citizens in it. She just has a castle on Crimson Island and lets her court stay within the confinements of it. Tyrion has the biggest kingdom, homing over forty thousand Vampyres. Tyrion's eyes slide to me and my skin immediately crawls beneath his stare. "Or maybe I'm wrong. Nothing is as beautiful as this work of art in front of me." A blush rises from my neck and blossoms on my face. A growl ripples through the room and I look to Molaris. She wasn't the source of it and neither was Acacius. The whole table looks to Lunan.

"Is something wrong?" Molaris questions her voice is poison in the air and I look between Lunan and Molaris. She doesn't want to make it obvious, but she is blatantly uncomfortable with the sight of Lunan. His Fae scent must be bothering her because it floods into my nostrils like a river dam breaking.

"What will I eat, Your Majesty?" His voice is like the rays of sun heating my skin. His golden eyes look to Molaris and a flicker of his irises tell me he is uncomfortable with her presence as well. He is a smart man for pointing out the danger in the room. Well we are *all* dangerous when I come to think of it.

"Tyrion, why did you bring the Faerie?" Scout asks openly in front of Lunan like he isn't there, but he is the elephant in the room. "He is nothing, but a distraction." *You're telling me.* For once I am glad that the attention isn't on me.

Tyrion doesn't look away from me and I try to look everywhere else, but my eyes don't listen and I stare back at him, in silent battle. "Lunan is the High Lord of the Day Kingdom and he brought some very special news that I thought would be best if it were shared from his lips." His voice fills the room. My heart picks up to a thrumming beat as all of the attention is dragged to Lunan. This isn't going to be good.

Now feeling as if he has to share, which he kind of does, he stands from the table and taps a knife against his goblet. When every pair of eyes is on him, he looks into his glass and promptly places it down with a frown. I look into my own cup and notice maroon liquid, that I doubt is wine.

"This past summer the Tree of Light was chopped down," Everyone gasps except for Tyrion and although I already knew of this, the words coming from someone else makes it shocking. I felt the shockwave of death radiate from the Tree this summer when I was still in Duke Rywell's cellar. The destruction of the Tree of Light stopped the mountain ash, laced in my shackles, to stop burning and I was able to free myself. I know that the Tree collapsing is devastation, but I need to thank whoever did it because their act led to my freedom. "The crime was committed by Evaflora Vox, High Lady of the Summer Kingdom, and also my mother." Everyone roars in a horrifying chorus. The courtiers hiss and seethe and why he added the last bit of information beats me, but I start to fear for him, until I notice Tyrion, smiling into his goblet as he sips the blood within. Lunan continues, louder this time to be heard above the hissing Vampyres. "Although Evaflora is my mother. I am not and will not be in partnership with her. She, on the other hand, is openly at brink of war with the mortal kingdom, now ruled by a Faerie, Equadoria. My sister is the queen and she is struggling against Evaflora and her forces."

"Why does the war between a Faerie and a Mortal have to do with us?" Aaron asks from his seat and Molaris is shaking so violently that she doesn't even sip the blood before her. She doesn't put her hands in anyone's line of sight as she stares down at her lap.

"You're missing the point," Tyrion chuckles. "The Mortal Kingdom is now ruled by a High Fae."

"How did Equadoria allow an immortal to sit on the throne?" Scout is equally confused and I look to Acacius who looks just as curious as I do.

"She died as a mortal, killed by her father. The princess' guard killed the king and the princess was reborn, as a queen, and a High Fae." Lunan's words crack like thunder through the dining hall. Everyone is silent with the dire news and I can tell I'm the only one who doesn't understand the importance of these people. But the idea of a human being reborn as a Fae is just unimaginable.

Aaron and Scout stare dumbfounded. Tyrion is beaming with glee and ready to jump out of his skin with excitement. Molaris, on the other hand, grows enough strength to stop her tremble and now glares openly at Lunan and Tyrion. "This is a great deal of news, Tyrion." She whispers. Her voice is like a thousand snakes hissing in unison, ready to strike, ready to kill. Lunan falls back into his chair and stares at me with shadows in his irises. I get the inkling that he isn't here upon his own will.

"I had found this out when I arrived to Abella in search for news on the lands current status. I sailed south and was met by a servant boy, walking along the coast, who told me what had happened after I compelled him. My first thoughts drifted to the prophecy," Tyrion drawls, waving his goblet around like a royal scepter. "Three Fae Druids unite together to defeat a common enemy. One can control flames," Tyrion's eyes glide over Lunan and quickly shift back to Molaris. "Another wields lightning." Acacius shifts in his chair and my beating heart hasn't calmed and instead gallops into a stuttering pound. My discomfort is obvious, well it feels obvious, as I keep a mask up of solemn features. I try to make it believable and as adamant as stone. Lightning threatens to erupt from my fingertips at the mention of my ability, so I sit on my hands. "Lastly," Tyrion adds, many minutes later. "A mortal with immortal genes gets reborn as immortal will control the Void. The prophecy is unraveling before our eyes and we know where two pieces of the puzzle are. One is right next to me and the second is in Equadoria, the third, is hidden somewhere on Abella waiting to be found." What they don't know is that the third piece is sitting right across from them. If I play my cards right, I'll never be found.

Acacius explains the legend behind the prophecy in my mind. *When the mortals learned of the immortal Fae and their powers, they became jealous and taught themselves to manipulate nature and control its growth and ways. Some of the humans were able to create balls of lightning through chants and rituals, or even make white-hot fire flow through the air. The use of such abilities isn't made for their human bodies, so each time a Druid, their name, uses power it harms them. If the human's take, they must give. The Fae became curious of their unique abilities and the Druids trained them, only three. The human druids were punished by death and the three immortals, named Fae Druids, were unstoppable. One controlled the lightning, another fire, and the third got selfish and continued the study of the druids and created a whole new type of ability that is only inherited by the prophecy. Only once every ten centuries are the three Fae Druids alive, and it seems, you are one of them.* His voice drifts away and the ghost of his words echo throughout my skull.

You are one of them. I never stop hearing it. I am a Fae Druid. I've always known that my powers made me different from many other Tempestatis Fae. My parents had abilities that varied, but related to elemental control. My father could summon mist that would make him vanish and my mother could control and manipulate water. When they came together they created a storm. Or was my mother a vessel for the prophecy?

Lunan bore his eyes into mine and I just stare right back, a challenge. I will him to know, to understand what I am. A gleam reflects over his eyes and a part of me feels like he already knows.

"So, what do you plan to do with this information, Tyrion?" Scout questions, vulgar assumption between her words.

Molaris jolts as if pulled from her thoughts, I've never seen the queen so unsettled. I don't get why the presence of Lunan has any effect on the situation at hand. Before he arrived with Tyrion, she was throwing me around like a ragdoll, controlling my blood, manipulating me at her will. She was strong and unyielding, but now, she is like a skittish animal who was hit too hard.

"I want the three pieces of the puzzle," Tyrion muses, and his fangs glimmer beneath the ornate chandelier. His eyes, wrinkled at the corners, fall on me. I lift the goblet of blood to my lips, the crimson liquid sweet on my tongue. I can play this game. "I want the three druids and I want to join the fight. I want to take all of Abella in the grasp of my hands and let the centuries of Fae and human rulings end. A new power will rise and Vampyres will have their reign."

The other three royals beam with excitement, even Molaris. Bitter cold trails down my spine and Acacius goes taut next to me. Lunan has the look of pure terror as he glances between the Vampyre kings, and queens, and at the rest of the grimacing courtiers. So many fangs reflect the light, feign smiles, evil intensions. They all whisper at the back of my mind as I stare at the room crowded with fake, conniving monsters.

I want to run, I want to scream, but Acacius keeps me grounded as he grips my wrist beneath the table. My hands are still firmly placed beneath me and the other Vampyres wipe their clean faces, symbolizing they are done with the meal, which they have barely touched. I would've liked to admit I was hungry, but now any appetite I had has left this island and took a swan dive into the churning ocean.

The hollow eyes and pale skin become a sickening sight, so I shake Acacius' grip off of my arm and rise from the table. Everyone looks at me with furrowed brows and I want to scream at them to look somewhere else. Keep their stares off of me.

"I didn't give you permission to leave," Molaris croons from her chair, hiding the unease that has become so constant for her since Lunan and Tyrion's arrival.

I didn't want to be a part of this Vampyre life and currently every part of me wants to be away from here, so I don't stop the violent retort. "And I didn't give you permission to manipulate my blood, but that didn't stop you, did it?"

Tyrion howls in laughter and Lunan hides his grin. Scout and Aaron snicker behind their porcelain hands. Molaris hisses from her seat. A strand of her ivory hair falls into her eyes and she pretends that it doesn't bother her. "We'll be speaking later."

"I'm jumping with joy at the thought," I fire back and Acacius grabs my arm hard enough to bruise. A silent warning to stop, and even though I don't want to be a part of the Vampyre court, Molaris is still my queen. I look to Tyrion who just grins in anticipation for what I'm going to say. "My name is Athena," the answer to his question at the start of our dinner and I allow myself one more look over Lunan before I leave the dining hall and drop my white napkin over the black handprints burned into my chair. I pray nobody sees or else I am going to be a knight in Tyrion's game of chess.

CHAPTER FIFTEEN

~Ariadae~

    Kane is Jax's brother, but it doesn't stop the unease churning within the pit of my stomach. I have been betrayed too many times by the people close to me that I've become unaccepting of the intentions of strangers. I went through too much to be innocently assuming everyone is kind and helpful. Nobody cares about a stranger's needs unless it benefits their own.

    Although Jax and Kane appear very different from one another, I notice the similarities. They both walk with a warrior's gait and both of them are...beautiful, yet I find my eyes catching on Kane's wavy dirty blond locks and tanned skin. They both have angular jaws and high cheekbones, but Kane has a slimmer nose and sleek brow bone that makes a blush heat within my body despite the bitter cold. After the blizzard, the snow has become deeper, if it's even possible, and much thicker. The flakes brush along my sagging arms and waltzing crystals still fall from the clear blue sky above.

His armor is white plaited leather and is sleeveless, exposing sun kissed skin and ink black tattoos. The gauntlets, chest plate, and boots of his outfit are lined with wolf's fur and a longbow is strung across his shoulder blades. A long sword is sheathed straight down his spine. With his large amount of weaponry and bulging muscles, even bigger than Jax's, I may not trust him, but they make me feel more than safe. I don't scan the surrounding trees as we ascend Archaic Mountain.

"What are your tattoos?" I ask and nod my head towards his visible biceps.

He grins with a white toothed smile and looks down at his arm. "This one," he points to the obsidian paint depicting an image of a howling wolf and dark swirls spiral from the animal's mouth and fade into his shoulder beneath fabric. "Is part of The Proving."

"What's The Proving?"

"It's a series of arena-style battles that prove that the heir's abilities are strong enough to rule our kingdom." His words dance with the falling snowflakes and I let it linger there, not wanting to seem too eager with my questions. I have never known anything about the Winter Kingdom culture because Jax doesn't talk to me about his home.

"I know Jax gave up his title as Heir, but did he participate in the Proving?"

Kane looks back at me, his sea-green eyes filled with a gloom and his previous pretty smile is gone. "He didn't give up his title. What made you believe such a lie?"

What? Jax told me he handed his title to his brother and became a warrior. After establishing his life in the Winter Kingdom as a warrior he ran through Elkwood Forest, down the mountain, only as a tiger pup, where my father stumbled upon him and brought him to me.

"He competed in the first three of the ten tests in The Proving," Kane adds and I grow more curious as to what he is saying. Although this is very intriguing, it makes me wonder what else did Jax has lied about. "In the fourth test, he was supposed to…spill the blood of an innocent. It's to show that even the strong can't be weak when on the throne. He lifted the knife to the girl's throat and dropped it to the ground. The entire court and Winter Kingdom was watching him."

I pity him; the whole Kingdom must've been either furious or ashamed to have him as their Heir. I've learned over my time in Elkwood and inside of a Faerie Kingdom that their traditions and standards are so much higher and dangerous than mortal customs. Two courtiers who hate one another could tear each other to ribbons at a ball and the other Fae milling about won't even mind it. That would be a good night for the Fae. Just that thought is sickening.

"What happened to him after that?"

"Well the kingdom and court were furious and so was our father. The High Lord decided to exile Jax from the Winter Kingdom."

It all makes sense now. The running into Elkwood. The reason he said I gave him a purpose. It was all because he is an exiled prince left to nothing. He never left me in my years growing up and even inside of Elkwood, after he was hurt, he came back. But now that Jax is an exiled heir, stripped of a title, that makes Kane the new heir to the throne and he participated in the Proving. I think of the fourth test and if I would be able to do it. If it really came down to the fate of my kingdom I would, but otherwise I'm glad I am not an heir in the Winter Kingdom.

"Did you participate in the Proving?"

"Yes, and I completed every task," his shadowed eyes burrow into mine. My gut twists at the idea that the last view the innocent he killed saw was those stunning eyes. I don't know if killing an innocent being can be justified for ruling a kingdom. "I'm not the little kitten that Jax is."

Kane's words end all conversation for a long, long time. We walk through thick and thin snow and small rivers descending the mountain. Rocks are scattered around the river bank where we stop for a quick break. The monthly demon was roiling with a thousand claws, hollowing my insides. I'll be fine in a short while. Kane waits by the flowing stream, crouching and staring into the glimmering water that looks like a thousand yards of iridescent tulle being shaken in rough winds. The pine which I do my business behind is extremely dry and it's dying. It confuses me because the surrounding trunks are alive and damp from the snow. Even if a tree was dead it should at least be soaked because of the gale that had hit Archaic Mountain last night. I saunter around the trunk staring at the layered bark and don't stop the gasp that escapes from me. Instantly Kane is on his feet, dagger drawn, moving towards me with a hunter's approach. I point to the pine.

"What?" he whispers, thinking it's a Forsaken, but when he gets closer he sees what I'm staring at. The bark, in a large dinner plate sized circle, is clawed away jaggedly revealing the white wood beneath. The vertical groves in the wood are stained with an onyx sap-like liquid seeping from a word carved into the trunk. *Iris.* That's the part of an eye that holds the color. It's spilling with the tarlike goop, with a high viscosity. It drips slowly like honey. "What is that?"

"An eye?" I suggest and he studies the tree. He grabs a twig from the rocks on the ground and pokes the dripping black. It glitters like a thousand stars and when he pokes the letter '*I*' within the word, the dark sap slithers and begins to coil onto the twig and up the wood, consuming it whole. "A new type of infection?"

Kane drops the stick before the night liquid can touch his skin. If it conquers and devours wood extremely quickly, I don't want to know what it does to skin. He wipes his clean hands in the river and looks back at me, brow furrowed. "Maybe it's a name." I just shrug and put my fiery hair into a ponytail before tossing my quiver over a shoulder and string the bow to my back.

"I don't know anybody named Iris, do you?" He ponders my words for a second, but just mirrors my shrug.

"Nope, it's an ugly name anyway." He says and I roll my eyes with a chuckle. I begin walking along the river, up the mountain. I notice the blue sky start bleeding to an orange, and I pray we reach the Winter Kingdom before night falls upon us. I'm not in the mood to be stuck here during night, with a Faerie I barely know, and the Forsaken haunting the surrounding woods.

"Will we make it there by nightfall?"

"Yes, but only if we move fast enough," his voice makes a tremble start in my hands and legs, but I push past my fear and surge forward with a new found energy.

"Well even if night comes, we should continue moving. It's not like we'd sleep much anyway."

He looks at me, eyes glowing, and smile gleaming. "You've got a point there, Your Majesty."

Night arrived without warning. The canopy of pines above my head blocked out the setting sun, so as soon as I thought to look up, night was upon Kane and me. He pulled the hood of his cloak up, shielding my eyes from being blessed with the sight of his features. My favorite part about traveling with Kane is that he isn't the snarky, cold, bitter Jax. Yes, Kane has a few sarcastic comments, but in all truth he is sort of funny.

"How is he?" My voice is loud in the silence of Elkwood forest, even on Archaic Mountain. Kane doesn't look at me as he pulls at a loose thread bordering the edge of his cape.

He instantly knows who I'm talking about when he says, "He arrived last night in a state of panic. He barged through the castle doors and interrupted our family's dinner. My mother cried at the sight of her son. It's been seventeen years," he looks at me saying it's my fault. I don't understand his desire to blame me for Jax's absence; they were the ones to exile him, his own family. "My father was surprised, but immediately became the High Lord he is and sent out the Frost Guard to search for you."

"Who is the Frost Guard?" I ask, my breath coiling in the dark air.

"They are the sentinels of the High Lord, and the Frozen Wardens are the guards of the Fae in the Winter Kingdom." That makes some sense. I never thought of different ranks of guardians having different names, but also who knew that Fae even existed. I didn't even know about the existence of Faeries and the Forsaken until I entered Elkwood Forest for the first time this past summer. Anything could be possible. Kane looks into the impenetrable night ahead. Darkness is roiling between two trunks of towering pines. A noticeable chill makes his body quake, as well as mine.

Two Arbors step out of the trees. The pine trees that I thought to be trunks rising into the night were really Arbors blending into their surroundings. Kane has his sword drawn and poised to strike at the Forsaken who stand, waiting for him to make the first move. My own Fae instincts rake down my back like claws, so I turn on my heels, drawing an arrow in my recurve bow, aimed into the shadows that were once behind me. At first I don't notice anything, but then there is a pair of clouded red eyes that wink open.

I hear Kane snarl before he leaps into battle with the Arbors behind me and I hold the arrow steady before me. I'm at a standoff with an Umbra who is only a rippling dark blob, blacker than the surrounding night. The scarlet eyes blink once, and suddenly they thin and become ovular. The scarlet bleaches to a deep ocean blue. The shadow grows porcelain skin from nowhere and pointed ears frame the skull. A chest swells and long, smooth legs stand in the snow. Moon white hair flows in the wind shielding the naked girl. She smiles with a demon's grin and I focus on her face. She is a Fae, but nobody I recognize. Crackling lightning surrounds her palms and I stand my ground, like the Umbra, both of us unmoving. I no longer hear Kane in the heat of battle, but I can't look away from the Forsaken before me. I will shoot when my Fae instincts tell me to. When I was first in Elkwood, as a human, my Fae instincts felt like a heavy stone in my chest and now that I'm a Faerie I understand what they are.

The Umbra doesn't move. The young beautiful Faerie is idle in the now glowing darkness, illuminated blue from her crackling lightning. An inkling of thought crawls into the back of my mind and it feels like a punch in the gut when I remember what Novid said to me the day I left Equadoria. *Meet the girl who sparkles like lightning and the male who blazes like a thousand suns.* Although I have no idea who the Umbra is, a part of me does. *The girl who sparkles like lightning.* Before I can ask the Forsaken anything about the apparition, it hisses, revealing a mouth full of blood and elongated fangs, longer and sharper than the Fae's. An arrow whistles over my shoulder and through the Umbra's middle, making it shatter into nothing.

I whirl onto Kane. "Why would you do that?" I shout and immediately notice the Arbors, now nothing but splintered wood scattered in the snow. Large ice spikes have risen out of the white mounds and are covered in shattered wood. Although Kane comes from the Winter Kingdom fire burns brightly behind his eyes. "You obviously weren't going to do it! I took care of the damned thing!"

"It wasn't going to hurt me," I gesture to where the girl was standing between the trees and even as the words leave my lips I know them not to be true.

"And curiosity *didn't* kill the cat," he rolls his eyes and I do the same, crossing my arms. "Let's just get you back to your boyfriend."

"He's not my boyfriend," I've never said those words out loud and for some reason, it feels good. Kane's brows furrow together in confusion.

"So, what *is* Jax to you?"

"It doesn't matter," I dodge the question and Kane throws his hands into the air, obviously finished with the conversation.

"Whatever," He strings his bow over a shoulder and I do the same. "I'm sick of talking to you anyway." Suddenly I don't like the presence of Kane over Jax. He is rude and doesn't understand what's going on with Evaflora and the Forsaken, then again neither does Jax. He still doesn't know about the Umbra attacking me as an image of Novid at the castle and telling me to "meet the girl with lightning and the male who burns like fire." I guess after this I'll have some news to share with him when I arrive in the Winter Kingdom. *If* I arrive in the Winter Kingdom.

Kane walks ahead into the night, ascending the forever lifting Archaic Mountain. I have no choice, but to follow. I understand that Archaic Mountain is the tallest mountain on Abella, but never did I expect to be climbing day and night! Jax and I had walked along the border of the Autumn Kingdom and the Spring Kingdom before we got separated. The High Lord of the Autumn Kingdom hates having trespassers on his land, but the High Lady of the Spring Kingdom is known to take traveling Faeries against their will, so we deigned to avoid both threats. Now that Kane and me are on the Archaic Mountain Range, we have no fear of any threats, besides the damn Forsaken.

"How far are we from reaching the top?" I pant through jagged breaths that slice my throat. Kane shakes his head.

"You're like a faeling," He mumbles and even though I just met him, I know him enough to be aware that his eyes rolled. So do mine.

"Sorry, Your Highness," I feign a gleeful courtier's voice making fun of his title. "Did I disrespect your graceful ride on your unyielding high horse?"

Kane answers with a growl that sends chills down my spine. I want to stop, but my mouth won't let me. I sort of find enjoyment in teasing him. "Or am I, the High Lady of a mortal kingdom not worth your righteousness?" His eyes flick to me, eyebrows knitted together in rage that flows off of him. I feel a wave of building heat from his skin, at least two yards away from me. "I didn't know that mortals were such inconveniences." His upper lip curls back revealing gleaming teeth.

"Jax shouldn't have wasted seventeen years of his life on you," His words are like a stab to the heart ruining any fun I was having. "I'd rather him bring home a human whore than whatever you are. Maybe he shouldn't have brought you back from the dead!"

My hand print is bright red on his face and the resounding smack that stings my hand sends ravens scattering into the night sky. He doesn't even lift his large hands to his throbbing cheek and tears threaten to spill from my eyelids. I will not cry. I will not give him the satisfaction of his words hurting me, but they did. No matter how much I want to deny it, I can't.

Kane's eyes immediately soften, his mouth opens, eyebrows curling upward in regret, sadness maybe. "I'm sorry, I shouldn't have said that. I just get hot headed when I'm scared"

A tear breaks past my barrier and I wipe it on my sleeve as I begin marching up the mountain. "No! Fuck you!" I hide my shaking breaths, but I still know he can hear me. Even if he does want to, he doesn't attempt to apologize again. These Archaeminza brothers are two peas in a damned pod! They both seem to pick arguments with me and also use their words as daggers. Fuck Kane and Jax. They're both assholes.

My body wants to fall into a deep never-ending sleep, but my brain is swelled, scattered, and needle-focused for anything in Elkwood. I won't sleep comfortably until I arrive in the Winter Kingdom and with thick walls between me and them, the Forsaken. Ever since that first attack with the two Arbors and the Umbra, I haven't been threatened by any Forsaken. I'm thankful for it.

I thought too soon.

A Troglodyte with blue scales breaks through the brambles to my left and on instinct I dash for the right. My ankles are at odd angles on the uneven slant of the mountain side. I stumble over my steps as the

Troglodyte closes in on me. Kane shouts from somewhere, far behind the Troglodyte now grinning at me with a reptilian grimace. My Fae instincts are screaming within me and I try to weave between trunk after trunk of the pine trees. I am now positive the trees lean in my way because it feels as if every two feet I'm changing and shifting my course around the bark covered trunks.

I hear the whine of a sword being pulled from its sheath and my body, extremely tired and full of pulsing adrenaline begins to tremble. Before I can quicken my pace into my screaming leg muscles, a sharp blade slices down my calf, making my scream howl into the night and my body to tumble to the snow. I follow gravity down the side of the mountain. My ankle twists and I cry out again, I think I hear Kane scream, but all I see is snow, darkness, white stars, a night sky, and pine needles. What seems like a thousand daggers stabbing into my skin, morrow deep, are the sticks and thorns from trees and brambles shattering beneath me. I'm rolling, trying to stop myself, but when I throw out my arms or legs to stop more sticks and thorns stab into me.

It feels like, long, painful, agonizing ages, I tumble down Archaic Mountain, until my back cracks against a tree. If it weren't for my Fae body, every bone beneath my skin would be shattered. My vision blurs at the edges and dark spots threaten to spread. Coppery

blood fills my mouth and I spit into the snow, staining
the white fluff with crimson. The tree stopped my fall, so
with quivering limbs I try to move. Pain sparkles like
electricity up my body. When my brain stops its heavy
rattle, I rein in my focus and notice I'm staring at the sky,
dark green pines loom around the opening of the moon
peeking through the canopy. I feel the trunk against my
back, but I'm lying down. How is this possible? I begin
to wonder if my eyeballs flipped in my skull before I roll,
begrudgingly, to my right and the tree trunk vanishes.
I'm falling straight down a twenty foot drop towards
knotted thorns. A scream tears my throat as the sharp
needles grow closer and closer every second with the
roaring wind of my fall. I need to try and save myself
from death, so I turn my body, not wanting to split my
skull open and let my back smack against the thorns
first. Sticks and vines shatter like glass and I fall even
further until my back smacks against a jagged surface
that feels like stone. My spine meets the ground, and a
skyward facing bone tears through my flesh on the left
side of my abdomen, going through me. My body
instantly arches against the shooting pain and feeling of
bone rubbing on bone. The sharp marrow, that rips into
my flesh and grinds against my ribcage, conjures the
memory of my father's steel sword reverberating against
my ribs echoing throughout my skull. My blood curdling
scream doesn't stop the agony and flaming pain that

makes me flush all over. Tears spill down my face and I don't want to move. The pain is enough to kill me and I start to think about the darkness that surrounds me in this thorn prison I've landed in. Trembling and hissing at the pain, flashing through every movement, is all I can do to withstand the agony. The bone that penetrated through me is stuck to the floor, so I have to lift myself off of it. The morrow touches my own making me shout and shake. My screams and sobs echo within the dark cell made of brambles and I hold a firm grip on the hole in my side. If I don't die from bleeding out than I'm going to die of either infection or starvation. For a moment, I feel sorry for Jax, never knowing what happened to me, unless Kane is fine and makes it back. After our fight earlier, I wouldn't blame him for going to the Winter Kingdom without me and saying he couldn't find me. And know that I am alone, bleeding out of a hole in my side, and a cut on my leg, and the thousands of splintered bark pieces stabbing into my clothes. I pray for a familiar face besides Novid or Gaston.

"Help," I call up to the hole in the thorn ceiling that I fell through. I see the tree that I fell from, suspended high above the drop. "Somebody! *Anybody* please help me!"

My voice drops to a whisper, but even in the darkness of the cave it echoes through the grotto. "Please…"

I look around me as I drop to my knees against the uneven floor. What I thought to be jagged rocks is broken bones, human bones. A sob escapes my mouth and so does a wail, "HELP!"

A rippling growl that sounds like rolling thunder booms from the back of the cave, in the darkest corner, and I finally realize that this thorn prison isn't a prison at all. It is a home. *It's a nest.*

CHAPTER SIXTEEN

~Ariadae~

    Somehow, I didn't lose my weapons in the tumble. I'm equipped with a quiver of arrows, a bow, and a dagger. I draw the dagger not wanting to release the pressure on my abdomen. Shifting steps and moving feet approach the shaft of moonlight, shining through the broken hole above me, shake the entire nest. I prepare myself for a Demised beast, the size of a castle, but instead, a tusk drags along the ground of bones. Grey, leathery, wrinkled skin emerges into the light and a smooshed face with large teeth protruding from the monster's jowls soon follows. The ginormous beast somehow fits within this grotto and it has become surprisingly cramped.

Large bones, erupting from its back scrape against the vines and thorns that make up the ceiling. An inkling of memory slithers from the jagged scar along my shoulder. I remember this monster's claws tearing open a wound on my arm with its talon from around a tree. What I thought was a startled white stag that saved me, is who I now know to be my mother, distracting the monster from killing me. She wasn't ready for me to die because she knew I'd find my way to the Tree of Light. That white stag isn't here anymore. I'm alone.

Its ink-well eyes are like orbs of glossy oil, hidden by the wrinkles of the beast's face.

"We have met before," My shaking voice doesn't hide my fear. I have nowhere to run and nowhere to hide and now am worse than before. I don't have my mother to save me. Even if she was here she may only fight the Akuji to kill me herself. The Akuji is the boogieman of the Fae. Parents of Faelings would use the Akuji to make their children go to bed or follow the rules and Jax recognized it. If I hadn't killed the Rune Witch then I could've brought this monster back to its tomb in the Rune Yard. It's too late now, I could have avoided this death, but I thought the Rune Witch was trying to release a monster that could destroy Abella, not trying to bring one back.

It answers with a nod and a humble growl. If growls can be humble. The Akuji doesn't rip me apart, or eat me, not yet anyway. I wait for my Fae instincts to shake, kick, buck before the pounce of the monster, but nothing comes. I look into the calm, adamant stare of the Akuji and the monster seems happy to do the same.

"ARIADAE!" A scream with thankful glee comes from above and I don't break my stare with the Akuji as I drop the dagger and fall to my knees sobbing. It was tall before, but now on the ground, the Akuji is the size of an average home. "I'll get you out of there!"

The Akuji's snarl ripples through the air and I can see the waves of heat from the beast's mouth in the moonlight shafting through the broken ceiling. The darkness closes around my vision, threatening to suffocate me as I stare at the obsidian storm cloud of the Akuji's irises. I'm losing too much blood. I don't see or hear Kane arrive, but the last thing I remember is the Akuji backing up into the darkness of the grotto as I lose consciousness.

A frigid breeze claws me from my sleep. I didn't dream about anything unless someone carrying me across the cobblestone streets surrounded by stone buildings towering high to the clouds that are so close I can touch them, was a dream.

I'm greeted by a pale, regal face with a crown of ice atop onyx hair, pin-straight. Her eyes are the same ice blue as Jax's and so is the dark hair, so I immediately know it's the High Lady of the Winter Kingdom. She smiles down at me, although her eyes are full of fear.

Feet scuff against the ground and wood scrapes against stone as suddenly Jax is looking down at me, his face in a panic. The white room is blindingly bright and the cold table beneath me feels as if it is made of ice. A chill makes me shake and the High Lady looks to her son, the exiled heir stripped of a title. "Do you have any food in Equadoria?"

Jax just ignores the comment and brushes the hair off of my forehead. A cold sweat clings to my skin and I barely feel it. I barely feel anything and I quickly fall into a state of panic. Jax hushes me but it doesn't stop the fear. I'm paralyzed!

"Watch out," the High Lady says with the voice of falling snow, soft and elegant. I don't feel anything, but my eyes droop until I'm sent back into an impenetrable darkness.

I lose track of the days. Each time I think I'm dreaming I'm awake and every time I think I'm awake I'm dreaming. The memory of the girl with lightning powers flashes through my mind with a distant thunder. Darkness will surround me and when I try to peer through the dark, I find nothing. But suddenly, in the distance, a warm flickering light appears, two, twin balls of flame. They illuminate dark colored pants that belong to a body, so I approach the being carefully. When I get nearer the flames vanish, and so does the man.

I know it's the male who burns like a thousand suns, but how I know, I'm not sure. Every time I see the twin flames at his palms I feel connected to him. As if my powers want to correlate with his. Not my Telekinae ability, but the Void. That purple smoke-like fire that burns inside of me is like a crackling, beating heart. The Void appeared when I was reborn as a Faerie. Somehow my new body unlocked another chest deep in the ocean of my mind.

A mist surrounds me as I stand in the open oblivion, not cold like death, but warm like a summer sun. I wear a white shift with a pale blue brocade across its papery fabric. I feel tightly wrapped bandages around my waist and my left calf, where the Troglodyte cut it open. A person cries out in pain before me and I run further into the dark towards the strangled groan. As if triggered by my location, Jeremiah appears and now it's my turn to cry out in pain. Tears slide down our cheeks as I take in his beaten, bruised, and cut body. His brown curls are clipped to the skin and I almost vomit at the reek of bile on him.

"Jeremiah," I sob into the dark. He raises his hanging head and looks at me. The wooden chair he sits in has his ankles and wrists shackled, but his eyes can still move. Their once warm chocolate is now shadowed dirt and full of agony.

"Help me," He whispers in the dark and his voice echoes a thousand times in my ears making another sob break past my lips. "Please."

I run to him, but the mist curls into a churning smoke beneath flaring fire that illuminates a stone wall, painted with an immaculate masterpiece. Jeremiah is gone and now I'm looking at the prophecy I saw in the Ravine of Wisps. My teary eyes lock onto the white hair of the Faerie girl, wielding lightning like a spear. Across from her is a male with fists of fire, the twin flames, and onyx cropped hair. His pointed ears symbolize him as being a Fae.

At the center, I stare into a mirror. Fiery red hair flows around a pale, delicate face. Green eyes glow and pointed ears peak between the orange waves. Purple, smoke-like flames surround the Faerie in dark robes as she seems to float on the battlefield. The Void whispers in the darkness from inside of me, *that's you.* The fire that illuminated the wall gets snipped out to nothing and I look at my hands. Small. Thin. Callouses embroider my palms and fingers where a sword and bow would sit.

"He's your brother." Rumbles through the dark and I jump at the familiar voice. More water instantly fills my eyelids and clumps on my eyelashes making my vision become a kaleidoscope. Her sun yellow hair glows and flows in the rippling darkness. Her blue skin isn't covered in holes or torn away like the other ghosts of my past. I smile at Seri. The Faerie maid in the Summer Kingdom who took care of me and told me what was happening. She was more of my mother than Evaflora will ever be.

"What?" I croak through cascading tears and heavy sobs. She is wearing a soft green dress, it makes her look alive. She steps over to me and hugs my shaking body, even with her swelled belly she holds herself elegantly.

She lifts her mouth to my pointed ear and whispers, "Lunan."

She's gone.

My eyes snap open and I regret it, the white stone infirmary blinds me and I cover my tear stained face, dry rivers of salt cling to my pores. Nobody is in the empty chamber and the table I lay on is grey stone which makes me tremble. My first thought is *where am I* and suddenly I remember Kane found me in the Akuji's nest. I awoke to see Jax and the High Lady. Unless that was just a fever dream.

It hits me like an avalanche.

"I have a brother," my whisper is almost mute and the words feel foreign on my tongue. The male who tried to help me escape the Summer Kingdom and danced with me at the Summer Solstice ball is my brother. Lunan had told me how to get to the Tree of Light because I had asked. He sold me mountain ash weapons my first day in my mother's kingdom. He had to have known all along. But how is he my brother? My father never slept with another woman, unless…Evaflora was born with the Tree of Light. She must be thousands of years old which gives her more than enough time to be promiscuous. Lunan Berdu Walsh is my half-brother.

The door clicks open and my eyes lock onto Jax. Relief makes his shoulders sag and he runs to me and grips me in a severely needed hug. I think of Seri and the warmth she brought to me.

"Ouch," I mumble into his shoulder through the pinpricks of pain and Jax tenses before releasing me in an instant. He holds my face between his calloused palms and he looks into my eyes. "I'm fine."

"I feared the worst." He kisses my forehead, then my brow, then my cheeks, and trails a line down my nose. He leans his brow bone against mine and we close our eyes. He heaves a sigh. "I'm sorry. For everything! I didn't want to lie about the Tree of Light," my chest caves at the memory of his lie. "I hated keeping things from you, but now, from now on, I'll tell you the truth and only the truth."

"Promise?" I click and he nods.

"Promise." He takes a seat on the table and rubs my thigh. He ditched the fur-lined leather armor for a silver tunic, embroidered with blue thread. Dark pants are tucked into leather boots and his hair is chopped off. He notices my stare and scratches the back of his head as a blush colors his ears and cheeks. "Do you like it?"

I grab his hand and hold it between my palms. I kiss each of his fingers, "I love it." His ice blue irises glow with happiness. He no longer looks like a shaggy warrior, but although I like the haircut, I wish it to be long again. But Fae hair grows extraordinarily fast, so the length will be back in a month or two.

"I love you," he whispers staring at my face for a reaction.

I feel quick to answer, but suddenly words slam against my mind. *He's not your mate.* I feign a smile and I physically lose the breath I was holding as the door opens. A Faerie with skin of grey fur wearing a white uniform tells me of her title as a nurse. She grins at me and flicks her brown eyes to Jax. She tries to hide her disgust, but fails horribly. "It'd be best if you leave." I wonder if she says this for my sake or hers.

Jax looks from me to the nurse, but I don't defend him. I have never been to the Winter Kingdom before, so I am not aware of their titles and ways of life. I, a High Lady of a distant Mortal Kingdom, am not going to start arguments or create a scene in a Faerie Kingdom. A part of me knows it won't look good to defend the exiled prince, especially if I do want the High Lord's army.

"I'll see you in a bit." Jax nods and leaves me to the stranger.

The nurse grabs my hand and says, "Your body is almost healed, take it easy for two days before doing any fighting or hunting. Have some tea and soup and stay warm or else the bacteria that got into your system will make you sick. Now be quiet." She makes quick work of changing my bandages and checking my vitals. She counts my heart beats and feels my blood pressure by just holding my palm. I've never seen a power like hers before and I wonder how she wound up in the Winter Kingdom.

The nurse leaves me for a moment to allow me to get dressed out of the uncomfortable shift and into my huntress, fur-lined, leather-plaited armor that I wore on my way to the Winter Kingdom. It's clean and relatively new looking. Once I'm in the outfit the hides and furs make warmth envelope me like a blanket.

The hairy Faerie tentatively knocks before entering and she gestures for me to follow and we walk down corridor after corridor, all of them are silent and made of grey stone. Each square of rock is engraved with beautiful swirling images that remind me of Kane's tattoos. "This way," the nurse calls pulling me away from the distractions as she grabs a torch from the wall and sticks it into my hand. "Go straight up those stairs, they'll lead you to the throne room where your…friend is."

"Thank you," I say, unsure of what to do in the growingly awkward situation. She waves me up the steps and I push on the flat wall at the top of the flight. The stone door scrapes against the floor and I see the dark blue fabric of a tapestry blocking my view of the room. Avoiding the fabric, I scurry into the large, open chamber and almost drop my torch in utter shock.

The High Lord sits on a throne of jagged ice. A crown of a similar style is fashioned to his dirty blonde curls and his sea-green eyes, Kane's eyes, flare like an unyielding storm, eating up the room and the hundreds of courtiers crowded within. His dark tunic, styled with a bright blue thread draws snowflakes across his chest. The High Lady is to his right on a smaller throne, but it is still a twin to his. She is wearing a diadem of silver snowflakes atop her onyx hair, which is slicked back into a tightly braided bun at the base of her neck. Her dress is a white glittering river that pools to the floor. Kane, looking nothing like the handsome hunter I met in Elkwood, is sitting on the opposite side of his mother. He looks regal and elegant, beautiful even.

The nurse said Jax is in here and I try to make my way through the thick throng of courtiers or citizens, which one I'm unsure of. They are all wearing either fur or silk, and all look to be warriors of some kind. Some of the women have arms the size of tree trunks. If this is what his citizens look like, I wonder what his army is like.

I place the torch into an iron holder that's fastened to the stone wall. The large ceiling is vaulted and columns rise up to the stone roof. Windows cover the entire wall opposite of me and the door is opposite of the Archaeminza family, the royal family. Midnight blue shades hang from the corner where the walls meet the domed ceiling. A glittering white embroidered snowflake, surrounded by small white spots, covers the fabric; I realize it's the Winter Kingdom flag.

"The exiled prince has returned." The High Lord booms from his throne and the crowd roars with anger, a chill rakes its claws down my back. I don't think Jax is here, unless the king is using him as a spectacle. "He arrives without invitation after seventeen years of being exiled. Do you think he deserves retribution?" The crowd screams *yes* with earsplitting hatred. My eyes scan the throng for his ice blue eyes, dark hair now short. I find nothing, so I excuse my way to the opposite side of the chamber. I start searching harder, faster, my fingers tremble. "He deserves a punishment for what he's done." The hundreds of courtiers jump with excitement. I try to peer between the heads and shoulders of the crowd and I see the king wave his hand before him.

"Seventeen lashes for seventeen years. Make it painful Reyluke." A fist rises above the heads and shoulders. The torchlight makes the bullwhip glitter through the air and the crack snaps within my ears as an agonizing scream gets drowned out by the roar of excitement from the crowd. *Jax.*

Panic controls me. I push through towering Fae that spit curses at me. One literally spits on me. "Watch out!" I scream and a woman with stone skin, like Rasgard, my dress maker, hisses at me. I duck under arms and elbow people's sides to get through. Nobody hears me excusing myself over the roar of the throng and the cracking of the whip. Two lashes have passed and a male that I try to move around slams his palms against my shoulders making me tumble to the ground. "Bitch!" he shouts and another lash cracks in my skull. Anger and fear become a burning war within me as I blast a wave of telekinesis at the Faerie. He launches into the air and lands on several people who shout and fall to the stone floor like dominos. The people between me and the High Lord notice the attack and immediately make a clear path to the dais.

I scramble to my feet and dash down the tunnel of people. I curve around them and ignore the male who pushed me cursing from behind. I fall to my knees and use my body as a shield over Jax's bare back. The white tunic torn to pieces is covered in blood at the bottom step of the dais. The whip snaps and a long cord splits the plaited leather on my back. I feel the sting, even beneath my layers. I hiss at the burn that clings to my skin.

The High Lord rises from his throne as does Kane and his mother. "What is this?" he shouts, I notice how quiet the crowd has suddenly become. Jax shakes beneath me and I'm careful to not touch the open wounds on his muscled back. Bruises cover his whole body like he had been beaten beforehand. What have they done to him? It was only minutes since when he left me in the infirmary.

"Are you alright?" I whisper and Jax nods, still trembling and I shake with him. He shakes with pain, I shake from the burning rage that floods my veins. I've never looked at anyone else with more hatred than when I glare up at the High Lord who stares at me in shock. Strands of my unbound orange waves hang in my face as sweat begins to bead on my forehead.

"Move," the Faerie holding the whip growls and I look back at him with the promise of death in my eyes. His pale skin makes his brown hair and eyes appear darker. His needle straight hair is braided down his spine and his dark cloak billows on an invisible breeze. He looks to the High Lord. "Shall I continue?"

The High Lord must nod in answer because the faerie raises his arm, the whip in hand and I barely have time to think as the metal strands at the end split the skin on my cheek.

"Father stop this madness," Kane roars and I decide to do that myself. I rise and project my hand forward, feeling Reyluke's heavy, adrenaline-filled heartbeat pulse through his thick neck. I begin curling my fingers into a fist and the male's dark eyes flood with panic as his supply of air is cut off. A dark red flush makes his neck become the shade of an apple and his veins become prominent between the crushing forces of my power.

"STOP THIS!" The High Lady screams in pure terror and the whole crowd begins backing towards the door. I hold the suffocating grip for a second longer, telling him to watch what he does next, before I release him. He pants and wheezes when he drops to the floor on his hands and knees, Jax still doing the same. I look at the High Lord. He stands on his dais, wanting to make his title clear. The whole Archaeminza family is standing on uneasy feet. Kane stares in disbelief and the High Lady's hands cover her mouth, muffling sobs. The High Lord however keeps a mask of adamant stone along his features as he looks me up and down, evaluating, calculating his next approach.

"Who are you?" He no longer shouts; his deep masculine voice makes my bones quiver and I straighten my spine. I brush the hair from my face and stare at him.

"Queen Ariadae Vox, High Lady of Equadoria."

He chuckles, "The mortal kingdom in the north?" He takes a seat instantly thinking I'm no threat. I try not to become angry with his assumption.

I notice the wheezing stopped. I turn faster than I should and pain slices through me from where the bone penetrated my side and I ignore it as I let the crackling sparks of the Void dance beneath my palms. Purple fire coils around my hands. Reyluke immediately drops the whip to the floor and backs away from me.

"Gods be damned," someone in the audience mumbles. More whispers soon echo through the chamber becoming a chorus of gossip. "What is she?" and, "The prophecy," floods my eardrums as more questions and answers are thrown around the room. More and more accusations begin to suffocate the chamber and I look back to the High Lord. Kane, who was so quick to fire retorts at me, doesn't even make eye contact. That damned prince saved me and just screamed for the fight to stop, but now has nothing to say. I have the feeling it's his father's presence that keeps his true thoughts from leaving his lips.

"Why are you here?" The High Lady asks and I let my Void vanish.

"I need an army," before I can explain, the High Lord begins laughing.

"You think I'd give a stranger my army? Even if I was debating the thought, what makes you think after your assault on my people you would receive any aid from the Winter Kingdom?"

My retort fires off my tongue before I can filter the words. "And what father thinks it's right to whip his own son because he didn't spill the blood of an innocent? Why would it be wrong for a Fae prince to have a heart, to be sympathetic of the innocent?"

"I'm giving him what he *deserves*. He is an exiled prince! He couldn't follow the tradition of the Proving, signifying his weakness of ruling this kingdom. If he cannot rule with strength and resilience than he is no son of mine!" The High Lady looks longingly at Jax and I notice the sympathy in her eyes.

"Jax protected me, he is loyal to me, and has always been there for me through thick and thin. Can you say that you did the same for him?" The words cut a wound in the High Lord. He looks away from me to Kane who just stares out the window, seeming bored.

"Be gone! Everybody leave immediately."

The courtiers vanish very quickly and the High Lord even sends away Reyluke who holds his throat feeling violated. *Good* I think to myself. I don't hide the smile as I notice the bruises now blossoming along his neck. The High Lord steps from the dais challenging me.

I stand straighter, if it's even possible. I look down my nose at the High Fae of the Winter Kingdom.

"Brennan," The High Lady whispers in fright at what her husband will do, but I do not fear what is to come. He hurt his own child just because of a heart beating within his chest. Maybe Kane isn't the nicest, but he has his own insecurities. He continues to stare out the window as if he is too frightened to look at or challenge his father.

Brennan, the High Lord, ignores her as he circles me and Jax, who is now rising from the floor. I don't risk making the effort to help him.

"You stole Jax's time these past seventeen years," he mumbles. He seems as if he doesn't know what to say or is pondering out loud. He decides to change the subject he brought up. "Why should I give you my army?"

Jax stands next to me and looks down at the floor, probably at the blood stains. I take off my cloak and wrap it around him, covering his naked torso. He needs to cover the wound before bacteria can get into it. But he hisses in pain and my heart stops as the silk touches his wounds. I cry out as I peel off the fabric sticking to the blood coating the skin on his back. "Can somebody please heal him?" Without question the High Lady jumps from her throne and rushes to Jax's side. She delicately helps remove the cloak and her hands frost over with a thin layer of snow. It glows and moves as she rubs the wounds on his back. He doesn't cry out or snarl in agony. The three lashes slowly close and I swear I can hear the creation of skin and the moist sound of it connecting. I glance at Jax's face which is stern, but his eyes are grateful for the euphoric touch of his mother. The first time she's done this in seventeen years.

I shift my stare back to Brennan who takes a seat beside his son, Kane. "This past summer Lunan," I choke on my brother's name. "Tried to help me escape my imprisonment at the Summer Kingdom, but he told me to stay, so I can learn the lies Evaflora was keeping from the other Faerie Kingdoms in Elkwood. I found out what she was keeping from you."

Kane looks up at me suddenly interested, but I don't look to his eyes, I'm too busy keeping his father's attention. Brennan even seems to lean in, waiting for the big secret. "She wants to enslave the mortals of Abella and become the singular queen of the entire continent." A tear falls from my eyes and the salt within burns the cut on my cheek. I wait for Brennan to answer, but he only stares at me. My beating heart leaps into an unsteady rhythm at the thought of him possibly wanting to team up with her. Two Fae armies- one Fae, one Forsaken- enslaving the mortals and conquering the continent. Another tear falls as a chill shakes me to the core.

A cold hand touches my cheek and I jump in surprise, but lean into the cool and soothing touch of the High Lady's healing magic. I silently thank her as Brennan looks to Kane, who doesn't look away from me. My eyes shift to him, as if he is going to answer and all of the breath leaves my lungs. My chest caves inward and a sudden crack resounds through my body and skull. Something, I never thought would happen, clicks into place. Kane chokes on his tongue as I realize he feels the same thing and I drop to my knees and vomit on the floor. The High Lady is quick to pull away her glittering gown, but Jax leans down, brushing away my hair. His fingers, dragging through my fiery waves feels so suddenly wrong.

I look up to Kane who just shakes and trembles like a kitten caught in a storm. He leans over to Brennan and whispers in his ear. Even my Fae hearing can't pick up what he's saying, but the High Lord nods, and Kane exits the throne room as fast as he can without running. Kane won't make a scene, not here, not with me. I'm sick to my stomach at the thought.

Another round of retching begins and Brennan's voice sounds distant. "It will take several days for the treaty to be written, feel free to enjoy everything the Winter Kingdom offers. And for now, Jax," he looks at his first-born son, for the first time in who knows how long. "You are no longer exiled from the Winter Kingdom."

I want to be happy, I want to hug Jax, but I know it's wrong. Everything I ever did with Jax is wrong and will always be wrong. Kane, the arrogant, rude, handsome, yet insufferable heir to the Winter Kingdom will make my living here for the next several days harder than I can imagine. Because he's my mate.

CHAPTER SEVENTEEN

~Ariadae~

 The accommodations that Lhys gave us are fit for a king. My bed is so big that I didn't even feel Jax on its other end. Jax slept with me and for the first time the two of us were in bed together, he didn't try to have sex with me. Even if he did, I would have denied it. Jax even being beneath the sheets beside me feels wrong. My heart knows it's not him I'm supposed to lay next to, but my mind speaks other things...or does it? Kane is funny, but a quick flaring fire. He is similar to Jax in that sense, but Jax has been around for longer although he lies. Maybe Kane lies too, but I haven't learned otherwise from his words. And besides, Jax left me in Elkwood.

I rise from the bed and head into the bathroom feeling sick to my stomach. It's hard to pinpoint the source of my sickness, but I feel as if the thought of recent news is the cause. I step in the stone tub filled to the brim with steaming water. I vomited three more times this morning at the memory of yesterday. I don't know why the thought makes me so sick. Just because I'm mated to Kane doesn't mean I *need* to love him. I'll do whatever I can to be with Jax, even if it means killing Kane.

I lean out of the tub as the acid floods from my stomach and splatters to the stone floor. Jax bangs open the door and I sink back into the water and hug my knees to my chest, shielding my body from his sight. "Are you alright? Are your cuts getting infected?" I shake my head and Jax grabs a rag to clean up the acid splashed upon the floor. I look away from him, away from his short black hair and ice blue eyes that make my belly spin. I peer out the clear windows that are along the side of the tub. The Winter Kingdom is made of stone, probably carved from Archaic Mountain itself. A large wall surrounds the many mansions, streets, and homes that go down the mountain side. Hundreds of wood-shingled buildings descend Archaic Mountain until they reach the wall that separates the kingdom from Elkwood. Just peaking over the other side of the wall are pine trees that seem to stretch on forever. I'm positive my window is facing south, towards the Mortal Kingdoms. A waltzing feather-light snow falls from the clouds that seem to be inches above the castle's spires. I bet if I climbed to the top of the flag mast, at the peak of the tallest turret, I could feel the water droplets which form the floating fluff that blots and moves through the blue sky. I feel as if I'm at the top of the world, but also at rock bottom.

For a moment, I forget Jax's presence, but the rippling water of the tub makes my head whip toward him, now naked, climbing into my bath. "What do you think you're doing?"

"Joining you," he laughs as if it isn't a problem at all, and he's right. He doesn't know what's wrong and I don't have the heart tell him. I have to start being better at hiding my discomfort. "Would you not like me to be with you?" a loaded question. Not a simple or normal question, but something pointed and waiting for my response. This decides if I forgive him of the lies he told in Equadoria. And I remind myself of the plan I created to love Jax and not Kane.

"No, you can join me," I mutter and uncontrollably squeeze my body farther into the corner.

He sighs as he stretches out his legs. His big toe rubs my hip bone and I barely hide the recoil from his foreign touch. He doesn't notice and I heave a sigh. This is going to be harder than I thought. I just need to remember I know Jax. He loves me; he even said so, before the mating bond. I begin to gag and choke the bile down. Jax doesn't even glance away from the window and the view outside.

"What happened?" His voice makes my bones shudder. He knows something is off, but how naïve was I to believe I could hide something from him. He watched me grow up and knows everything about me, and he could likely smell my unease.

"What're you talking about?" I play dumb as a ploy to pull his attention off of me.

He lifts a brow and looks into my eyes. "After I went to look for the fire wood I got lost, how did you find your way to the Winter Kingdom with my brother?" I almost cry out with relief that he isn't questioning my current feelings, but instead what happened in Elkwood.

"I tried to find you, but then he found me," I leave out the detail of the Umbra's shifting into Jax and making me choose. I won't tell him or anybody the choice I made. Kane had saved me from an imminent death from the Umbra.

"Then how did you end up having a gaping hole in your side and almost bleeding to death?"

I don't have to hesitate, my answer practically springs off my tongue as fast as a Dreag's pounce. "We were attacked by a Troglodyte and it chased me. Your brother and I got separated and I fell, far down the mountain, off a cliff into a nest." I also refuse to say my mate's name. It'll only make me sick and I don't think I have any more stomach acid left to give up. "When I broke through the thorns, I landed on a bone and it went through my side," my hands shake at the memory of the feeling of morrow on morrow. I can still remember the reverberations of steel on bone from when my father killed me.

"What was inside the nest?"

"The Akuji," I whisper his name as if I said it any louder the monster will arrive.

"WHAT?" He jumps from the tub and stands in the water, his manhood hanging a little too close for my liking. I ignore it completely and look up at his eyes. "How are you even alive?"

"I don't know," I mutter and look into the water. His body is reflected on the surface and I close my eyes, no longer wanting to stare at him. "I don't remember much after that."

Jax crouches down next to me and grabs my chin trying to make me look at him and I shake out of his grip. "What's wrong with you today?"

I keep my back to him, covering my breasts with my arms as I climb out the tub, the air is frigidly cold against my skin. My body reacts with a thousand goosebumps and I quickly wrap the soft towel around myself. "I'm just sick of talking about it. *And* the bath." I leave the bathroom and hear him sink back into the water before heaving a sigh.

I wring out my hair as best that I can and quickly get dressed into a long dress that fades from white to bright blue. It has a small train and hugs my curves nicely, my ribs stand out prominently and my breasts have become shamefully small since my reign as queen. Now, I understand why the High Lady had asked if Equadoria ran out of food when I awoke. At the thought, my stomach rumbles, begging for food, so I throw on a silvery blue cape, lined with brown fur. The cut on my cheek from the whip is gone and I pull up my hood and run from the chamber before Jax can follow me.

I don't know how I'm going to deal with these never-wracking problems. My mother is preparing for war, I found out I have a brother, my army has been murdered as was my court, I am trying to get an army, I almost died, my mate hates me, and I have an alliance growing with the Winter Kingdom. Although the latter isn't a problem, it's more of a necessity, and it still surprises me that Brennan was so open to the idea of creating the treaty.

Kane must've told him about us being mates because why else would the High Lord of the Winter Kingdom ally with Equadoria? My kingdom sadly offers nothing in return for his good graces, besides thanks. I don't have much else. Not that I would admit that to

Brennan until after signing the treaty. What he doesn't know won't bring harm to him.

I easily get lost in the maze of the Winter Kingdom castle. Its forever turning hallways and descending and ascending stairwells make the building impossible to map out. From somewhere off in the distance I hear Jax call my name, so I break into a sprint and find the nearest maid. The Faerie servant is human-like, besides the pointed ears and ethereal features. She reminds me of a Faerie version of Desirae, my personal servant back home. They have similar brown eyes, Jeremiah's eyes. My gut twists and before I can begin to gag the servant takes me into a hidden passage, most likely used by the help, and we descend spiraling stairs to a wooden door. She opens it and the dark, musky servant's passage fills with light flooding from the entrance hall. The grand chamber has a pyramidal ceiling with two curving flights of stairs meeting to a platform and spitting off hallways in different directions. Every stone block that makes up the walls and ceiling and fills the floor, are engraved with images; stories. Different swirls and spirals make me spin and scan every stone. I see the depiction of a hand made of fire touching the ground from the clouds. *Prometheus.* He gifted mankind with fire to further their advancement of life and later created the Tree of Light.

I move along the chamber staring at the different artworks of the gods. I find an image of a young woman; a coronet of blooming roses encircles her head of rippling hair. *Amare.* I'll never forget the face of the goddess of love and beauty.

"Ariadae?" My memories vanish in a flash and I glare up the stairs where Jax stands scanning the entry hall, looking for me. I am thankful for the hood of my cloak hiding my features, but ruling out the servants and males all around is making the scrambling crowd smaller and easier for him to find me. I mutely sigh and keep my head down as I basically run to the front doors that I pray exit the castle.

The outside air on the peak of Archaic Mountain sends my body into a state of shock. Ice freezes my veins and my lungs feel as if shards of glass have crawled within them. My body is frozen, morrow deep. I don't understand how the other Fae that are happily milling about can wear tank tops or shorts, unless they were maybe born within the Winter Kingdom and the ice is already in their blood. Their bodies must be accustomed to the cold and chill that is permanent so high up the mountain.

I ignore the idea of myself being mated to the heir of the Winter Kingdom and focus on the tall grey stone buildings that seem to reach for the clouds. I can't get over how close together they are.

I pull my cloak tighter around me and begin walking down the cobblestone road full of wagons, Faeries, and stores. The first shop I take interest in is a small café. What really draws my attention is the hearth in the corner of the wooden interior and I find myself walking through the double glass doors before I can look at any other stores. The warmth crawls along my bones and leaves pinpricks on my fingers and face. It feels like I'm using the Void, but when I check my hands they are clean of the purple smoke-like flames.

A rack next to the door holds what seems like hundreds of jackets, coats, cloaks, and capes, so I hang mine up along with them. A hush falls over the room and a chill slithers through my pores. When I turn around every pair of eyes is trained on me. None of the Faeries are trying to hide their stares, but instead sit openly and dominantly looking at me. I can't read any of their faces. I ignore them even though it's a lot harder than I ever thought possible, and walk to the small bar where a doe-eyed Fae barista stands, waiting for my order.

I glance over the menu very fast and pick the first thing that sounds remotely good.

"A small cup of the holly bean tea," my voice is barely a whisper. I try to call for the queen voice within me, but it doesn't come. The barista's soft features contort to complete disgust. "What's wrong?" I begin to wonder if the order isn't good.

She shakes her head like a wet dog and replaces the disgust with a feign smile that doesn't meet her eyes. "Good choice," she answers. I hope so. I wonder what made her react so violently. I check my clothes and wipe my face before leaving the counter.

I find my own seat on a small sofa beside the hearth. Wool blankets are draped over the furniture and I pull the train of my dress around my legs on the couch and lay the blanket across my shaking body. In what feels like mere seconds, I'm again greeted by the barista with a steaming cup of holly scented amber. I thank her silently with a dip of my chin and stare into the liquid, a small holly leaf floats atop the surface and the glass saucer clatters loudly against my cup. More eyes flick my way and I put it down. It's so cold on top of the mountain even the blanket and warm fire beside me don't shake the chill from my bones. It's irritating. I can't wait to sign the treaty and head south where only two seasons exist; Spring and Summer. It'll be dry and wet instead of frozen and bitter. It'll be easier and harder all the same. The weather will be easier to travel in, but getting the Mortal Kingdoms to align with us will be almost impossible. But there is still a possibility, which is what's dragging me all the way out here. And even if I don't get a large army, I have to find soldiers to get Jeremiah back to me.

The door swings open and a roar of laughter fills the café. I, and every faerie in the chamber look toward the door. I'm greeted by a beautiful face. Eyes of ocean green flick around the room and hair of curling blonde-brown waves bounce with life. Kane is here. My mate has found me. I pull my eyes away from him and focus on the flames that are dancing between the logs in the stone fireplace. The slithering, orange-blue fingers spew a plume of dark smoke into the chimney which I can only imagine puffs the dark clouds into the sky. The fire burns thick and bright, like my hatred for the male now ordering something at the counter. The once silent café is now full of chatter and a piece of me is relieved for the attention he takes off of me. I inhale deeply and take a long sip from my cup. The holly bean tea was a good choice on my part. The sweet liquid is spiced with a sour flavor that makes an interesting blend of tastes bless my tongue.

Kane takes a seat across from me and my joyous sip chokes in my throat. I explode in a coughing fit and put the cup down before I spill all of the contents within. Of course he would sit right near me because he can finally look at me without his father around. His angular jaw and cheeks become flushed with worry. "Are you alright?" I nod and wave away his question. I don't need his sorry excuse to seem kind or interested in my well-being. "We need to talk." Not a polite question, but a demand. Although I almost shake my head in denial, I find my head nodding through the silence that follows.

"What is there to speak about?" *Please don't say it.* I don't want to talk about the snapping connection that bonded us, and continues to make me want to move closer to him. I love Jax, I want Jax, I think…

"Last night," he whispers and looks around the room to make sure nobody is listening in on the conversation. "We mated." *Shit.* I can't avoid the truth anymore. Even if I push the questions away they'll still come around later in time.

"You felt it too?" I ask trying to be a little oblivious. I don't want to lead him on in anyway.

"Of course."

"It doesn't mean I love you, Kane. If that's what you are here to discuss." I'm in love with Jax. Never will I betray Jax for his brother. That would be a cruel torture, especially now after everything he's been through; the whipping and the punishment that will probably come one day or another.

Kane has the audacity to appear surprised, a lop-sided grin grows on his face and I want to claw it off with my grimy nails. "Why? Am I not good looking? From what I've been told I am quite the handsome fellow around here." I scan the café and try to ignore the females, blushing and eyes full of lust. I roll my eyes.

"If this conversation is about your commenting on your own obsession with yourself, I'm going to either leave or vomit on you." Kane wails with laughter and heat floods my cheeks and neck. Why is he even being nice after what he said to me in Elkwood? "Stop acting like we're friends."

"Are we not?"

"No, we are not friends. You are a sadistic asshole!" Someone gasps at the table behind me and I fight the urge to growl at the Faerie. Kane's smirk vanishes and sorrow knits his brows together. I can tell I've hurt him and I hate to admit that I feel sorry about it. The words sigh from my lips, exasperated and tired, "I'm sorry, just after what you said in the forest, I find it hard to be open with you."

"I'm sorry," he whispers. His eyes fall to the cup of liquid in his lap, a prominent frown on his face, "I didn't mean what I said in Elkwood. You were just judging me for something I am ashamed of and I didn't know where else to strike besides the throat."

I almost gasp with shock that he is insecure about killing the innocent faerie. It seems that both the Archaeminza brothers have hearts and have more in common than most would believe. "I can forgive, but I can never forget." The same rule I have with Jax.

He looks up at me, his blue-green eyes filled with a blissful glow. "You really mean that?"

"Sure, just don't do something stupid to make me hate you even more." He smiles and sips from his cup. I do the same.

He finishes his tea in a single gulp and I savor every bit of mine. For a moment, I don't think we'll speak again, but then his voice floods my ears. "So, you really don't think I'm gorgeous?"

"I said no such thing," I try not to smile, but fail horribly. He winks and all I can do is laugh in answer. I keep catching myself getting lost in his blue eyes. His full lips that look soft to the touch and his giant hands dwarf the second cup of tea that he orders. Our conversations vary from my father, which leads me to tears, then to what happened in Elkwood this past summer. I describe to him how I ended up in the war with Evaflora and how I adventured across Elkwood to save my father and eventually I learned of the twisted truth about how the curse wasn't created by the Tree of Light, and was instead conjured by my mother, which left Kane gasping with surprise.

"So, when you arrived back to Equadoria, hoping your father was free from the curse and back to himself, he truthfully wasn't and killed you?"

"Yes," I nod and sip from my own second cup to hold back a sob. He is on his third and I begin to hope he doesn't get sick from all the tea and sugar, my own stomach churns with anguish.

"What was it like...the afterworld," he asks, his words a bit unsure if not shaky. The question floods my brain with the memories of the dark bridge between worlds; the light of Nirvana on one side and the darkness of the Underworld on the other. I still remember the faces of the soldiers I killed, my friends who died, their skin peeling away revealing rotting flesh and even bone. "Novid and Gaston, the soldiers I entered Elkwood with, who died from the Forsaken, tried to drag me into the darkness. I'm glad I'm alive, but every day, I am haunted by my demons."

"Does Jax not chase them away?"

"He tries," I whisper and think of the first few days after coming back. I didn't sleep for a week because Novid and Gaston were always there, waiting for me to trip up or be alone. Jax would tell me to say they weren't real, but for a while it never worked. It was traumatizing seeing them over and over again. Never was I haunted by Seri. My maid from the Summer Kingdom kept me safe there and seems to be doing so now. I smile at the thought of her face in my dreams after falling in the Akuji's nest, normal, human-like, in a way that Faeries can look human. She told me Lunan is my brother. Lunan helped me in the Summer Kingdom as well, but I wish the birdbath of starlight in Evaflora's garden, which told me she was my mother, told me Lunan was my brother. I would've had so many more questions for him. I might even have taken him with me on my traverse through Elkwood.

"Have they haunted you since your arrival a week ago?" Shock floods me at the realization I was here for a week already, but only really woke up yesterday.

"Now that I think of it, no, they haven't. But has seven days really passed when I was being healed?" Kane nods. He finishes his third cup and places it on the low table between us. After the attack during the Winter Solstice ball and the healing process in the Winter Kingdom, it seems I am unconscious more than awake.

"I've been meaning to ask you about the nest."

"Oh, thank you for getting me out of there. I'm sorry for not saying it earlier," I mumble between sips of my tea and Kane's head cocks in question.

"What're you talking about? I was going to ask you how you got out." Kane's words makes my heart start to thrum and my brain spin with confusion. I remember little from the nest, but I do have a vivid memory of Kane seeing me and calling down to me before everything went dark.

"What're you talking about? You found me and brought me out. Didn't you?"

Kane shakes his head and a chill slides like a finger down my spine.

"You were passed out on the tree that you fell from." My stomach flips and I double over emptying my stomach on the floor. All I remember was fainting in the nest with the Akuji. My body shakes at the possibility that the Akuji lifted me up onto the tree like a gift for Kane to find. Kane rises from his seat and wraps my cloak around my shoulders. "Look away everyone, nothing to see here." He leans down into my ear. "Are you alright? Here let me take you back to the castle."

I get off of the sofa and avoid the liquid bile. I wipe my mouth on the corner of my cape. Embarrassment floods my every pore as Kane grabs napkins from the barista's counter to clean up after me. Everyone is looking at me disgusted and my stomach spins again. A vile flavor hangs in my mouth and I inhale before running from the café. Nobody outside in the frigid air knows what happened, so none of the citizens pay me a second glance. The eyes finally off of me are comforting. From a block away, I hear Kane running to catch up to me and I don't quicken my pace. I don't know why, but I want him to catch up. *He's your mate. That's why.*

"Sorry about what happened back there," I apologize when he gets within earshot. I keep my hand over my mouth so he won't smell the regurgitated tea. He pants a little bit as if not expecting me to leave so quickly. "I didn't mean to run, I was just embarrassed."

"Don't apologize; anybody would be in that situation." His not being disgusted makes me feel a lot better about myself. I see what he wants to ask begin to rise onto his lips and I jump to the answer.

"I'm fine. I just wasn't feeling that well earlier, that's all. I'm perfectly okay now." I even end the almost true statement with a smile. He doesn't seem completely convinced, so he removes his doublet and wraps it around me beneath my cloak. His chuckle flutters through my ears and I ask, "What?" as he looks away from my face towards the city around us.

"Nothing," He breathes.

"Just say it!"

"You could use a mint." I punch his shoulder before pulling his coat around my arms. The warm heat from his body clings to the jacket and I relish in its warmth. Kane on the other hand, is only wearing a tank top and doesn't seem bothered at all by the cold. His vein-ridden, tan arms are swelled with bulging muscles that flicker with every movement. My mouth goes bone dry. His skin is covered in dark tattoos, some are swirls that tell stories and others fade into jagged sharp spikes that have to be some kind of language. I know the Faerie language, but this, this must be ancient.

"Promethean," Kane grumbles as if he read my thoughts. He twists his arm around so I can see better, tree-trunk sized biceps ripple making the jagged language wave like water. It's strangely contradicting. "The tattoos are the language used by Prometheus himself when writing the Rift."

The question passes my lips before I can even think to ask it. "What is the Rift?"

"It's the sacred text written by Prometheus and his pantheon. It's the religious rule that Druids and monks follow."

Before I ask any more questions, I notice we have arrived at our destination at the castle and what seems like hundreds of courtier's sprint through the chamber to Kane in a screaming howl of excitement. Kane's face flushes bright red and I am immediately pushed and shoved by the throng of silk and fur, Faerie and Faerie, skin and hide. A hand palms my back strong enough to leave a bruise and fingers grab a length of my hair and tug, unexpectedly strong. Many shrilling voices shout, "Kane!" or "I love you!" One girl somewhere in the back is ambitious enough to scream, "Fuck me!" After the chorus of whines for attention a particularly stunning Fae with a dress of periwinkle turns her bronze eyes on me. Fires from a thousand suns burn with fiery rage behind them, the anger pointed at me. She lurches toward my face with a snarl and before I can jump away, her manicured claws rake down my arm. I cry out at the sight of crimson blood instantly flooding from the four slices along my forearm, branding me. Kane doesn't see what happens, but hears my scream. He cuts through the crowd, pushing Faerie girls half my age to the floor just to get to me. He doesn't reach me when the same periwinkle dressed courtier leaps onto me, smacking us both to the tile. The girl growls as she bears down on me with nails as sharp as knives. I feel like my skin is being ripped away by a Dreag or a Wendigo, not a damned courtier. For a moment, when I close my eyes, I'm thrusted back into Elkwood Forest. The shrill screams are howling Forsaken and a distant voice calls to me. Kane or Jax, I'm not sure, but I can't stop the urge that floods through my veins with the speed of a viper.

Like releasing a breath of air, an outward explosion of telekinesis sends my bronze eyed attacker and her fellow mistresses flying and sprawling through the air in the chamber. I rise on shaking legs as the screaming girls thud against the floor like beating drums. A song of cries and the flicker of sparkling tears fill the entrance hall. Maids, Lords, and Brennan himself run into the chamber. The father's and servants are quick to look to the courtiers, but the burning slashes on my arms and chest feel like hundreds of cat scratches. Scarlet blood stains the white part of my gown; the bottom fading to blue only has some violet droplets spattered across it. The cuts leak profusely and my Fae hearing picks up on the echo of blood dripping off my hands onto the floor bouncing around the chamber.

"Ariadae!"

I look to the voice in front of me, the male on the stairs, still where I left him as if he never moved, the Fae I know so well. Jax runs down the last flight and crosses the chamber in seconds. Faeries scurry out of his storming path and he immediately grabs my shaking arms. "What happened?" he whispers only to me. And for a second it feels like we are the only people in the room. But suddenly I notice the male that was the start of the whole attack. My eyes look over Jax's shoulder to Kane. Jax follows my glare.

"What did you do to her?" Jax's question is more of a growl than actual words.

"What did I do? I think you should ask what she did!" Kane points at me and I'm taken aback. He is blaming me for all of this even though the courtiers were screaming over him. What happened to the male putting his jacket over my shoulders? At the thought, I drop his doublet, torn to pieces by the attack. Kane notices. So, does Jax.

Brennan marches over from his place next to the stairs where he was talking to, I assume, one of the courtier's fathers. His cloak of midnight blue billows behind him like a gale of rage and fury. He shouts at Kane, Jax, and me. "The three of you, get in the throne room now!"

None of us look at one another and I begin to panic. I hope he doesn't stop the alliance and creation of the treaty because of this. It was just a stupid mistake and an assault on me. Brennan slams the throne room doors behind Kane, as he is the last to enter, and the High Lord doesn't even take a seat on his throne.

He turns to Kane first, his sea-green eyes promising a punishment greater than I can imagine. "What happened out there?" I don't know Brennan's relationship with Kane, but I'm not sure I want to know of their dynamic.

"Well I was at the tea café where I saw Ariadae. We delighted in conversation and she didn't feel well, so I, being the gentlemen you raised me to be...," Kane is really trying to pull the best from his father or he is being a smartass on purpose. I can't tell which it is. "...Guided her back to the castle. When we arrived, the Winter Kingdom Ladies must've heard of my initial departure and waited upon my return."

"What happened when you arrived to the threshold?" A threat waits in his words, a promise of punishment. The High Lord is waiting for the part where his Noble's daughters were found on the floor in tears. I shake uncontrollably.

"They swarmed us like hungry hounds to fresh meat."

"So how did they end up injured and on the damned floor?"

I completely forgot Jax was in the chamber until he jumps in and gestures to my still bleeding arms and chest. "You think they are injured? Look what those feral things did!"

Brennan finally looks me over. He isn't fazed by the blood, but I find it impossible to avoid scratching the already puffing and blushing skin around the slashes. I jump to the words recalling my memory, expecting his oncoming questions, "I was stuck in the middle of the hoard and a particular courtier sought me out. She leapt on me, pinning me to the floor and cut me open like a birthday present." It's almost impossible to not raise my voice as the whole scenario is idiotic, but I am a guest in the Winter Kingdom and I need to be respectful. And if I want his army than I want to keep my sanity so I don't tell of the triggered memories that arose from the assault. "I couldn't take the abuse much longer, so I simply got them off of me the best way I could."

"Your damned Telekinae abilities sent them flying across the fucking chamber!" Spit flies from Brennan's roaring mouth and I shield my face from his rage. Silence hovers over the four of us for what feels like hours until he finally mutters to Kane, "Get Lhys. We need someone to heal our guest." Just as the chamber door shuts I drop my bleeding arms in exhaustion and look to Jax.

I flick my gaze back to the High Lord of the Winter Kingdom, who is now somewhat composed and again regal looking. "I'm so sorry for my outburst. I promise it won't happen again."

I should be thankful, for the High Lord taking pity on me. His voice is a threat as it cuts like a knife through the air in the room, "If something happens again, expect an altercation to the treaty, Your Majesty."

CHAPTER EIGHTEEN

~Ariadae~

With Brennan's threat hanging over my head like the clouds above Archaic Mountain, I didn't leave my chambers until after High Lady Lhys healed me. Her ability to heal is truly astonishing and she tried to explain to me how she can manipulate the ice, born of her fingers, to replicate the skin cells quickly by freezing parts of the small miniscule skin, duplicating the cells. It basically copies the skin around the cut and pulls the pieces together by replicating the healthy cells. It seems impossible to do with ice powers, but centuries have taught her the very rare gift of a healer's touch.

I sit on my bed and wait for Jax to roar at me, hate me, destroy me at the seams for being with Kane in a café, alone, and he does just that.

"Are you fucking kidding me?" Jax shouts loud enough to shake the castle. Our bedroom doesn't seem like a private enough location to have this conversation, but with Jax's voice I doubt anywhere will be safe from listening ears.

"I had stopped inside for some tea and to sit by the fire to get warm," I try to excuse myself and lesson his anger, but it doesn't seem to be working. "Kane showed up minutes after I settled and trust me, I wasn't too welcoming of his unplanned arrival." And although I was upset at first, I'm glad that he kept me company.

Jax's eyes roll to the back of his head as he taps his skull in confusion. "But why did you speak to him, why did you go alone in the first place? You left so fast after our bath that I felt as if you wanted to get away from me."

"I just wanted some space, that's it," I continue speaking the truth and I hope he hears it.

"What is happening to us?"

"Nothing," I lie. "I just don't want every moment I spend with you to be fucking!"

"Am I not good enough?" He asks and tears seem to prick the corners of his eyes. I almost roar at his obliviousness to what I am saying. "Are you still mad about me lying because I kept that secret from you because I knew it would hurt you?"

I find myself not even being able to look at him anymore. The white-hot anger just floods through me and I have long forgiven him for his lies, but I will not forget them, not ever. "*Please* Jax," I huff as I rub the ache from behind my eyes.

"There's nothing more I can do than say sorry!"

"*Jax.*"

"And why can't you just forgive me, and let things be how they used to!"

"STOP," My throat burns as I scream making feet shuffle in the hallway beyond the door. We have an audience and I was expecting that, so he, spitting the distrust within my kingdom, won't sound good in Brennan's ears. "Jax that's enough, I've forgiven you long ago, but we will never be how we used to. You lied and that's the end of it, you ruined it. So stop trying to fix what is too broken for restoration."

Jax doesn't say another word before running to the chamber door and swinging it wide. I know he wants to run away, be alone like I wanted, but Kane's smiling face stands in the hallway, his fist lifted as if he was about to knock. "Is this a bad time?"

Jax snarls and I walk up to the doorway as I place a hand on Jax's shoulder in a piss-poor job of calming him. "What do you want?" I ask trying to keep the attitude from my voice and Kane lets his hand fall into his slacks.

"Your presence is requested in the dining room where we will speak about the treaty," He explains and my heart skips for a moment. How so soon? But instead of questioning, I stay optimistic and walk with Kane and Jax through the winding corridors where we say nothing.

Lhys shows none of the friendly self she was when healing me and sits, stone-faced next to Brennan, with Kane on the opposite side of his father. They sit on one side of the table while Jax and I sit on the other. The finished treaty lies on the table between us. I don't make to move towards the feather pen wading in the inkwell until I read the terms because a High Lord like Brennan doesn't simply hand over an army of the Winter Kingdom.

The High Lord waves his hand at the parchment, solemn on the oak table. "Take a look, Ariadae Vox." The rest of Brennan's court stands behind him witnessing the monumental event of a Faerie Kingdom aligning with a Mortal Kingdom. Although Equadoria is ruled by a Fae, the origins of the kingdom don't change. Magic was banished from Equadoria until my rebirth as an immortal and it's time for a new age. It's time for the bridge between immortal and mortal to be built. The treaty is only a blueprint in the grand scheme of things.

Jax pulls the paper towards us and I read the first article. It is full of information that I thought of myself, connecting the ties between human and faerie. There is other simplistic things that are obviously game changing, but beside the point of what's at hand. I let Jax do the bulk of the reading and I notice his breath hitch. I flick down to the fourth paragraph where his finger is frozen. It reads:

The alliance between Equadoria and the Winter Kingdom of Elkwood will only become aligned if the Majesty of Equadoria completes their terms and conditions stated. Ariadae Vox, current Queen of Equadoria must compete in the Proving. The five trials will test Ariadae's ability to be fit as a ruling leader of the Frozen Army. She must complete the five trials to tie the alliance between the Winter Kingdom and Equadoria. If the Proving is not completed, than the Frozen Army will not be placed into the hands of Equadoria and no alliances will be attempted at a further date.

"No," the singular word I voice claps like thunder in the silent council chamber. Jax grabs my arm and tries to pull my attention before my reaction can get violent. The courtiers gasp with shock at my quick retort, but I will not be a puppet in these courtly games.

"Ariadae," he whispers. I glare at him from the corner of my eyes. "The only way we can get the army is if you complete it. It's our only chance."

I stand up and so do the High Lord, High Lady, Kane, and Jax. "I will not participate in Winter Kingdom culture! We can get an army from the Mortal Kingdoms," I spit venomously and the rest of Brennan's court doesn't mumble or move. Smart. Hunger roils in my stomach which begs to be filled.

Kane looks at Jax and I, utterly surprised. I barely refrain from hurling a wad of my spit onto his face. Kane shouldn't let this happen! He is my friend, I am his mate!

Jax grabs my arm again, pulling away my glare. "No," He growls. "If the Mortal Kingdoms don't believe us, we have no army. If we have the Frozen Army, even without the Mortal Kingdom soldiers, we would still have a fighting chance to stop your mother."

I want so badly to fight back. I want to roar at the sun, the sky, Nirvana, and Prometheus himself. Why can't he strike down Evaflora and save me from this downward spiral? After this summer and his helping me, I have a feeling he has no reason to step in. He is just watching the game unfold before his eyes and enjoying the sight of it. For the first time in centuries the gods will be entertained with the song of war. But the only way that'll happen is if Equadoria partners with the Winter Kingdom.

"The offer is only on the table for as long as you sit in the council chamber," Lhys whispers and I see the apology in her ice blue eyes, Jax's eyes. She has nothing to do with this and I can't help but think Brennan made this alteration after the courtier accident yesterday. He said if it happened again. Not that he would alter the treaty.

"I thought you weren't going to change the treaty," my assumption is thrown down upon him like a dagger that kills the silence.

Brennan smiles wickedly and I can't help, but to see Evaflora's face painted on his. A monster is a monster, a beast is a beast. I'll never leave the horrors of Faerie Kingdoms or Elkwood Forest for as long as I am alive. "Ever since you revealed that you have two powers and your title as Fae Druid of the Void upon your arrival, I have been waiting to see what you can do."

"You are a sick bastard," Jax mutters.

"Watch your mouth outcast!" Reyluke, Brennan's personal guard, and the sentinel who had whipped Jax in the throne room shouts. Some of the court members flinch at the roar of Reyluke and the growl Jax bites back. I grab his wrist. He calms for a minute and faces me.

I decide to play with the rules of this treaty. I look down my nose at Brennan, even though he is a full head taller than I, and voice my compromise with a voice of a queen who is powerful, regal. "I will participate in your Proving if you lift the exile on Prince Jax Lycus Archaeminza."

Brennan's smile taunts me and I want to leap across the table and smack it off his damned face.

Reyluke's thunderous howl shakes the chamber. "DO NOT GIVE HER WHAT SHE WANTS!"

Lhys glares at her husband's personal sentinel and maybe even acquaintance. Reyluke is instantly ashamed of his outburst and becomes a whimpering puppy with his tail between his legs.

I never break my glaring match with Brennan who is happy to oblige.

"Do it father," Kane whispers to his High Lord. Brennan doesn't peel his stare away from me.

"Let it be done then."

I dip the feather twice, the dark ink reflecting purple off the firelight. The pointed tip fluidly swirls my name onto the thick parchment and two drips of ink follow the final letter before I place the pen back into the well.

"Your first trial is tomorrow."

CHAPTER NINETEEN

~*Ariadae*~

The eve of the Proving is a night of parties for the Faeries of the Winter Kingdom. This is their tradition that comes only with a new heir or royal, entering the family, so it's not often that they get to celebrate this wildly, or so I hear.

I sit in a small garden overlooking the city at the back of the castle. I stumbled upon the small balcony courtyard during my walk through the seemingly endless halls. I couldn't sleep no matter how much I willed my body to relax and settle, but my brain is alive with fireworks. The sound of people celebrating outside doesn't help me either. I have no idea what the Proving entails, but I do know that Trial Four is shedding the blood of an innocent. I knew about it when I signed my name on the treaty, but I feel that I may not complete that Trial. I've already failed and I haven't even started the damned thing yet.

The cold stone bench beneath me makes me shiver in my fur coat. I know it's my fault that I'm cold because all I'm wearing beneath the wolf pelt is lacey undergarments, but I don't want to go back to my room because I fear Jax might be awake. After I signed the treaty all he did was hug me while I cried. We didn't speak about our fight before the meeting and I didn't shed a tear until I left the council chamber, but now my eyes are all dried up. I want so badly to cry away the pain of Jax and I's inevitable falling out, but no tears come. I bet even if I *did* cry the salt water droplets would freeze and break before they even hit the ground.

The whole garden is covered in grey cobblestone and is surrounded by a black wrought iron fence. The glimmering fire lamps that illuminate the streets of the Winter Kingdom make the whole city radiate and aglow with life. Joyful shouts and laughter rise into the air and my stomach twists. How can anyone find entertainment or excitement in the Proving? I sure as hell am not excited for the trial tomorrow and what makes everything worse is I don't get time to prepare. It doesn't matter. I wouldn't know what to even prepare for.

"The Winter Kingdom is gorgeous before the Proving," Kane says from behind me and I am not in the mood to turn around or even engage in conversation. The only sound I make is a heaving sigh. "I remember the night before my Proving; I had sat right where you are now and stared at the stars, trying to ignore the joyous shouts of happiness."

"I'm not doing this for myself, Kane," I break my silent promise to not speak. He knows how to get right beneath my skin like a burrow beetle. "I'm doing this so my mother doesn't enslave the rest of the humans on Abella. I'm doing it for *my* people."

I hear Kane's shoes scuff against the stones and I smell the odor of anger. Its putridly sweet smell is disturbing to the senses. "You are nothing, but selfish and childish! I had the disappointment of my brother's failure weighing me down, so I had the stress of a thousand lives in the Winter Kingdom burying me six feet under!"

I whirl to the Faerie prince. He stands shirtless in the doorway, his face is shadowed, but the glow of the city makes rivers of tears burn brightly on his cheeks. I thought tears wouldn't come again, but now they threaten to spill. He had to do his Proving and so do I.

We both have our reasons to complete the ten Trials, although very different, they are exactly the same.

"My people need me," My broken words croak inside my throat. "My army was decimated in Solaria and I was left with a legion of one hundred warriors at my home. The borders of Equadoria are being attacked by the Forsaken and Evaflora has attacked my castle and murdered my court. I want nothing to do with the Proving, but for the sake of survival and the life of mortals on Abella, I need to do this."

Kane runs a hand through his hair and stalks over to the balcony overlooking the city. He pulls a cylindrical tube from his pocket and holds the end of it to a torch, lighting the cigar. He holds it to his lips and blows away the sour, but also sweet smelling smoke. "I know," he mumbles and a part of me isn't surprised. "Before your stay at the Summer Kingdom the five other Kingdoms of Elkwood had been meeting and talking. We invited Evaflora, but she denied the invitation to speak with the High Fae. We knew she was keeping something from us."

"I know most of the High Fae in Elkwood are aware of the threat of my mother, but do you know what made her want to plan and conjure this path without consulting with the rest?"

Kane shakes his head and blows another cloud of smoke. "Once you learned of her intentions and told

Lunan, the High Lord of the Day Kingdom, he came to each Kingdom and gave us all the news. We still aren't sure why she would suddenly want to remove the life of mortals, but we have reason to believe she is inspired by the eastern continent Pangea."

If mortals are treated as slaves on Pangea than how have the humans there not rebelled? How could the humans even let the Fae take control? Suddenly I remember a letter Samuel had read to me before he died. "Before the death of my court we had received a request for aid on Pangea."

"Was it the mortals rebelling?"

"No, they fear a dark force that wants to conquer their land," I whisper and stand closer to Kane on the balcony and stare out at the glinting lights of the city that seem to blend with the stars. I can't see where the Winter Kingdom ends and the sky begins. It's alluring and magical. "I had to deny the request because I have nothing to offer." And I have my own war to fight.

Kane holds out the cigar to me and I shake my head. "Smoking helps me relax sometimes," he whispers and his words blow away the odor that quickly vanishes on a passing wind. "It started before the Proving."

And although I don't think him to answer I find myself asking, "What can I expect tomorrow. What's the first trial?"

"I can't tell you what it is, Ariadae. Mate or not," he scoffs. I look down at my bare feet in an attempt to hide my shameful blush. "But I can tell you that it will test your strength. You're a Fae now, so my father wants to see your power. He wants to see how far you'll go for his army. "

"He wants to see what my powers are?"

Kane laughs outright. "No, he wants to see your ability in hand-to-hand combat."

A shudder fills my bones as I remember the sight of the citizens in the Winter Kingdom. The males are gargantuan and the women have biceps as big as tree trunks. Compared to them I am just a brittle twig.

"Who am I fighting?"

Kane tosses the finished cigar over the railing and it plummets down to a slanted roof far below. The height of the balcony makes it seem like the castle is on a mountain itself. He looks to me, lips in a thin line and shakes his head. "You need some sleep. You've got a big day tomorrow." And before I can object his end to the conversation, he saunters through the garden door and leaves me to the chill night.

A part of me wants to go crawl back into a bed warmed by a large body, but another part of me knows the quicker I am asleep the faster tomorrow will come. If I really think about it, it's only hours away from daylight. I breathe in, kissing the night goodbye, and wander back to my chambers. Tomorrow is my first trial and now with Kane's hint, I'm mentally prepared. Well as prepared as I could ever be.

The Proving is something special to Winter Kingdom culture. Most of the Fae that are eagerly jumping and running into the entrance didn't believe they'd see another Proving for the next twenty centuries. Now, many are present as they herd like cattle into a large hole in the side of the mountain. The wrought iron gate is spiked at the ends and jagged lines and angles of metal work make images of snowflakes across the bars. The entrance into the arena is at the heart of the Winter Kingdom and I walk with Jax and six Frost guards. The tall sentinels keep the crowd of people from coming too close to me, and I am genuinely surprised by the amount of protection Brennan has given me. I understand that I am a Queen, but to these people I am nothing but a guest in their home. I guess Brennan knows how to treat his guests.

"Are you ready?" Jax asks into my ear, his breath on my skin is hot and clammy. I nod, not ready to give away my words. I know if I talk I won't be able to hide my fear and as I peer toward Jax at the corner of my eye, he seems unable to hide his as well. He anxiously keeps wiping the sweat from his palms onto his pants and his dark brows seem to be permanently knitted together. He notices my stare and I look towards the guard at the entrance who lets us go by. He must know who I am because he doesn't even make a second glance our way. Jax leans down again and I grab his hand in mine. His fingers tremble a little and I know it's not because of the cold. "I need to go, but I'll see you tonight, I promise." His whispers vanish and he disappears into the throng of people. The mouth of the mountain swallows me whole as I cross beneath the portcullis hanging above my head.

The sentinels guide me into the vestibule, full of bustling Winter Kingdom faeries, and direct me to the far wall that leads further down the tunnel toward the arena. Or stage. I don't question our change in course, but just as the six guards and I squeeze into a servants passage I want to turn back. It's a downward stairwell that spirals into the rippling darkness. I can't see anything, but obsidian silhouettes shifting in the tight space.

One of the guards from behind pokes my back urging me forward. The descent down the mountain is extremely unpleasant. "Move," he mutters his voice void of emotion or a care in the world. "I want to get out of here." I don't argue and ignore my internal pleas to turn around and push onward.

In my descent, I pass torches that seem to be randomly scattered throughout the stairwell keeping a mental track of each one. I don't see any other doors leading off the servant's passage, but just in case, I'd like to know my way out of the mountain. I've already seen sixteen torches mounted on the thick jagged rock. The stone isn't grey cobble or placed tile. The walls, ceiling, and floor are brown jagged stone and look as if the tunnels were carved into the mountain. A chill slithers across my skin at the thought of all of the weight of the Winter Kingdom and snow atop my head. What if it all came crashing down?

"Keep moving," a sentinel grunts and I didn't even realize I had stopped. Shaking away my fears I ignore the growing burn in my legs and thighs. "We're almost there."

"Oh thank the gods," a voice whispers from the back and it makes what feels like humor bubble in my gut, just scraping beneath the fear that burrowed itself into my skin.

"At least someone shares the same feelings," I call out into the dark and know everyone will hear me. My voice even carries down the passage and bounces back echoing. The servant's passage is echoing everything and making our whispers louder and a part of me wonders if it's on purpose. Too often do servants and the help see things and whisper in their quarters. If the High Lord placed a spell on the tunnels so all secrets could be heard I have to wonder what incident gave Brennan the reason to do it. I would ask my guards because they seem quite personable, but the stairs round one last time and I'm staring at an open doorway. Fear floods my body like a warm flush and I run out of the tunnel.

A thousand screams make the mountain shake and I literally jump at the sound. I peer around the Proving center and look down, down, down, hundreds and thousands of feet below to Faeries talking and laughing, arguing and kissing. A billion faeries fill the seats of the colosseum that has to be the size of the whole Archaic Mountain range. I barely see the dust sized faces at the opposite side of the dirt stone seating that descends into an ominous pit, the size of an ocean. I wish I was exaggerating, but there is an entire valley within the pit. Green hills roll from a thick forest at the north end of the arena. Sapphire rivers glitter between the green like snakes in grass. Snow covers the southern end of the valley which is to my right and my mouth goes dry at the sight. A whole kingdom could fit into this mountain, who am I kidding, the whole Winter Kingdom is here beneath Archaic Mountain, ready to watch me complete the Proving. *If I can complete it that is.*

A sentinel of the Frost guard who brought me down here grabs my upper arm. I look to his tawny curls and cold grey eyes. His pale blue armor is plated leather and covered in the swirls that have become common imagery in Winter Kingdom culture. "You need to get ready, Milady."

I nod. "Where should I go?"

He answers with a slender finger pointing to a wall along the walkway that appears to wrap around the whole arena. A slim door is the target of his pointing and I nod my thanks. I abandon my personal guards and enter the brightly lit chamber. The space flickers with a glow as bright as the sun from the many candles openly burning around the square room. A table is at the center and I see my clothes for the Proving and small ivory bowls full of creamy liquid in every shade of blue.

I strip off my deer hide shift and fold it onto the table where my new clothes are. The overseers of the Proving must've been told of my arrival because two young women, frail and thin compared to the many muscular women I've seen in the Winter Kingdom, walk into my changing room. They smile at me and with the flickering candle light the symbols and swirls of paint on their skin shimmers like sunlight bouncing off of lapping waves. A memory of the ravine in the Summer Kingdom flashes through my mind and I ignore the sound in my ears of the turbulent waves that churned beneath the bridge like a roiling beast.

The twins, I realize, dress me into skin tight brown pants, black hide shoes with fur leg warmers. My top is dark brown like the pants and a braided pattern of blue yarn creates a thinning triangle descending down the front. A cropped black top is placed over the shirt and I admire the midnight blue stitching creating the beautiful swirls. The short top is slanted across my shoulders making it a tank top and the twins wrap my hands in brown bandages that cover my knuckles, palms, and forearms. My exposed upper arms are pale white from the winter and I shrink away from the cold silver armlet they place on me. I shiver at the chilly metal and the twins laugh in sync with one another. I shake harder, but not from the cold. One twin braids the top of my hair letting the rest of my fiery waves fall around my shoulders. The other twin takes the ivory bowls and begins painting triangles, swirls, and dots of electric and midnight blue patterns on my face and arms. I can only wonder how good I look, but assume the twins are proud because they hug one another, and then me. Never do we exchange words as they kiss my cheeks, avoiding ruining the fresh paint, and guide me back towards the walkway I came from. I want to ask where to go, but that's when I notice their thin lips and hollow cheeks. They don't have tongues.

"Welcome to the Proving," a deep male voice says pulling my attention from the twins and back towards the colosseum. The twins vanish into the changing room and Reyluke smiles down at me. I roll my eyes and he chuckles. "I didn't want you to do this, so don't start giving me attitude."

I turn on my heels, already sick of this conversation and begin walking towards the northern end of the arena. I barely mind saying, "Says the male who has more venom in his words than a viper."

Reyluke laughs harder and matches pace with me. "I'm here to tell you about your trial."

"I'd rather go in blind," my words bite into him and I watch his big hands become fists. He can't hold back his rage and I smile to myself. He looks down on me and I hear the quietest ripple of his growl. Even the roar of the talking faeries can't subdue his true hatred towards me. I'm glad the feeling is mutual. He has no reason to hate me, he just hates Jax. "I'll never forget what you did."

He knows exactly what I'm talking about as he reaches for his belt as if the whip is coiled there, but for my sake, it's not. I doubt Brennan would allow Reyluke to escort me with a weapon. The High Lord knows how I feel about Reyluke and how Reyluke feels about Jax. Reyluke whipped him and then me! He wants nothing more than to see me gone. If I have any reason besides retrieving an army to compete for, than this is it. To show Reyluke that he cannot overpower me, Jax, or other people.

"What I did was ordered by the High Lord. I was following my commands."

"My father wanted me murdered, but none of his sentinels followed through with the order," I fire back and I have no idea what Reyluke's power is, but I feel a wave of heat smother me. I choke on the hot air and stifle a cough.

"You're mortal guards are weak and unloyal. If you were dead you'd save Abella a lot of trouble," He shoots back and I can't help but feel the blow. I want to deny his words, but at the end of the day they're the truth. I played a big role in kick starting this oncoming war. My mother was planning to enslave all mortals in Abella, but what I did when I attacked her kingdom and tried to turn her people against her had caused her to move twice as fast and aim her first target at me. And the only reason I'm getting this army is to defeat her, to get my best friend back. I'll deal with the Solarians when I reach the southern Mortal Kingdoms and ask for their assistance.

I don't retaliate against Reyluke and focus on the path. We have reached the curve of the oval colosseum and are only northwest on a compass, but a long staircase to our right descends straight down to the arena floor. Reyluke bows for some dramatic effect and follows after me when I start the never-wracking walk towards my first trial. The roaring faeries start to hush one another as I walk by in my Proving getup. The last woman to be seen competing in the Proving was Lhys, the High Lady of the Winter Kingdom. I know she has healing powers, but I wish I was around to witness that performance. Lhys seems like a force to be reckoned with, even beside her husband.

Kane, Jax, Brennan, and Lhys, greet me at the floor of the arena and I receive a hug from Lhys which I wasn't expecting at all. Her dress is made of jagged ice and her skin is painted like mine. Kane wears a Barbarian style fur getup and even his tattooed body is adorned with more dark paint. The High Lord Brennan wears a fur tunic, black pants, and a billowing blue cloak. His face is covered in electric blue spots across his cheeks, nose, and forehead. Jax is the only person not decorated in paint or regal fashion. He wears a simple shirt and pants; his cropped hair has grown on me the past couple of days. And although I want to wonder why Jax doesn't have the patterns of the Proving painted onto his skin, I know without asking only past competitors wear the symbols.

"Good luck," Kane says and gives a thin lipped smile.

"You'll do amazing," Lhys whispers and rubs my arm reassuringly. Her touch makes my skin rise in goosebumps. It's comforting, yet unsettling.

The High Lord, instead of offering wishes of luck looks out to his people, sitting in the stands waiting in anticipation and I look to Jax as Brennan calls, "Let the

first trial of Ariadae Vox, Queen of Titanium Antlers'
Proving, commence!" Some magic he uses allows his
vice to resound clearly over the colosseum and the
roaring I heard before is nothing to the ground
shuddering quake of excitement that comes from the
Winter Kingdom. I cover my ears in shock and Brennan
only laughs. Jax grazes my forearms with his fingertips
and I smile at his touch, he mouths, "I love you" before
placing a kiss on my forehead, avoiding the drying paint.
Brennan gestures me forward and waves a dramatic
hand towards the archway leading into the valley. As I
pass Kane I notice his angered stare of jealousy and I
look away. I know he's my mate, but it's becoming easier
to ignore him. At least that's what I keep telling myself at
least.

I step through the open doorway and drop five
feet into the dirt floor of the arena. Another earsplitting
scream shakes the mountain and I don't feel the need to
cover my ears, now I am somehow used to the roar. I
take a step towards the lush trees that fill the northern
part of the valley and I watch them twitch and shudder.
After a decent amount of time wandering through the
forest in the arena. The boughs crack and snap, shedding
the bark revealing ivory branches. Skulls sprout at the
end of every branch; even some that are finger thin,
grow and hang from the ends. White wax rises from atop
the skulls and candles wink to life. The hundreds of

candles, one for every person in the colosseum, make the arena as bright as midday. I walk through the maze of bone trees and try to find a way out of the forest. Each ivory trunk makes me think of another person I killed, another death I caused, a different life I stole. Every skull stares down at me, the open eye sockets full of slithering darkness. I look away from the roiling shadows that are between the boughs and trunks. Somewhere in the distance hinges whine and iron scraping on stone makes a horrifying song. The crowd screams with excitement and over the screaming people I hear the guttural wail of an abomination I have met many times.

My first trial is defeating a Dreag.

"Silence! Everyone we do not want to startle our participants," Brennan shouts above the faeries that become instantly mute. I smell the carrion on the air and I hear the rattle of chains. The faster I defeat this Forsaken the quicker my trial is over and I can move on. I follow the sounds of the Dreag and head to the eastern wall. I weave between only three bone trees when I finally get a good sight of the Forsaken. My stomach turns. "This year is different! Ariadae will face altered trials and will have to complete all five, instead of ten, in twenty four hours!" My chest caves in. I duck behind an ivory trunk and look at the Dreag again. The typically frail and skinny abomination is taller with veined muscles. The sight is sickening and I watch the beast drop down onto all fours like a hound. Its dark eyes scan the forest and I look away in fear that it might see me.

I need to complete this trial faster than I figured. I only have about four hours per trial and if I'm timing this correctly it's already been thirty minutes of my first hour! I take a deep breath relaxing my panic and ignore the questions I have for the alterations of the Proving. A crackling breath pants next to me. I glance in my peripheral vision and regret it. The Dreag is standing five yards from me. It sees me. It stands on its hind legs, the grey wrinkled skin of the monster is taught against the rock hard body. The Dreag's claws click in anticipation, blood lust.

It launches forward. Claws out, teeth bared, leaping through the air and I stumble around the tree using an ivory bough to swing my body around the thick bone trunk. I hear the claws slicing the air like blades and land on uneasy feet. I lurch into a staggering sprint as fear makes my body shake violently. Adrenaline has begun flowing through my veins making my muscles work better, any shaking subdues, and any unease vanishes. The Dreag's bounding chase shake the earth beneath my feet and I continue weaving throughout the bone forest, dodging tree after tree as they leap in my way.

I think of my powers and let a part of me uncontrollably call to the invisible chest within the dark ocean in my mind. I dive into the dark waters and swim deeper and deeper into the flowing waves of my past, memories, regrets, promises, and many more. I need to pass it all and make it to the chest buried at the bottom. There are two and I need to open the right one or this can all go wrong.

I feel the Dreag leap, the absence of ground shaking pursuit and I leap to another bough and swing around the side of the trunk. I run back towards from where we came and before the hulking Forsaken can start its chase again, I jump onto a trunk and pull my body up onto the branches. The bones crack and shake as I climb higher and higher up the ivory, the smooth, soft texture is a foreign feeling against my calloused hands. Though I'm exhausted from the stairwell and the fast moving sprint from the Dreag I don't feel any burn in my leg muscles. All I can see, hear, and feel is the pounding of my heart as the Forsaken approaches. It stalks like a cat, close to the ground, ready to pounce. It sees me and smells me within the tree, but I also see and smell the abomination. It reeks of carrion and I calculate the distance.

Within my skull I whisper now and tear open the chest of invisible bubbles that fly to the surface in unfathomable speed and explode outward from within me. I feel the trunk of the tree with invisible telekinetic fingers and crack the bones. I lean on my thick bough and an earsplitting crackle pops into the air as the world tilts. The skulls fall from the branches and the Dreag howls as the hundred bone pikes penetrate its muscled skin and hold the Forsaken against the dirt. I hang onto my branch and lift my toes which dangle inches from the dead Dreag, pinned to the ground by the bone branches of ivory, now stained crimson. The silence in the colosseum makes me sick and I quickly climb out of the cage of bones and walk away from the corpse. I take my time weaving through the forest of marrow and within minutes I leave the ivory trees behind and the faeries howl with excitement. They stomp on their stands, cheer, jump, and even scream my name. Brennan keeps to himself, Jax runs into the pit and grips me in a body crushing hug. Lhys cheers beside her husband and Kane stares everywhere, but at me. I want to ask him why, but the threatening glare I get from Reyluke is too euphoric.

One trial down. Four to go.

CHAPTER TWENTY

~Ariadae~

I barely have time to take a drink before I'm being shoved back into the valley. They dragged me and Jax out of the pit after the first trial. I sit on the stone seating that is offered to the thousands of faces watching the Proving.

"Why the hell are there alterations?" I curse out before gulping a large amount of water.

Brennan just smiles to himself and Lhys looks furious. I begin to wonder if she was aware of the alterations or not. "Brennan changed the Proving for *you*," Lhys growls facing her High Lord and I keep my eyes away from him. I'm afraid my rage might snap and I don't want to do something I'll regret.

"Yes, well the Winter Kingdom court agreed to the changes and have approved each one I made," Brennan turns his stare to me and approaches me like a prowling wolf. A part of me knows beneath his skin, he is a hound. "My kingdom has seen the same trials be completed three times before. If the Proving is only completed every so often I might as well start changing the trials."

"But why is *this* Proving the first time you're doing this?" Kane rises from his seat and saunters up to his father. Brennan glares down at his son and Kane matches his stare. I can feel the tension taut within the air, so I focus on continuing to hydrate myself.

"You know damn well why he did this!" Jax leaps down Kane's throat and I drop my bottle in an attempt to hold Jax back from his brother whose sea-green eyes shift to him. Jax growls and Kane bears his teeth.

"Enough," Lhys hisses at the two brooding males. Brennan tries to hide his smile, in some twisted way he finds enjoyment in all of this. "People are watching. Remember we have an image to uphold."

Before I can ask any more questions or request more water Reyluke itches with excitement to get me back into the pit. "It's time, High Lord."

Brennan nods and guides me to the archway leading to the valley. He looks out to his audience and announces, "Let the second trial begin!" The crowd jeers with excitement. This is the first time they are seeing trials back to back let alone different from the past Proving's trials. I understand their enjoyment of the affair, but I can't shake the feeling of being humiliated. I am on display for all of these people, to show them what? To show them that I deserve their army? A part of me wonders if a different agenda is my reason for playing the Proving.

Two Frost guards walk up to me and begin binding my wrists and ankles. My hands are bound in front of me instead of at my back. I jerk away on instinct and Brennan is quick to hold me still. "Don't struggle," He whispers in my ear. "This is all part of the second trial." What in the god's could test me with my hands and feet bound? I can barely do anything! I hiss at the tightening cords of rope that constrict my skin. The rope surprisingly burns, even beneath the wrapping on my arms.

I look over my shoulder at Brennan. His wrinkled face has stubble growing along his jaw and his sea-green eyes, Kane's eyes, look down at me. I swallow my pounding heart that slams against my ribcage and ignore the voice telling me to run, or hop away.

"What is my second trial?" I choke on the words and ignore the Frost Guard adding more binding around my ankles. Brennan smiles and looks to the valley. The song of iron gates rising fills the mountain and a roar drowns it out. Not a roar of cheering, but instead the rushing flow of unyielding power. The salty smell overpowers the scent of dirt and stone within the mountain and I shiver at the sight of the valley being swallowed by churning blue waves. The dark waters remind me of the ocean within my brain and I feel as if I'm drowning already when the forest of bones, the hills, the snow covered plain are drowned by a manmade ocean. The lapping waves crest like a storm and pool onto the lower levels of the colosseum seating. Even the four foot walls surrounding the twelve foot drop into the pit don't stop the water from rising above the edge. Some faeries around the chamber shout at the water splashing onto them and others rejoice in it. I can't tell if it's cold or warm, but I take my time saving my breaths. I need to relax. I need to prepare myself for what I'm going to do.

I inhale deeply.

Hands slam against my spine and I tumble over the railing and into the midnight blue water. I almost lose my mouth full of oxygen by the extreme cold that bites through my clothes. My skin instantly becomes ice and I try wiggle towards the surface. The only light within the dark ocean, but I am being dragged down. I fight against the pulling force which does nothing due to my bound hands and feet. I look to my toes, the dark shadows at the bottom of the manmade ocean, and realize that no abomination is dragging me down. A large anchor is woven through the cords of braided rope around my ankles. I shake beneath the surface and try to avoid panicking. I should've focused on what the Frost Guard was doing, so I could see how to unlatch it. Instead I let Brennan distract me; I let him talk me into doing this damned Proving. How can I win?

I have to get free, but I feel the building pressure in my chest. It feels like the stone I once had while being a mortal, but instead of becoming heavier its expanding. It's widening and growing with every passing second and I waste many seconds trying to wiggle my hands free. No matter which way I twist the cords, they seem to become tighter instead of looser. Pain roils within my gut like a coiling snake drawing the air from my lungs. *One, two, three.*

I yank in opposite directions and I literally feel the tightening rope. Within the dark, cold water I expel some pressure in my lungs, subduing the pain and send a waltzing throng of bubbles to the surface. My breath of air is still big enough to last me a bit, but is depleting quickly. I sink down further, my anchor is settled on the bottom and I see the thousands of dancing lights flickering down through the surface. It partially illuminates the dark. The salt in the water burns my eyes, but I ignore the pain and try to reign in my focus on my ankles. If I can pull myself free from the bindings, or the anchor, I can get more air. I try to pull against one of the cords, lifting up with all my strength and grab at another. If I can maybe pull different cording of rope it will loosen the binding, but at the back of my ankles I feel the ropes tighten. I try a different side and then the opposite tightens. If I pull right, the left side tightens. I never find an equal ground. My pounding heart becomes a hammer banging against the bones in my chest and a drum in my ears. The floating feeling that overcomes me is shocking. My mind feels light, but I know my limbs are heavy, even with the anchor at my feet.

The ropes around my wrist and ankles tighten like constricting snakes and I thrash around the water. The burning in my lungs and throat is excruciating and finally I cry out in frustration. My breath leaves my mouth as I scream and bubbles rise. I try to save some, but it's barely enough. If only I could somehow untie the cords I could rise to the surface. Wait! Why didn't I think of this before?

I dive into the twin ocean of my brain and swim to the closed chest. It's only been about an hour since I used it. I unlatch the dark golden lock and the bubbles rise and seem to actually form around me, within the actual water and not just in my mind. They move and spin, attaching themselves to the cord's grooves and braiding. I use my telekinesis to wiggle space between the bindings with the bubbles and the moment my invisible hands touch the braided cords it tightens more and I whimper. My head becomes lighter and darkness grows at the edges of my vision. The burn in my chest is making me feel as if I'm on fire beneath the surface and the rope rubbing against my skin is stinging like a cat scratch.

All the burning reminds me of my other power. If my Telekinae ability can't untie the rope than maybe I can burn it. I know the Void starts fires and burns through anything, but it doesn't move like flame, it isn't flame. My mind opens up with the chest inside and purple smoke rises to the surface, my fingertips, and winks out the moment it touches the water; the water swallowing the Void. I would cry if my tears wouldn't be swept away by the shifting undercurrent. The fire in my chest is too much. The pressure makes my vision blur and focus. Black spots smudge my eyesight in the dark water and I scream beneath the midnight blue waves. The bubbles of my last breath escape into the manmade ocean and dance around me. Some fly straight up and others flurry around, lingering for a bit. My air is gone and soon I will be. I won't be able to save Abella or the mortals from my mother's wrath. She'll take every living human on the continent and make them do her bidding and she'll kill anyone who stands in her way. Now accepting the inevitable, I watch the last of the bubbles that linger rise. One tiny pocket of oxygen clings to a crevice of my layered binding at my wrist. The golden braiding is glowing within the bubble and I feel the space within it with my telekinesis. My internal chests of power are still open within me and I am careful not to jerk or move with excitement. I will survive. Using the bubble of oxygen and my invisible fingers I delicately expand the air and watch the pocket expand to an orb swallowing my wrists whole. Purple smoke-like fire slithers from my fingertips and around the bindings in the safety of the bubble surrounding my hands. It eats away at the cord and my vision vanishes. My chest pops. I scream and water floods down my throat. Everything drowns in darkness.

Cold air flushes into my chest filling one lung and creating another. I cough out the last of the salt water and Lhys stands over me, her ice covered fingers touch my chest forming new lungs within me and heals me from the inside out. "What happened?" I croak through a throat of dried salt and Jax and Kane jump down by my face and pour a canister of foul tasting water into my mouth.

"Somehow Ariadae, you completed the second trial," Kane whispers. "I don't know what gods you worship, but you better thank them. We thought the worst." Kane's eyes water and I know he is trying to hide his feelings, but it's hard when your mate almost dies. I wouldn't know the feeling, but I would have to assume it would feel like losing a piece of me. Of who I am.

Brennan is somewhere because I hear his angered words, hushed and hidden by the bustling audience. I only catch bits and pieces of what is being shared, but I understand enough. "Twenty hours left," and also, "How?" and the last thing I hear clearly is "Raid."

I expect some kind of ache or burn, but all I feel is the ghost of Lhys' healing touch. I feel my new lung working to fill my body with fresh air. No longer am I surrounded by the churning dark waves that have abandoned the arena. Some sort of magic has drained out the water in the arena and all of the trees, hills, and snow is back in their rightful places. I pull my focus from the pit and pay attention to my trembling legs as I lift my body from the cold stone ground. People cheer and a smile spreads across my lips. The reason for their applauding is sort of sickening, but boosting my confidence at the same time. Kane and Jax hold me up and I'm glad to be between the two of them because if I wasn't, who knows what fight would erupt. Lhys brushes the dust from her dress and Brennan stops his conversation with the brooding Reyluke. The High Lord gives me a thin lipped smile that doesn't meet his eyes and I don't understand the sudden change in atmosphere. He turns to the valley and opens up his arms to the people of the Winter Kingdom. "Due to some unexpected issues we will be skipping the third trial and moving straight to the fourth!" I am thankful for the skip of the third trial, but suddenly I realize that my exploding lung was the difficulty and what the fourth trial is; spilling the blood of an innocent.

I approach Brennan and reach towards him to get his attention. Reyluke snaps toward me and grabs my wrist in a bone crushing fist. I cry out and he laughs as I fall to my knees in pain. Jax growls, but to my surprise Kane leaps, with a flash of light shifts into a snarling wolf, and slams Reyluke to the stone floor. I rub the pain away from my wrist and watch as Brennan grabs Kane's collar and throws him off of Reyluke. Kane quickly shifts back to his human looking form and Reyluke brushes the dirt from his wrinkled uniform.

"What the hell was that?" Brennan is quick to turn on his son. I look at Jax who eagerly wants to jump in, but I notice Lhys has her hand around his wrist, leashing him from the fight. I'll thank her later.

"He hurt her," Lhys answers for Kane who glances between me and Reyluke. If it weren't for Brennan, I don't think the fight would've ended so quickly. Four Frost Guards descend the steps and look to their High Lord.

"Is everything alright, Your Majesty?" Brennan glares at Kane and then Reyluke.

"Yes, Alwen. Go back to the entrance, the others need you there," Brennan orders and the four sentinels seem to sprint back up the hundreds of steps. I wonder why there would be a need for them at the entrance, but then again more people might be arriving, but with the amount of people already filling the seats around the mountainous colosseum, I doubt anymore could squeeze.

"Ariadae," Brennan draws my attention away from the crowd and to his sea-green irises. His tone becomes suddenly serious. "This is one of the hardest trials, but you need to be fast! We are running out of time. And remember it's just a test." He turns away from me and towards his people. The hundreds of faeries go silent and wait for their High Lord's command. "Let Trial four begin!"

I look towards the pit. No longer do the trees, green hills, and snow fill the valley. Now it's just all flat dirt and at the center is a hunched figure standing, waiting for my arrival. I approach the body. I step into the arena and don't peel my eyes away from the innocent at the center. The broad shoulders and thick chest tell me it's a male, but the thick cloth bag over his head makes my stomach twist. How do they find a volunteer for this trial? Or does Brennan order an innocent against their will to complete it. My stomach twists into a thousand knots tighter than the cords that bound me in my second trial. I feel like I'm going to be sick.

In what feels like hours I am finally standing before the male. His dirt covered tunic shows signs of him being a vagrant. A tear spills from my eyes when he hands me the curved dagger. He knows what is coming and he willing handed his killer the knife. My lip quivers. I feel like I'm making my first kill again. The memory of the arrow flying through the sprinting Summer Kingdom guard flashes across my sight like lightning and I hear the smack of his body on the cobble stone square. The memory, the kill, although created months ago is as fresh as if made an hour ago. How did Kane do this? How did Brennan do this? I noticed the paintings on Lhys' skin show her completion of a past Proving, but I refuse to believe she drove a blade through an innocent's heart for Brennan. Or did she do it for her people?

With shaking fingers I grab the smooth hilt of the curved dagger. Its silver blade flickers off the floating lights at the top of the peaked ceiling and I see my reflection. The war paint is somehow intact even after being beneath water in my second trial and my eyes are red, filled with tears, wet stains cascade down my cheeks. The reflection is me. The reflection is a killer. I have killed people for self-defense because I had no other options. I only kill for necessity, not desire. Every part of me says to drop the blade. I don't need to kill him, I can find another way to get an army, but I think of the scarred faces of the slums in Equadoria. I remember the houses torn apart from the Forsaken. I remember the absence of Jeremiah. My people need me, they need an army. *I* need an army. My brain knows what I need to do, but my heart makes it a thousand times harder.

"Make it quick," the male says and my eyes snap to the fabric covering his face. I know his voice. I remember his height. I yank the dark cloth that shielded his face and stare at the man I love. *Jax*. I feel as if I receive a knife to the heart. Brennan wouldn't make me kill his eldest son, but when I look back to the stands I notice the missing body. How did Jax slip by me into the pit?

"I can't," my voice is shaking uncontrollably. "I can't do it!" I cry out and cover my mouth with my free hand.

Jax's ice blue eyes grow sorrowful and his brows furrow. He lifts a large hand to my cheek and wipes away a descending tear. "You have to do what I couldn't. Remember, it's only a test, Ariadae." *It's only a test.* Suddenly I put the puzzle pieces together. The foul tasting water isn't just from the Winter Kingdom wells, it's an elixir. I lift the blade and stop my flowing tears.

I drive the knife into Jax's chest and he cries out. Blood spills from the wound and waterfalls down the front of his shirt. I second guess myself for only a second until I look to Brennan, smiling at the railing beside Lhys. Kane stands next to his mother and Reyluke is opposite of Lhys beside Brennan. My heart begins pounding and I sprint towards the royal family. Did I make a mistake? Did I drive the knife into the real Jax?

"Jax!" I shout up to the High Lord and his family. Suddenly boots shift and familiar, cropped, black hair rises from behind the railing and a lopsided grin greets me.

"I'm glad you caught on," Brennan winks to me and I fall to my knees in a mess of tears and cries and sounds I didn't even know I could make. "Don't drop out on me yet. You still have one more trial."

"I know," I choke out through sobs. I don't even know why I'm still crying, but I just laugh at the happiness that I was right. I'm glad I didn't make the biggest mistake of my life. I'm so emotionally drained I just pray that I get the chance to breathe first. I need a moment to calm my heart, to lesson my raging fear.

"Trial five, the last altered trial shall commence!"

"What?" Lhys questions to Brennan who only smiles at Reyluke. "She is exhausted and drained, Brennan! You can't expect her to immediately compete in the last and hardest trial?"

"Sure I do," Brennan grimaces and anger erupts through me like a raging forest fire in a dry summer. The

High Lord looks to his personal sentinel who saunters with a killers gait past his master and down the steps into the pit. I rise from the ground and back away from the prowling monster, stalking towards me, his chosen prey. I back far enough away that Reyluke stops approaching and stays about a hundred yards away from me. His tall muscular body matches my stance and, although I am lean, I am no longer frail and weak. I was able to bring Reyluke to his knees before with just one of my powers, I am not afraid to use both this time around.

Brennan's laugh bounces off the walls, magically amplified. "The fifth trial is known to be a performance of power, but this Proving's alteration is making it a battle of power. Reyluke Samos, my most talented and trained warrior will battle the Queen of Titanium Antlers. Let's see who'll rise above. Just so everyone is clearly understanding, the loser dies." I thought this Proving couldn't get any worse than it already has. It appears I am wrong, as usual.

Reyluke decides to show his powers first. He throws out his hands like preaching the sky, but suddenly his skin vanishes to shadow and he's gone from sight. My pounding heart patters and suddenly a force slams against my spine throwing me into a tumble across the hard floor. I grunt and stop my barrel roll before I travel too far. I already feel the forming bruises. I look around the arena and nothing is in the vast empty space just dirt and shadows, everywhere. The dark rippling forces seem to surround me in the center of the arena. A night-dark shadow stands out amongst the others and it flies at me with surprising speed. I scramble out of its path and dodge Reyluke's blow. I rise onto moving feet and run towards the wall. If I can keep my back protected I can focus on the shadows.

What feels like a brick colliding with my moving legs is Reyluke sweeping me. My face slams against the dirt and I spit the dust from my mouth. I ignore the speckled crimson scattered in my spit and try to stand. A pointed boot cracks against my ribs and the tear-jerking pain makes a scream erupt from my lips. Adrenaline pumps through my veins like venom and soaks into my pores. I project a spinning fan of telekinesis around me, protecting me, feeling for him.

Reyluke's jacket grazes an invisible fingertip and I grip the fabric with my power and throw the sprinting shadow to the ground. Reyluke appears at my feet and he kicks my feet out from under me before pinning me to the ground. His fists pound like my heart beat, *boom, boom, boom, boom,* against my face. A crack tells me that my nose is broken and my eyes water. I throw my hands up in an attempt to stop the blows, but he unsheathes his claws and rips them through my skin. "Why won't you die," He spits and the words slither into my skull and unlock a primal rage that I didn't know I had. I have been in the afterlife and never again will I be attacked by the people I loved and the ones who want to bring me to an alluring darkness that steals everything I am. I will never again be clutching at the arms of life.

Reyluke flies up into the air from my powerful shove. The crowd gasps and I push my telekinesis against the dirt and ground of the arena to fly faster, higher, farther than he. I meet him high above the arena floor. Reyluke twirls through the air and the spinning world slows down. Everything moves in slow motion as the searing pain of my Void trickles through my veins like lightning dancing on water. A long burning javelin of purple smoke sharpens to glinting points. With all the force left in my immortal body I throw the beam and it strikes down like thunder, cutting through Reyluke's chest and straight into the floor. A relief I never felt before floods through me and the crowd, witnessing the murder of the best Winter Kingdom warrior, stares in silent awe.

I land like a cat, graceful and silent on my feet. I look at Reyluke, slumped against the javelin that is rising from the floor. His body sags and crimson blood soaks the purple Void that has seemed to harden to a crystalized material. Blood dribbles from his lips. I look down at the male that took joy in whipping Jax, and wanted to see me dead. "It's ironic isn't it?"

He chokes out more blood and makes gurgling sounds, his only way of answering my question.

"You wanted the Proving to kill me, but all it did was kill you."

I hear Reyluke's last breath leave his body and by the time I look away from his corpse and stop smiling the High Lord is staring at me with a grin plastered on his face. "Ariadae Vox, Queen of Titanium Antlers has completed the Proving!" The crowd roars with excitement and Jax runs to me wrapping his arms around me. "She has allowed herself access to the Frozen Army and…" I look to Kane who stares at me with eyes full of tears. He mouths "I'm sorry for this" and then I feel the whip crack between us. Like a crashing wave inside me I feel Kane's sadness and I fall to my knees at the shock of it. My senses are on fire and my Fae instincts roar over the screaming crowd.

"What's going on?" Jax questions and looks around for answers.

"Ariadae Vox has proved her power to rule for the Winter Kingdom and accepted the mating bond of Kane Archaeminza."

I don't have time to scream as Jax shows enough anger for the both of us. A single tear cascades down my face and I barely have time to look to Kane before an arrow flies down from above and rips a hole through Brennan's throat, spraying his blood all over everyone.

CHAPTER TWENTY-ONE
~Ariadae~

Lhys' scream of terror rips apart the roaring mountain. I look up at the many entrances throughout the colosseum where faeries try to flood out, and Forsaken flood in. Dreags crawl across the ceiling and drop down on unsuspecting women. Males fight hard against the Arbors and Troglodytes, so do the Frost Guard. Wendigoes join the party and so do Wood Nymphs who claw and target the faelings. Mothers of their children become fearsome beasts and attack the abominations with claws and teeth. Nobody comes between a mother and her baby. Lhys is no acceptation. She forces Kane and us into a small bubble of swirling wind around Brennan's corpse. Jax must get his powers from her, but I've never seen Jax heal. Kane flinches at every arrow that breaks against the barrier.

I stare down at Brennan, blood pooling beneath him as he chokes and gargles on the scarlet leaking from his neck. I want to wonder how we didn't see it coming, but we did, *he* did. After my second trial I awoke to Lhys healing my exploded lung, but I overheard Brennan talking to Reyluke. One of the words shared was "raid" so they had to have known. That would also explain why my Fae instincts were freaking out while he was announcing my triumphant feat. Was I supposed to win? If I had died and Reyluke didn't, then he could've saved his High Lord. Now, Kane, my mate- I feel his fast beating heart and the grief blooming in his stomach, or maybe it's my own- he is now the High Lord of the Winter Kingdom.

Lhys cries and shakes from the heavy sobs. "Don't leave me, Brennan," she screams down at his pale white face. His blue eyes no longer glow; instead they grow shadowed and fill with gloom. So many times I've seen those darkening eyes of death. "Don't leave me to do this alone!" She cries and Jax doesn't look at his dying father. Kane grabs his mother's shoulders, pulling her away from the corpse, void of a soul.

"You aren't alone, mother!" Kane pulls her face close to his as he whispers to Lhys. She cries and I even see a few tears slip past the warrior's glare. "I'm standing right here and," he looks to his brother who paces along the barrier, itching to fight for the people who exiled him or maybe the wolf inside the bubble. "Jax is right there."

My hands tremble and I'm not sure from either shock or terror. I fear the death of Brennan. I fear the hundreds of Forsaken murdering people around me. I fear what will come of Jax and me. I am full of rage and hatred for Kane. Jax didn't know that Kane and I had mated, and yet the bond was completed between Kane and me. How did he get my approval without me actually agreeing to the bond? Suddenly I put the puzzle pieces together. How could I not have seen it before?

Ariadae Vox has proved her power to rule for the Winter Kingdom and accepted the mating bond of Kane Archaeminza. The Proving is completed by the Fae who will be ruling the Winter Kingdom. It was created to prove their ability as a High Lord and High Lady. Kane told Brennan, the night Jax was whipped in the throne room, right after we felt the bond, about our mating. The High Lord decided to make me be committed to his youngest born, through love or not, I cannot deny what's now in my blood. But I can always avoid it, the reality of it. I will ignore him until he dies of a broken heart.

"You tricked me," I speak my racing mind, more to myself than to anyone, but Kane's ears perk at the sound of my voice. He pulls away from his whimpering mother, an emotional heap on the ground, and looks to me. I stare right back at him and I hope he sees the hatred burning brightly in my eyes. The anger that has come of his manipulation. "You had me believe that I needed to complete the Proving to have an army, but instead you just wanted to be mated with me."

"Ariadae," Kane winces and I can see the physical cringe. Lhys looks up abashed at my words and seems to completely forget her husband's corpse beside her.

"You did what?"

"Father wanted-," Kane starts but Jax's warning growl ripples through the barrier bubble.

"You've done enough, Kane." Jax's claws are erected and he looks as if he is about to shift into the white tiger I grew up knowing.

"Jax is right," Lhys agrees and looks to me, her eyes full of sorrow. "I'm sorry for what has been done, but the bond can't be broken once accepted." A stab to my heart has me holding my chest and stifling a sob. I know my partner of many years hasn't died, but I still feel sick at the idea that a relationship died today, and it isn't just Brennan's and Lhys'.

"Ariadae," Kane steps toward me, hand outstretched as if he wants me to take it. I am mentally revolted, but physically I want to lean into his form. "I'm sorry." His sea-green eyes flood with tears and Jax snarls bearing his teeth.

Jax leaps into the air and I don't even feel connected to my body when I send a telekinetic blast at him, throwing his body against the barrier as he slumps to the floor. Kane looks thankful, but I also feel ashamed. I shouldn't have stopped Jax from attacking Kane. He deserves everything Jax would do to him, but I still hear the crying women, screaming children, and howling Forsaken just beyond a barrier of wind. We can't forget what is going on around us.

My eyes flood with tears as I look at Jax who just stares at me, mouth in a sneer. He looks as repulsed as if I were a beggar asking for sex. I feel every bit of hatred in his eyes like a thousand swords to the chest. Each blade slices my organs and especially my heart. What has Kane done?

I turn my glare to my mate, the Fae who burdened me with his being for the rest of my immortal life, the Fae who damned my relationship with Jax. The Faerie Prometheus birthed me to love. "I'll never forgive you," I say, not a whisper or a question in my tone. It's a promise.

Before Kane can answer an Arbor slams its fist against the wind wall. Fury burns in the dark pits of its hollowed eyes. The dark bark of its skin looks damp like it had waited in the snow. I can't help but feel responsible. The Forsaken had most likely followed me here, it wouldn't be the first time they followed me either. I still remember when my mother and her army trailed Jax, Zube, Jeremiah and me to the Tree of Light and chopped the source of magic down. It still haunts me.

"Let me take care of this," Kane storms to the beast. He does a small twisted jump and projects his hands toward the Arbor, projecting a large, horse sized icicle to draw from the snow flakes, fluttering within Lhys' barrier and penetrate the beast's middle. Bark cracks and shatters as the Arbor is lifted into the air from the sturdy spike of ice, glowing bright blue in the lights of the colosseum.

Jax rises from the ground and Lhys does everything in her power to not look at Brennan, but she's failing miserably. So am I. The High Lord is gone and now, the new High Lord is fighting for his people instead of mourning his father. I feel the seed of sadness within my gut, but I can't tell if it's mine or his.

Lhys looks to the fighting Faeries of the Winter Kingdom. Some are attacking the Forsaken and others are running. What I don't understand is why a thick parade of marching Troglodytes begins to descend the stairs I had walked towards the pit. The adrenaline rush from the battle with Reyluke hasn't gone away yet and I let the familiar pinch of the Void pinprick my hands. The lizard men march in unison and one of them at the front wears a flowing cape of raven's feathers and what I assume is a sentinel beside him carries a large barrel. Never have the Troglodyte's worn clothes, or carried themselves with grace.

"Are they learning to *be*?" Kane drawls, his question floating into the air. We want nothing more than to fight back, but we're frozen still in fright and confusion. "Are they learning to be coherent?"

The Troglodyte sentinel stumbles on a single step and the barrel tumbles down, faster and faster, approaching the bottom. Bouncing against the stone, the barrel lifts into the air skipping chunks of stairs at a time and landing, hard. Each smack against the stone is another splinter in its wooden surface. I cringe and wince at every bounce and every flip of the large cylindrical barrel. I try to ignore it and focus on the parade and I notice that every single Troglodyte carries one of the wooden barrels.

The Troglodyte with the flowing cape of feathers, as black as its large amphibian eyes, turns to the sentinel who dropped the barrel and with a croaking, voice shouts, "You imbecile! What is wrong with you?" A chill slides down my back. I see the physical shiver on the three other people in the barrier. I assumed that the Dreag being, faster, stronger, and smarter in my trial was an alteration made by Brennan, but now I understand that he found the Dreag in Elkwood. My mother is teaching and altering her army to be better, stronger, and a step ahead of me. This is a never ending game of chess, but I never make a move.

I draw my focus back to the barrel as it smacks against the final five steps and the momentum carries it right over the railing and into the pit, a twenty foot drop, and shatters about thirty meters from the barrier. Black, oil slick liquid erupts and puddles around the splintered wood. Somewhere above, in the seats surrounding the pit, an arrow flies from a bow and strikes the cord holding a chandelier. The large crystal and metal work falls until the glasswork smashes against the oil and the hot candles, still lit, touch the inky black. Fire plumes into the air and I barely have time to throw up a telekinetic shield before the flames shatter both Lhys and I's barriers and launch us all into the air with the debris, glass, smoke, and flame. The mountain shakes and my body slams against the dirt floor, hard. I can't hide the pain that flashes through my body and any reign I had on my power vanishes. I hiss at the burn along my skin, but when I look to my hands, no red skin or black charcoal is there, but when I look towards a hissing wince I see the red blisters already formed on Kane. I want to run to him and make sure he is okay, but I can't pull my eyes away from the burning black wax. Blast wax. It was used during the immortal and mortal war centuries ago to start never ending fires in Elkwood Forest. I don't understand why the Troglodytes are carrying so many barrels until I notice how many there are...hundreds if not a thousand. They are becoming smart and they formed this attack and are planning to bring down the mountain, with everyone inside.

Although I still can't find it in my right mind to move, I watch Lhys, covered in dirt, burns, and blood dripping from a cut on her temple, scramble to Kane and heal his burns almost instantly. Jax is gone from sight, but large hands, lifting me from my arms tells me he's still on my side. No matter what Kane did to ruin our relationship, Jax and I will find a way to work together. I work to get my feet under me and mumble my thanks. Jax doesn't answer and just hands me a bow and slings a quiver on my shoulder. He leans down into my ear and watches the Troglodytes flood into the pit. They scatter and begin stacking and placing barrel upon barrel around the outskirts of the mile long pit. The blast wax at the center is still burning making the depiction of the Troglodyte with the raven cloak flicker between the flames. It is a horrific, but somehow beautiful sight. The wide mouth of the green scaled abomination is grimacing at me and the hair on my arms stands on end. With shaking hands I knock an arrow onto the curving shaft of the longbow.

Kane helps Lhys onto her feet and Jax stands in front of me, protecting me. Although we both know I don't need the protection I am not going to deny it. The High Lady and her second born son, the new High Lord, runs to Jax and I. I look out into the colosseum seats. Forsaken bodies cover the space and black blood runs in rivers, staining the pale brown stone, night black. Other bodies, Fae corpses, seem to be easily visible throughout the hundreds of seats. My stomach flips and flips for the people I can't help. Smoke from fires scattered throughout the colosseum cloud the expanse beneath the Archaic Mountain Range with black plumes, and waltzing, bleach white ashes, that fall like snowflakes. The parade of Troglodytes is still leaking into the arena and the stack of barrels, in a matter of minutes, has grown to a large hill. I can no longer see the first five rows of seats beyond the railing that is now hidden behind the wooden tubs of blast wax. If *one* barrel can cause a ginormous explosion that shattered two shields, threw all of us into the air, and shook the mountain, and is still burning with bright blue flames; that number of barrels can surely split the continent in two. We can't let that happen.

I stand onto my toes and mumble to Jax, who doesn't break the glare from the Troglodyte leader, "We need to do something." I glance back to the Winter

Kingdom Faeries still battling and the legion of Frost Guards diminishing. "Preferably fast."

Before Jax can answer me, the Troglodyte wearing the cloak of feathers, shouts across the pit to us. "Thank you for this lovely welcome to the Winter Kingdom!" A hissing laugh wheezes past his lips. "If you haven't figured out what is happening, let me explain. I am the General of the Troglodyte legion of High Lady Evaflora's army! We have learned of recent ties of the Winter Kingdom and the Equadorian kingdom. Now the Winter Kingdom is openly at war with the Summer Kingdom. Now we are ending this war before it can begin!"

If he thinks he's ending this war he is wrong. He is starting the rife between the Winter Kingdom and the Summer Kingdom! The Winter Kingdom hasn't even gone after the Summer Kingdom and Evaflora has gone out of her way to hurt me. She is doing it without even touching me, but she is easily harming my people and my friends. I feel the boiling rage build up at the thought of everything my mother has done. She murdered my father, stole my human life, attacked my people, and is now attacking my only ally. I'm not going to let her destroy another chance of leverage I have.

"Shield the barrels," My words spiral into the churning smoke that is building up beneath the mountain. I pray either Jax, Kane, or Lhys heard me.

"The demise of the Winter Kingdom will open up a path to the Mortal Kingdoms of Abella, which Evaflora would like to acquire," The general starts talking again. My ears grow sick of the sound of his croaking voice. "I am following my queen's strict orders and now for the grand event. My Troglodytes will now light the barrels and bring down Archaic-,"

The Troglodyte's words are cut off as a long, blue feathered arrow slices into his mouth and out of the back of his skull. He falls like a chopped tree in the wood. Kane, Jax, and Lhys all turn to me, my bow empty of the nocked arrow; their faces show the pure shock of what they have seen. I will not let my mother destroy my only ally in this battle.

I stalk past my companions and approach the gaping Troglodyte parade, who doesn't even notice the almost invisible layer of ice, covering the barrels, protecting them from any oncoming spark. The abominations look from me to their General, a corpse on the ground next to the still burning blast wax. I smile a devilish grimace at my attackers and stare every single monster in the eye, my voice sounds like a mighty warrior shouting over an army. "Tell your queen that nobody fucks with my kingdom. Not anymore! Now I will reign as queen and rise above my mother. Equadoria and the Winter Kingdom are officially at war with the Summer Kingdom! May we start the rife of your ruin!"

Before the words can sink in, the doors explode inward and large Faerie warriors wearing thick, ice colored armor and brandishing an array of weapons storm into the colosseum. The Frozen Army, *my* army, has arrived.

Faeries cry and shake as we leave the Proving arena. Plumes of smoke lift out of the large open gate and Forsaken bodies lay everywhere. It's as if the soldiers Brennan had sent to the gates were protecting the colosseum for as long as possible. I place a kiss on every Frost Guard's corpse that lay near the gate, thanking them for what they had done, what they sacrificed.

A howling mother pulls my attention, I run to her before I notice the devastation in her arms. She falls to her knees and I sit with her and cry. I close the faeling's blue eyes and pull her into a hug, very aware of her child's body between us. I'm sorry; I silently say because the words can't leave my mouth, they can't get past the rock lodged in my throat. These people didn't need this to happen to them and it's entirely my fault. The only reason Evaflora came is because of my being here. How she found out about my travels, I don't know, but all I do know is that she needs to pay, she needs to lose this war, and I want her blood on my hands.

I help the wailing mother to her feet and refuse to hold back my own sobs of grief, as I guide her to a light-blue armored Frozen Sentinel. He nods to me and walks further into the city. I try to offer my help, but then I see him, Jax, limping with his mother under his shoulder. Kane follows behind, but is sure to stop and help anyone with a single smudge of dirt on them. Lhys is crying louder than the mourning mother as she moves through the bustling crowd of panic, pain, sorrow, and loss.

I raise my hands to Jax to pull him in a hug, but he turns away with his mother leaving me to fall onto my knees and cry out the aching feeling within my chest. I feel like I did this, but it was my mother, my blood, my own creator who caused this devastation. I watch as another wave of injured Fae get carried out, limp out, or walk out of the dark grotto. Another tear slips down my cheek as I make a silent promise. *I promise that Evaflora will get what she deserves. And I promise that I will never hesitate tearing her head from her damned shoulders, Prometheus help me.*

CHAPTER TWENTY-TWO

~Ariadae~

 The aftermath of the attack on the Proving was
pure devastation. No other word can describe the raid.
Sixty two faelings had been murdered, taken from their
parents. Large mourning shrines have been erected
throughout the Winter Kingdom and candles burn
before portraits. Flowers cover the sidewalks and
cobblestone alleys. The Winter Kingdom is mourning.
The grief hangs like a cloud over the city. The number of
Faerie deaths is beyond counting, but many mourn the
children. It is very rare for Fae women to become
pregnant let alone give birth, so the faelings are very
important to sustaining the life of the kingdom. Many

children are still alive, but not enough to complete a generation.

After the clearing of the Forsaken and the removal of the barrels within Archaic Mountain, I sent word to Equadoria of the attack and the alliance with the Winter Kingdom. Zube had left his position at Equadoria to one of my father's sentinels and came straight to the Winter Kingdom to help us, within a day of travel. It was no surprise to see his rushed arrival, but he immediately felt the loss of the city the moment he walked through the gates two days ago. Now we, the Archaeminza family, Zube, and I all sit silently at a long wooden table in the dining hall in the castle. Iron chandeliers illuminate the otherwise dark chamber, the flickering shadows make my heart flutter, the memory of the Umbra still a fresh one. I fear the darkness, shadows, and oblivion that come with death and the Forsaken. We haven't even spoken of the abominations or the attack since the moments it was over. Now, in this room, we, as allies, need to decide the fate of our kingdoms and what we will do to better our chances in the war I started with the Summer Kingdom.

"I am no longer High Lady," Lhys says, her voice dreary instead of her typically light-hearted tone. She flicks her ice blue eyes, Jax's eyes, to me. I still can see the stains of where tears lay along her cheeks. *"You are."*

"I don't know how to be a High Lady," I admit and I wouldn't have the title if it wasn't for Kane who forced me into it. This trickery and lies will end tonight. "No longer will we lie, manipulate, or plan behind one another's back. From this day forward I wish that the allegiance between the Winter Kingdom and Equadoria be honest." I slide my glare to Kane who only pushes the food on his plate around like a child plagued by boredom.

"You don't get it," Jax growls from beside me. "*You are* the Winter Kingdom. You are the High Lady, you are Kane's equal. You can create laws and obliterate them. You have even more powers than just your Telekinae abilities and the purple flame you can conjure."

I look to my hands and ignore the sound of the Void whispering sweet nothings. Now that I think about it, no longer does the cold bite at my skin, and I even feel the bitter ice, nipping in my blood, but it isn't pain, it's like a comfort or a firm hug. The thought of training and controlling this new power inside me makes my stomach twist. How many powers can a Fae have? I know now that I am part of a prophecy, I am the Fae Druid of the Void, but what else will I be? Immortal Queen of Equadoria, Queen of Titanium Antlers, High Lady of the Winter Kingdom. What other titles must be added before I can defeat my mother?

I play with the fur cowl covering my pale shoulders and stare at the midnight blue silk, studded with glass that looks like a night sky. The gown is regal and was waiting for me on the silk chair in my bed chambers. There was also a diadem of blue crystal snowflakes. I deigned to leave it behind. "I don't know what it's like to be a Faerie queen of a Fae kingdom. I've only been an immortal queen of a Mortal kingdom for eight months. I can't believe it's already February," I mumble to the table and Zube gives a condescending smile and pat on the shoulder. How many times will I change before I am finally able to sit and be lazy? I just want a world where I can be comfortable and not worry about my safety or others. At this rate I doubt I will have a moment to read a book before I'm dead.

"We need to discuss what happened," Lhys mutters to the table ending any spark of normal conversation. "The Proving was attacked by Evaflora's army, or at least a piece of it. Thanks to Ariadae acting quickly a General of her Troglodyte legion is dead." Everyone nods their heads towards me in thanks. I was only stopping a threat before he became something more or worse. I don't feel like getting bit in the ass again. "Now, Ariadae has declared war on the Summer Kingdom even though the Frozen Army is all we have." Lhys glares at me. "Why start this war, Ariadae?"

"My mother plans to make all mortals on Abella be slaves and die beneath her rule," I mumble. I feel like I've explained this a thousand times, but nobody understands the true threat my mother poses. "She is willing to attack the Faerie Kingdoms to do just so! The Troglodyte General said it himself. She wants an easy path to the Mortal Kingdoms and we were in her way."

"Why do you care so much for the mortals of Abella? Wasn't it a Mortal Kingdom that decimated your army in the first place?" Lhys question seems absurd. How does she not care for the mortals? But I realize that she doesn't get it, she's never been a mortal and truly feared death. Maybe she has had a few brush ins with dying, but never will she die of age or disease or even starvation.

"She is an immortal with a human heart," Kane says to nobody in particular, but I can't help but agree with him.

"I was born a human, as was Brennan, and Evaflora! The mortals were created by Prometheus first and your husband was chosen to lead a new species! The Faerie Kingdoms were built on mortal origin and now as the Fae, we owe them our lives. They gave us life, so many centuries ago, and now we need to help them keep theirs." Lhys is silent at my statement. I fear bringing up Brennan was too soon a wound to open up, but she needs to understand the necessity of saving the humans.

No matter how she may disagree, it doesn't matter! I am the High Lady of the Winter Kingdom.

"What do you suggest we do then?" Zube openly asks to me and maybe even to Kane.

"We gather an army and defeat the true enemy in this war," Kane proposes and stares me in the eyes for the first time since the end of the Proving. He really looks at me, and I look at him. I see the agreement and rush of confidence within him and it's contagious as it floods through me. I hate him so goddamn much, but he knows what I want and agrees with it. We both rise, our chairs scraping against the stone floor. Jax, Zube, and Lhys rise as well showing their agreement with what is to come. "Your mother."

CHAPTER TWENTY-THREE
~Fayla~

I expect the gift at my doorstep to be from Lunan, but instead my stomach twists at the sight of the jagged letters of the uneven sentences that seem to run on. He is the Vampyre King of Vampyra, the island off the coast of the northern peak of Abella. The sad part of the whole situation is that I didn't even get a moment, after my dinner with the Vampyre royalty, to take off my dress before the package arrived. A small leather box, cold between my fingers, is tightly shut with a golden latch. The shimmering metallic rim makes me think of Lunan's glimmering eyes. He almost ruined everything during the dinner when he growled. I do believe that Molaris has become suspicious of our connection, although she seems very distracted by her own connection with the High Lord of the Day Kingdom.

I open the small box and within the leather gift is a necklace of braided black cord and hanging down the sides is curving, ivory fangs. At the necklace's middle is a large ruby, uncut and jagged like a large rock. The size of the stone is a toddler's fist, making it worth much more than it appears to be. A small torn piece of parchment within the box tells me that rubies are a symbol of love, and when a Vampyre gives you another Vampyre's fangs they are very interested in you. As flattered as I am at Tyrion's liking in me, I don't feel a bit of regret as I snap the necklace, the fangs flying across the room, and throw the ruby in a bin within the bathing chambers. I don't need gifts from a Vampyre when I have a High Lord that I'm mated to.

"What on earth have you done?" A male asks from my doorway and my heart jumps at the thought of it being Tyrion, but instead it is Acacius. Relief, a human emotion, flushes my cheeks. "Molaris is furious with you. Now you need to have a Vampyre King enraged as well? How do you get off?"

I roll my eyes. I'm sick of these Vampyre rules and court manners. "Please, the King only wants to bed me and have me bear a child. I'm not some cattle he can use for his pleasure."

Acacius closes the door to my chamber and a gloom shadows his blood red irises. I take a step back from his approaching gait and he whispers, "What is going on with Tyrion wanting to control the Fae Druids?"

I've been meaning to ask Acacius the same question. "Do you think he knows about me? Us?" I toss the possibility into the air and Acacius takes it and runs with it.

"It would explain why he is suddenly creating Fae allies and becoming more independent from the other Vampyres, but he must being using Lunan for an ulterior motive."

"Like what?" I press on and look towards the door in fear that someone might be listening. "Molaris wants to speak with me about what happened during dinner. Will you go with me?"

"I can't," he mumbles and I want to slam my fist against his face. "She hasn't summoned me, or you, yet."

At mention of a summons the door opens and the man with bleached hair is staring at Acacius and me. He glares at the two of us and I know he remembers that brawl we all had before the Vampyre royals' arrival and I can't help but smile at the thought of the broken nose my maker had given him.

You'll be okay, Acacius whispers in my skull and I look to him. *Hopefully.*

I walk with the man who leads me everywhere. I don't care to know his name or even ask because I know that once I learn it I'll be cursing the damned male. I am in enough trouble as it is from my cursed mouth. The last thing I need is both Molaris and her personal servant to want me dead. I am under her roof anyways, so it's hard to slip by easily without being punished for my actions.

I ascend the stairs into the throne room and I already hear shouting from Molaris on the other side. I can't even think of who it might be before I open the doors and am gifted with the sight of... of someone I didn't expect. Lunan stares at Molaris, who looks down at him from her dais. She has ditched the gown from dinner and wears all black, oil-shined leather armor. Her typical coronet of silver stars lay around her skull and the large, thick, midnight colored cloak is illuminated by the pulsing lights in the throne room. She looks regal, but crazy. Blood trickles from her nose showing signs of no sleep during the day and her ivory hair is unbound and tumbling around her shoulders in knotty clumps and whisking strands. She looks like the fierce, blood-thirsty queen she is.

"Why did you really come here?" She seethes at Lunan who looks a bit bored of the Vampyre before him. They don't notice my presence until the bleach haired servant of Molaris' closes the doors behind me, locking me in with the feral beast. I smell the vile tang of Vampyre blood dripping from her nostrils and I assume Lunan does too. He looks at me, his eyes wide with surprise. I wish to say that I should've warned him, but now is not the time. "Why else would Tyrion bring you if not to torture me?"

"AND YOU!" She screams and points to me, descending the dais in a storming gait of rage. She is losing it, truly crumbling from the inside out and I can't tell if it has been from over time or if it has started since Lunan's arrival. "You can't seem to keep your damned mouth shut! And you have every male in my Kingdom pawing after you, and for what?"

"Acacius would concur with your statement," I say with a sly smile and I feel the separation of my soul from my body. I feel as if I'm watching my death come. The way I'm talking right now seems like I have a death wish. Or maybe I just don't care for a lunatic queen. "And maybe I just have something to offer the men in return."

An exasperated growl rips from her throat and it sounds painful. I wait for the feeling of my bones going taut, of her controlling my blood, but then I start to wonder why she hasn't used her power on Lunan yet, unless she is so drained from not sleeping during the day that she is too weak to conjure her ability and make people bend to her will.

"Why would you think I arrived with Tyrion having a different motive," Lunan asks. The sound of his voice makes a euphoric, life-giving chill rattle my body. Lunan makes me feel alive without even touching me.

"Because of our past," Molaris whispers and my ears perk. A part of me knew she had known him from somewhere else, but to hear why she is so shaken around him would be a great insight to her life. "When I was still a Faerie in the Summer Kingdom and you were living with Evaflora, we had sex." My eyes flick to Lunan who stares apologetically at me. In what gods damned hell covered earth would Lunan have sex with this blood thirsty, manipulative bitch? Why would he even do it? "We had something," Molaris adds, her fingers trembling as she approaches Lunan with a hunched back and bulging, blood shot eyes. She wants him so badly to remember, but all I want to do is forget what I've heard.

"Molaris," Lunan mumbles like he is comforting a small child. "We never had anything. My mother arrived and tried to kill you, but instead branded me with this scar," He gestures to the jagged line from his scalp that descends through his brow, skips his eye, and starts up again on his cheek bone, dragging along his cheek to his jaw. Even with the brutal line marring his face, he is still inexplicably handsome and beautiful. Like a High Lord should be. "You ran off and were never seen again."

"You should've come after me!" She shouts as if he actually cared about her. "You never tried to save me from the fires in the garden or the wrath of your mother!"

"He never loved you, Molaris," I hiss, quickly protecting Lunan from the Vampyre queen's growing rage. She may be upset with him for their past, but I have been boiling the water beneath her; I set the fire under her chair to spark this anger. He doesn't see what's coming, but I have been at the other end of her hatred and anger and I don't want him feeling the full extent of her power, and rage. Even if she is weak, she is still a twenty thousand year old Vampyre. How weak can she truly be?

"You shut your mouth, you immortal bitch!" Molaris spins on me and is snarling in my face in seconds. "Don't make me finish what I started the night the others arrived." Her threat doesn't scare me as I know she is in an unstable moment of anger and Lunan would burn her to ashes before she could tear out my throat, or at least I hope he would be fast enough.

"Don't harm her," Lunan warns with a rippling growl. Even I feel the crackling threat in the rumble of his snarl beneath my feet. The floating stars in the throne room seem to gloom over and dim from fear of the Fae Druid of the Solar. "I'll do to you what my mother tried so many centuries ago."

Her eyes flood with crimson tears. Her bottom lip quivers as she looks at me, her face inches from mine.

"You don't mean that," she whimpers and I see Lunan's fingers begin to illuminate with embers and coiling smoke.

"But Molaris, I do."

I feel the shift of my blood around my heart, the shudder in my steady beat. Before Molaris can explode my organs, my hands sparkle with bright lightning that rockets into Molaris making her scream and shoot across the room. Her burning cloak makes her look like a flying comet among the stars. Lunan's hands erupt in flames and the doors bust open and slam against the walls, the boom echoing through the chamber. I feel the pulse of my power as I arch a bolt of lightning across the throne room; the blue cords sparkle like a whip and crack against Molaris' servant's face, burning his skin clean off. He shouts and screams and some phantom wind slams the throne room doors shut. Lunan sends a ball of red hot flame to the servant and ignites the Vampyre turning him to black ash on the ground. It only took seconds for the growing argument to turn into a raging battle.

Molaris uses her throne of chrome spikes to lift herself from the ground. Her coronet of stars is gone and her blood tears stain her face and hair as she shudders and quivers like a possessed mortal. With a devilish smirk, cackling laughter pulls from her throat. A shadow steps into my peripheral vision and I turn to the cloud of black smoke. I go to strike it with my palm of netted lightning, but a dark hand grips my forearm stopping me. Lunan goes to attack the assailant, but stops himself when the shadows ripple and Acacius emerges from the darkness. He can manipulate the shadows. We all look to Molaris who is still laughing by her throne, but we begin to back away as lumps begin kicking and bucking from her shoulder blades beneath the fabric of her leather armor. As if a person is stretching their arms beneath her clothes, two large tents rise from her back and she twitches even more than before. Her smile widens and the blood leaking from her eyes and nose stains her teeth. Fabric tears and she unclasps the midnight blue cloak revealing large, membrane wings. A glinting talon peaks both and she stops her quivering and lets her wings flutter.

"Lunan, Athena," Acacius mutters grabbing our wrists. "It's time to go." He doesn't break his stare at Molaris as he begins dragging me and my mate from the scene and towards the doors. She leaps into the air, the wings flapping, lifting her into the shadows covering the top of the throne room and I don't see anything in the darkness above. I fear her descending upon us, but before she can do so, we slam the throne room doors behind us and take a large torch rod and stick it through the iron handles, locking Molaris within. It won't hold for long, but it will give us time to leave and escape.

"Let's go," Lunan says as he runs with Acacius down the first flight of steps to the landing. My maker and my mate stop to look at me and notice I'm not following them. My feet, firmly planted in the floor. "What's wrong?"

"We need to get out of here, Athena," Acacius warns. "We don't know how long she'll remain withheld in the throne room!"

"I need to do something first," I say to my friends, my warriors, my family.

I knock on the dark oak door and in seconds it swings open.

"I knew you'd come soon," Tyrion mumbles gesturing me to enter his chambers. The rooms may as well be a manor on their own. The center room is only a large chamber with seating before a hearth, burning brightly in the chilly room. Many doors lead off to different rooms for different purposes that may serve Tyrion well. "Did you like my gift?"

"I loved it," I lie as I saunter towards the love seat and rest my body on the silk sofa. Tyrion smiles and sits on a twin across from me. His grin appears more like a grimace from the shadows and the flickering flames. "Thank you, but it isn't why I'm here to talk to you."

His thick eyebrow lifts at my response. "What did you come all of this way for?"

I feel sick to my stomach as I pull the lacing off my golden bodice. My breasts seem to fill the fabric quickly without the restraint of my corset and I try to ignore Tyrion's eyes, devouring my revealed skin. "I've been very lonely in this castle."

"As I would be," he mutters, completely distracted by my slow and alluring undress. Women have the power to manipulate men, but men have the ability to overpower women, so the line I am walking is a dangerous game of my past and what I intend to do.

"Please," I whisper. I look to the large flames burning brightly and stand up pulling a lounge blanket with me. I drop the thick cotton onto the floor and remove the large overdress and lay down onto the blanket beside the fire. "Join me."

As if I put Tyrion under a spell he rises from his seat and squats down beside me, his face coming too close to mine. He smells my skin and the sweat beginning to bead on it from the heat of the fire. I try to avoid thinking of where Molaris is and how much time I've already wasted. All I have are seconds to complete what needs to be done. I quiet my beating heart in fear that with such a close proximity he will hear it.

I lean on my elbows and let the King of Vampyra climb on top of me. My skin crawls and the Fae instincts still within me buck and scream with urgency and growing panic. "Have you ever been with a male of my title?" Tyrion whispers and I choke on the thought of his being on top of me. I try not to retch as I stroke a hand on his stubble covered cheek.

"No, but I also never plan on it."

"What?"

My sparks slice through his skull, quickly paralyzing him. Only burning a Vampyre or tearing them apart can kill them, so I wrap the cotton blanket around his stiff body. His black eyes dart around the chamber and look from me to the large flames burning next to him. I pull myself out from beneath him and kick the corner of the cotton blanket into the crackling embers. I squat down and place a kiss on his forehead. "Save a place for Molaris in hell," I whisper with a lover's purr and stalk out of the chambers before locking the door just as his clothes begin to catch fire. I won't have these damned monsters chasing after me in my life beyond this hell.

I run through the hallways and west wing of the castle with lightning speed. The feeling of being a Vampyre and Faerie is something I can't describe. I can only die from being torn apart or burned, and I am faster and stronger than my Fae brethren. It's something that only Acacius and I will feel the power of and I doubt we'll be creating any more hybrids within these next two centuries. Besides, I'm not ready to be a maker.

When I reach the throne room I stop my sprint and begin to run down the steps, taking two at a time. Lunan and Acacius wait at the doors of the castle and gesture for me to hurry up. Just as my left foot reaches the landing of the stairwell the throne room doors explode and wood flies everywhere through the chamber. I shield my skull. The sound of beating wings and the screams ripping out of Molaris are deafening.

"YOU WILL NOT GET AWAY FROM ME!"

I let the lightning Prometheus gave me crackle to life in my fingers and the electric blue bolts dance across my body. I feel Molaris' fingers graze my head and she screams in agony as a thick cord of electricity races through her nervous system. She retreats to circle high above and I notice her starting to descend for Lunan and Acacius. My pounding heart begins smashing against my chest in an uneven, painful rhythm.

"RUN!" My throat rips as I scream through the entry hall and I know that every Vampyre in this damned castle, on this island, has heard what is going on and is awakening to see the ruckus.

Molaris dives. Wings flap and push her downward so fast she seems surprised. Acacius darts forward and jumps against the wall. Lunan follows. I realize that the wall isn't a wall at all. Instantly, as if they vanished, the doors to the castle fly open and Molaris, unable to stop herself, soars right through the doorway into the bright, noon sun, burning in the sky.

Her blood curdling cries makes my skin crawl and my blood run cold as I join Lunan and Acacius to walk through the doors. Molaris tries to use her wings as a shield from the sun, but all it does is cover her large black membrane wings in large red, bubbling blisters that seem to grow and pop as quickly as boiling water bubbles. I look at the glistening lake and the cliff that is to my left.

"What have you done?" Molaris chokes on her words as blood fills her throat. I've never seen a Vampyre die in the sunlight, but I'd enjoy today to be the first time.

"I'm ending what you started," My threat falls onto her like a blanket and she sighs. "Never did I want to kill you, well that's a lie, but I never would have done this if you hadn't made me."

Acacius walks over and grabs my arm, "We need to go."

Lunan comes up behind me and begins pushing me with Acacius to the woods. I yank myself free from their gentle hands and stare at them in disbelief. "Don't you want to watch?" I ask the two of them. I know Lunan may not, but I am positive Acacius does. He spent centuries sharing her bed against his will and he was never able to break free of her. Now he is getting the chance to be separated from his maker and never be burdened with sharing her bed. But instead he grabs my wrist and starts pulling me again.

"As much as I'd love to see her die," He glances down at Molaris who is now crying beneath the dome of her boiling wings. He releases my arm. "We have to go, now."

A part of me doesn't understand why he is so desperate to leave, but I look into his eyes, the scarlet irises are getting ready to beg for us to leave, so I grab Acacius and Lunan. I close my eyes and ignore the smell of boiling flesh, thinking of green grass, tainted by the salt from the sea. I imagine the feeling of rocks and sand beneath my toes, and then I see the spot where the ground meets the horizon in my mind.

Light flashes like lightning before my closed lids and my feet slam against stone like I had jumped. The sound of grass whispering in the wind kisses my face and fills my ears. I focus on the noise of the churning waves. When I open my eyes I see the cliff meeting the horizon and for a second I think I imagined the wrong spot, but when I spin in a circle, looking past Acacius and Lunan, who stagger on uneven feet, I know I have reached the right spot. No Molaris will plague us or reach these lands, hopefully. I walk, step by step, closer to the cliffs edge and let the wind rustle my wavy black hair. My lacey undergown is thin and peasant-like. My pointed ears can be hidden by my hair and I look out at the clouds kissing the horizon. No longer does the ground meet the blue sky, now dark blue churning waters clap against the pale blue veil that is surrounding the bright yellow sun.

"Where are we?" Acacius questions and I'm surprised he doesn't remember. When I turn away from the cliff I see Acacius and Lunan looking around them, but neither of them notice the looming shadow about ten miles away. The rolling grasses of the eastern cliffs go on forever. Until they reach the mortal kingdom Alpri, the place where Acacius created me in an alley when I was dying. The eastern cliffs border the eastern coast of Abella and Alpri is about ten miles inland from the cliff's edge. Farther east, across the sea, is Crimson Island, the place we just came from. The distance is so far, yet too close for my liking. As if suddenly coming down with the flu, my head becomes light and my vision blurs in and out of focus. Everything is twisting and turning and I hear Acacius jumping to my side "Are you alright?" He mutters in my ear.

Lunan's hands are beneath my head as the world twists and the clouds and sky become all I see. "The jump was too much for her," he tells Acacius and I want to say Lunan is right, but my lips can barely move. All I feel is a subtle drip of liquid from my nostrils and ears. I know its blood because I can smell the sweet aroma slice through the salty air. My view of the sky vanishes and the ringing begins in my skull. Everything goes black and my body becomes numb. Suddenly, before I even realize what is happening, my body is being moved, dragged, touched, tended, and I can't even say the words that I am awake and I feel everything, but see and hear nothing. I can't do anything. Whatever I did in trying to get here has been a mistake. I begin to wonder if I have died, but then my nose fills with the scent of an herb and I am pulled back to consciousness.

Part Three
GARDEN OF FIRE

CHAPTER TWENTY-FOUR

~Ariadae~

The fate of the Winter Kingdom was left to Lhys as Kane, Jax, Zube, and I begin descending Archaic Mountain. The pine trees that cloak all of the Archaic Mountain Range rise high above our heads, blocking out the blue sky, dotted with white tufts. The snow is denser, moister, on this side of the mountain because now we are heading south, towards the Mortal Kingdoms. February has past and it is the dawn of March. Spring will be arriving soon in the northern region of Abella, but as for the south, the heat never dies. Winter for the mortals is just chilly nights and warm days with nipping breezes, lucky humans.

"It feels like old times," Zube mutters, looking down at his thick boots. Sentinels within the castle in the Winter Kingdom offered him armor and thicker clothing, but he denied, though grateful for the offer. He currently wears a night blue tunic, white shirt, and the large heavy supplies in bags and satchels on his back. All of us have received multiple types of clothing for our trek across Abella and we even took precautions bringing crowns, a symbol of power only mortals love. The human kings and queens see the accessory as power, wealth, and strength. The High Fae only see the crowns, coronets, and diadems as what they are, accessories. I once believed that the crown was my father's shining jewel, but now I can only imagine the coronet of dark thorns he wore within his final days. My stomach pangs and bile rises in my throat. I push aside the thoughts of the man who killed me and look over to Zube.

"But now, we have much better odds," I chuckle, smirking to myself. No longer do we need to fear the Foresaken and the horrible monsters within Elkwood. Now we are beyond the enchanted forest of Faerie's, monsters, and magic. We have arrived in the human, boring, bland part of the world. Zube being here reminds me of the one person we are missing, Jeremiah. I want him back in my grasp and I want to hug him so tightly that he could never be taken again, but I can't get him with no soldiers. I can't bring this group of warriors back into the Summer Kingdom because I don't know what we would find there waiting for us.

Jax chuckles as does Zube, but Kane just looks down the mountain, watching his footfalls for roots and rocks that make the uneven terrain beneath us. If we were to fall and start rolling it would hurt like hell. It's been about two weeks since the Proving and I still hate Kane. A part of me understands what he did though to have me become his mate and accept the bond. It's not like I would've accepted it otherwise and I've grown to start liking the High Lord, but he doesn't deserve forgiveness for what he lied about. I am his equal in every way and it feels good. I am not beneath or above anyone; we are one in the same, two sides of the same coin. We are connected forever through our mating bond making us allies forever, well work partners forever. The bond is supposedly stronger than marriage and love, but I will not be marrying the male who lied to me and manipulated me to be forever bonded to him. It's unbreakable though and will last as we ascend into Nirvana and join Prometheus' pantheon.

I gallop a few steps and match my gait to Kane's. He smirks at the ground.

"Hello," He mutters and I feel the excitement flutter within his chest. How he thinks this could be a good thing, I'm unsure. "How is my mate on this fine morning?"

I punch his arm and he chuckles and rubs the already forming bruise along his thick bicep. "Don't call me that," I whisper and flick my eyes to Jax. He has changed since the Proving. There were multiple brawls between him and his brother before we left the Winter Kingdom last night, but I understand why. Kane, although having good intentions, still manipulated us and basically ensnared me into his love. It's not even that I love Kane, it's just I can't ignore our connection, our bond. Jax was my past lover and I know it pains him to see me with Kane, but the High Lord of the Winter Kingdom and I haven't even kissed, or touched one another, besides punching or hugging. The day after the Proving I had broken down to tears. Sick horrible sobs that had me trembling beyond control and I sat before a faelings portrait in the street, surrounded by the burning candles. I couldn't stop the onslaught of sadness and grief, but I thought I was alone. I wasn't. Kane had come walking by and saw it was me on the ground. I didn't ask questions or even recoil when he wrapped his arms around me and just held me as I wailed like a child. I was still mad at him for what he did, but at that moment it didn't matter. We haven't even discussed what happened that night. Nor do I want to.

"Where do you want to go first?" Jax quirks from beside Kane, holding up a yellowed parchment, inked with the locations and kingdoms across the jagged rhombus that is Abella. "We could go west to Janari. It borders the western edges of the Archaic Mountain Range and we could stop at Febrei afterward, making our way down the continent." He trails the path with his fingering stopping on Janari; a small black castle is roughly drawn onto the paper. Then he loiters on Febrei, a slightly different, but similar castle. Then he crosses Marzia, adjacent to Febrei at the center of the continent, and cuts straight to Alpri, a trading capital and an overall wealthy kingdom. The large citadel, ruled by a High Priestess, is growing along the Eastern Cliffs.

"Or maybe we should start at Alpri," Zube cuts in, peeking over Jax's shoulder at the map. They seem to keep focusing on the northern Mortal Kingdoms that border the divide- Archaic Mountain Range- but what they aren't thinking of is how I plan to reach Lunaria, at the southern peak of Abella and the bordering kingdom to Solaria, the enemy kingdom that decimated my army. I plan on ending the feud between our kingdoms. I don't need my mother knowing of our rife and going to the king of Solaria for support. I also can't handle more than one enemy at the moment.

"What's that?" I hear Zube click and I look ahead. Between the trunks rising into the sky and the melting snow I see what he is talking about. A large wooden structure is straight before us on the path. I quickly jog over to the strange structure. The ground beneath my feet changes from dirt, snow, and roots to smooth cobble. A long path is traveling farther down the mountain; it's a road for merchants and may have been the path my father followed to speak with his allies amongst the mortals. The wooden structure, which is as tall as me, is actually a toppled over wagon. On the light gray stones are envelopes and boxes and threadbare sacks tied shut with tawny yarn. I look over the packages and wonder how this huge cart would've spilt or toppled. That's when my eyes lock onto the large slashes and claw marks down the side of the wood. Blood is speckled along the driver's seat and the mare that would've been pulling him along is long gone.

"Look around," I say, spitting orders to my friends for the first time in a long while. "Whoever was traveling through here was attacked."

"But from what?" Jax wonders out loud.

Kane looks from Jax to me, then to the span of trees opposite of the road. "Isn't it obvious? Evaflora attacked the Winter Kingdom, which is only about a mile up the mountain from here."

Zube sniffs the blood and claw marks on the wagon. "Human," he mumbles.

I pick up one of the water-stained envelopes and flip it over. A blue wax seal of a crown in the center of a large star isn't broken, telling me that the attacker had no need to commit this act. What makes matters worse is that I know the symbol. My heart begins thudding repeatedly and I crack the wax quickly and unfold the paper. I skim over the words and read every paragraph of the warning.

"Zube," I mutter. "Do you recognize this?" He glances at me, eyebrow quirked. Kane and Jax continue circling the scene looking for more pieces of evidence that may be lying around. Zube stumbles over the mess of letters and packages and finally reaches me, pulling the letter from my fingertips.

His eyes read the first line before he glances up at me. His hazel-green irises, flecked with brown, are filled with every inch of the panic and grief I feel. "Yes," He stutters on his words. "These were the letters I was going to have delivered to the Mortal Kingdoms before your arrival."

"What?" Jax comes around the side of the wagon. He looks toward Zube and me and to the warning of our oncoming arrival between us. "Zube you sent those over two weeks ago."

"Yes, I know," Zube mumbles. His throat bobs. "Janari is only twelve miles from this rendezvous point."

"Guys!"

We all look in the direction that Kane had vanished.

"Come here," He calls. "You're going to want to see this."

We all leave the wagon and the attack scene. Whoever Zube had deliver those letters is dead. The innocent mare is gone, but likely murdered. But what makes matters worse is that only twelve miles away is a city full of mortals. If the attack on the wagon happened last week...I shake the horrifying thoughts from my mind and weave between the tall pines until I see Kane staring outward. I pick up my pace and run past Zube and Jax and I would've kept going if the sight hadn't stopped me. My knees slam against the cold hard earth. Tears swell into my eyes and Kane just looks at the mess with a glazed over face. His eyes unreadable.

Children, human, hang from large iron hooks in their middle amongst the trees. Blood paints the forest floor, staining any leftover snow red. Women and men's corpses are scattered around the forest clearing in different states of decay like the Forsaken had brought the humans out here over a series of days. I thought my mother was trying to enslave all the humans on the continent, not make them into paint and toys to be thrown around. I understand that she has hatred towards the humans for the curse the Tree of Light placed on the Forsaken for killing mortals, but why go on a vengeance parade? The curse transformed the succumbus Fae centuries ago! No human still alive today would know what those beasts are unless they travel through Elkwood, which is unlikely. If this is only a few miles away from Janari than what does the kingdom look like?

Kane lifts me off of my knees and pulls me away from my living nightmare. Jax and Zube can't peel their eyes from the sight as we all charge off into a sprint towards the Mortal Kingdom. This happened a week ago and how many Forsaken made that horrific killing field; graveyard more like it. The wagon was relatively intact, so maybe there wasn't too many Forsaken, but if only a few abominations created that… What could an army of thousands do? What did my mother create to defeat me in this war we are waging? We have grown to bigger and larger attacks on one another. There will be an oncoming day where my mother and I shed the blood of one another, a day when our armies will fight against each other.

I thought the clearing of dead children, women, and men was bad, but now my stomach rises into my throat and my heart sinks. I've never seen Janari, but when I break through the forest and officially get off the descending ground of Archaic Mountain, I know what's before me isn't right. The Troglodyte General I killed said he needed a passage into the Mortal Kingdoms and the Winter Kingdom was in my mother's way. Apparently that's not so because the Forsaken have reached the Mortal Kingdoms. The Troglodyte horde that entered the Proving colosseum wasn't the only parade carrying blast wax. They were just the distraction.

I step towards what's left of Janari, a human kingdom of innocent lives. All that's left is a finger deep layer of grey-white ashes.

CHAPTER TWENTY-FIVE

~Fayla~

A sour liquid flooding down my throat yanks me from the impenetrable darkness that had taken over me. I spit the vile juice from my mouth and look around the dimly lit room. All I'm wearing is a white shirt, with the sleeves removed, and a pair of tight, smooth, brown pants. I don't recognize the chamber or even the clothes I am wearing. I try not to panic as I roll on the table I lay on.

"Glad to see you've awoken," a female croaks from the shadows and I roll off the table completely and try to land on my feet, only to clatter to the floor. "Oh! Dear! You are much too weak to be walking about!" She runs around the wooden table and grips my shoulders. With surprising strength she raises me back up onto the wooden slab and as much as I want to fight, kick, and attack this stranger, I can't focus on anything, but the heavy exhaustion that is bleeding through every part of me.

My throat feels like steel beams keep me from swallowing, but my lips split from the movement as I choke out, "Who...are...you?"

"Compared to you?" She lifts a dark brow and tosses her knotty grey hair over a shoulder. "I'm nobody, but a generous healer wanting to help an injured Fae. I'm little more than a peasant in these streets." When I look at her wrinkled skin and dark eyes, I see the wisdom and full life she's lived. I haven't seen a human since I killed Duke Rywell's brother in Alpri. But what amazes me is that even though humans live within a century, they achieve so much and experience so much more! I feel as if I have seen nothing of the possibilities of the always changing world. I mean, I was trapped in a cellar for *thirteen* years, but that's beside the point. I remember as a child being envious of the mortals.

"Where," I begin to ask where my maker and mate are, but I feel as if maybe something happened to them. What if this human isn't healing me, but poisoning me instead? Revealing the names of the ones close to me is something I'm not ready to reveal yet. The healer stares at me, waiting for the question and I just decide to ask the one thing I already know the answer to. "Where am I?"

She chuckles and looks down to a different table of tonics and bubbling potions and green herbs. "You're in Alpri, immortal one. May I ask you a question?"

I sit up and swing my feet over the end of the table and look at the healer who makes me a bit uncomfortable. She is wearing long dark robes and I assume her to be a witch rather than a healer. Although I don't trust her, and I really don't care about her well-being, I can't ignore the sugary scent of her blood. I can eat human food, but blood is like a drug to the part of me that is Vampyre.

"What is it?"

"What species are you?"

My heart skips five beats. Suddenly the room feels small and although I can't die I feel as if I will. Acacius told me to never reveal what I am, but I feel as if I can tell this hag anything. The way her dark eyes stare at me makes me believe she already knows the answer.

"Why would you ask such a thing?" I decide to pull up an impenetrable mask of oblivious confusion. If I play my cards right I may be able to leave this chamber, but I have an inkling that she won't let me if I try.

"Well," She waves her hand like a witch would a wand. She starts to aimlessly wander around the chamber while she begins to list off everything on her fingers. "I noticed your pointed ears, so I thought Fae, but that's when I noticed the two x scars on your neck showing a Vampyre bite. When I looked into your mouth I saw the elongated canines of a Faerie."

On the instinct of a threat, my Vampyre fangs snap down.

She pauses. "And that happened. So I decided to take a test, so I into cut your arm, extracted the blood before you could heal, faster than any Faerie. I poured a mixture into the vile of your blood and it turned obsidian, the only time that happens is when the herbs react with traces of iron."

I try to silence the fast pace of my galloping heartbeat, but fail miserably. I peer over my shoulder, looking at her out of the corner of my eye. She seems to wait for an explanation. "Iron is common in Faerie and Human blood."

"Unless the being's blood is half iron, then the blood wouldn't turn black. You were healthy a week ago." I've been asleep for a week? "I needed to run more tests and see what you are. You're a hybrid. Born Faerie turned Vampyre. You are one of the immortal *nightwalkers*, but also a *daywalker*. You are a Vampyre *and* a Fae." The healer's words just barely pass her lips before I grab a large beaker of some dark green concoction and throw the mixture behind me. She ducks beneath the flying glass and the strange potion as it smashes against the wall staining the dark wood neon green. For her age I'm surprised at her speed. She sprints to a counter and pulls a syringe full of a dark blue liquid off the surface. I clamber off the wooden table at the center of the room and let the wood remain between us. I knew she wasn't just a simple healer! I reach onto the table and grab a large cutting knife she must've been using to slice the herbs that appear to be growing by a window to my right. "You're not getting away from me," she seethes.

My first thought is to jump, somewhere far away, but the memory of the feeling that took over me after we arrived on the Eastern Cliffs is too fresh. I don't want to jump to some alleyway and blackout again where she can find me. It's not like my trembling legs will get me far anyway, but they sure as hell won't make me unconscious.

I feel for the cold thrumming power within me and all I find is a small, weak cord of blue light hopping between the fingertips of my left hand. The knife is tightly snug in my right. I stare at the mortal hag as she shifts her weight back and forth and wheezes her panting breaths.

"You want me?" I smirk with a swagger I didn't know I had within myself. "Then don't be a meddling coward, come and get me."

She dives and rolls across the table. Her robes fall away revealing a frail naked body covered in red scars on bone white skin. Her golden teeth gleam as she leaps towards me in the candle light. I scramble to the right, towards the large pots of plants. She lashes out with the syringe and catches my shoulder with the endpoint. I instantly fear the sedative being inside me, but when I look to the needle it is still full of the blue liquid. I shoot the weak cord of electricity and it leaps from my fingertip onto her bare skin. She shudders and begins to laugh.

As she trembles her grey hair falls before her face and she doesn't even seem bothered from the strands of corded, knots of hair that hang before her vision. "Magic gives me such a rush," she breathes and then is sprinting at me screaming at the top of her lungs. She approaches meters in single steps, and with my Vampyre speed the world slows. She is flying through air and moves slowly across the chamber as if beneath water. I move out of her path and circle around the table of herbs and lift the large knife that never left my fingers. I hold the gleaming blade against her throat. Her body begins to twist and her legs start to fly forward as I hold the back of her head and yank the blade across the wrinkled skin of her neck. I smile as blood spews everywhere and showers the wall, window, growing herbs, me, and the floor in scarlet warmth.

I stop moving quickly and her body slams against the floor. Her momentum causes her to roll into the wall. Blood, surprisingly still leaks out of her neck and is pooling around her, staining her pale skin with a scarlet hue. With a grin on my face, I lick the mirror-like blade and sigh at the eruption of sweet, warm flavor on my tongue. Oh how I love the taste of blood. I have only drank from one mortal before and I killed the poor girl. She was young, and in a strange way, beautiful, but I didn't care about her death. Nor do I care about this wicked, dark-hearted healer who is well past dead. No longer do I need to fear killing my food, so I just drop the knife to the floor and crawl down to her naked form, huddled beneath the growing plants and illuminated window, clouded with dirt and dust. I shiver at the euphoric feeling of my fangs slipping ever so easily into her neck.

The door bangs open and two pairs of feet come stumbling into the chamber. I pull away from the body and crawl away, acting as if scared. My fear has long passed, but I don't need Lunan and Acacius thinking that I killed her because I was hungry.

I stagger to my feet and look to the two males, humans. They look at me in horror and glance around the room in utter terror. "Sorry for the mess," I mutter and shrug. The odor of their emotion slams up my nostrils like a brick and I stalk towards the men who begin to actually shake in their shoes and I blatantly stare down at the large wet stain that is continuing to grow on one of their pants. "And I'm sorry that I loosened your bladder." One male whimpers and the pisser just stares at the window. They must've been in training or maybe customers of the healer, but whatever it is, it doesn't matter anymore. I have my friends to find somewhere in this Mortal Kingdom and I'll need to do it on foot.

I leave the two humans in the room, basking at the scene. I don't know where I'm going, but I aimlessly walk down the hallway and quicken my pace as I get to the stairs. I don't know what type of security Alpri has, but I'd rather be gone before the kingdom guard arrives. They don't need to know of Vampyres and Fae wandering through the streets. The stairwell drops me off in a small, unwelcoming threshold and I notice two large wooden doors before me. I clatter through them and stumble into an alley. Dark swirling puddles of sewage are scattered in the shadowed alley and I avoid the whispering vagrant at my feet. He hisses at me and I hiss back, bearing my blood stained teeth. He recoils and whimpers like a struck hound. A flowing wave of moving people wearing different colors and styles of dress pass the entrance to the shrouded alley. I approach the bustling people and try to stay in the shadows as I peer outward to see what all of the crowding is for.

Merchants of different skin tones, wearing different clothes, bear a variety of items. Awnings shield carts full of weapons, blankets, potions, rocks, and even clothing. Iridescent khalats draw my eye, but that's the opposite of what I want. That's when I notice the dark, skin tight, silk outfit nicely folded on a merchant's cart. The awning is striped blue and white, and from the glow of the sun on the fabric I can see the metallic shimmer of embroidery on the uniform. I look at my own outfit. My feet are bare to the elements and my threadbare shift is stained with blood, sadly, so is my face and hair. I almost shout with excitement! The onyx dye that stained my hair on Crimson Island is gone and now the moon white waves are back and softer than before.

I hug the wall as I leave the alley and sneak behind a female merchant who is bargaining her clay jars of water from different locations around the world. I personally find the idea a load of dung, but anybody will crave for the taste of magic nowadays. These humans seem hungry for something different, change, culture. Whether the water is from a faucet next door or a secret island off the coast of Pangea, I swipe a jar of the liquid and quickly douse myself. My sodden hair is cold along my skin, although the moist, summer-like heat is overpowering. The air is thick and wet, but it is only March.

With my face cleaned of blood and my clothes hiding the blood, I approach the merchant across the square that has the neatly folded uniform I was eyeing. I look down at the black silk and admire the golden swirls that seem to twist into stars that twinkle on the fabric.

"How much for this?" I ask touching the suit and looking to the man with pale white skin. His dark hair tickles his brow and his soft grey eyes seem to glow beneath the shade of his cart's awning.

The corner of his mouth lifts as if I may have made a joke. "The item is sold," he says sounding more like a woman than any man I have met. I start to wonder his gender when I realize *she* is using the majority of her weight on her hip poking out in a way only women do. And yet they still conquer gender conformities. They make me think of the Faerie culture and practice of loving another Fae for their personality and never their gender.

"How is it sold? It's sitting right in front of me."

"The customer who purchased it is retrieving their money," The merchant growls like a want-to-be queen with a shit poor attitude. Apparently this human, who I actually liked, is a royal bitch.

I glance around the bustling square and make sure nobody is looking at me. I turn around and in a fluid motion snatch the bitch's collar and yank her towards my snarling face. I let my elongated fangs twinkle in the sunlight. She doesn't even scream. The merchant's breaths come out in panicked pants and she looks from my fangs to the square. "If you don't give me the damned uniform I will split you from snatch to chin and greedily enjoy the taste of your blood."

A single tear falls and I push the merchant away. She holds her chest and doesn't meet my eyes as she scurries towards another merchant's wagon. I grab the beautiful outfit and slide into it. Thank the gods for my luck because I notice a box full of silk slippers. I put on a pair of black ones and then yank a cloak of bright silver from a hanging rack. I can't help, but smile when I hear the bitch's cries from across the square. The merchant doesn't say a word when I let my billowing cloak fall over a table of blades. My fingers hook onto two large daggers with night-dark handles and the silver blades are etched with the Faerie language.

I feel as if I'm flying when I let my Vampyre speed take me across the city. I scale a wall in seconds and I'm hopping from roof after roof until the noon sun falls and descends behind a heavy gloom of black clouds. I feel the crackling lightning above the clouds and far away. It feels like a pulse, a beating heart. It sounds like a drum in my veins and I know it is still miles away. I can't even hear the booming thunder from Alpri. It's alluring and making my strength ascend. I feel this growing energy within me and I want nothing more than to feel its true power.

I feel my mate. Lunan is nearby. I don't know where, but I can feel the wire between us snare me and begin to pull north, towards the storm, toward the castle. I follow the path, it carries me over roof after roof and with my incredible speed I build enough momentum to let my body fly into the air and right over the wall that surrounds the castle. The storm tingles in my bones and I feel the clouds split and the lightning crack to the earth like greedy fingers reaching for gold. I inhale the scent of electricity and I scream with thrill as I land on my feet and roll, stopping the momentum. Alpri shakes as the roiling thunder rattles Abella. I can't help the smile on my lips as I feel the thrumming electricity. It is only a few miles away now. It's traveling hard and fast.

Another flash of light and my attention is thrown to the shadows at my right, hiding amongst the thickets that surround the castle grounds. I am in the garden; the many towering hedges make the place a maze. I try to ignore the uncomfortable inkling in the back of mind that something is wrong, as Lunan rounds the corner. Acacius is at his back and they duck behind a fountain. I wonder who they are hiding from, but I don't want to risk being seen just in case. I crouch down and run over to them.

Lunan grips me in a hug, instantly relieved. "We have been looking for you everywhere," He whispers and places a kiss on my brow. Although I still feel uncomfortable, I'm unsure why; my heart flutters at the softness of his lips.

Acacius jolts with fear and then suddenly starts to act like a father figure. "Now is *not* the time," He seethes.

"Why?" I question and look around the garden for their attacker, but see nothing but flickering shadows when the lightning crackles, followed by booming thunder.

"We couldn't find you," Lunan jumps in, too excited at the sight of me. His face is a sight for sore eyes and I can see the warm glow of his golden irises in the dark. Those eyes will guide me, a torch in the night, and the light at the end of a path. "We had left you in a small shack on the outskirts of Alpri and when we came back you were gone."

I look at Lunan and grab his wrists in an attempt to calm his fluster. "A hag took me and was doing tests on me," I look at Acacius. "She knows what we are, well what I am. I got rid of her." I don't need him panicking about someone knowing. The way I killed her, there is no chance of her coming back.

"What do you mean, Athena?" Lunan questions and I forget he is even talking to me. I have been known to my mate under a false name. I don't answer Lunan, so he looks to Acacius. "What is she talking about?"

"We'll discuss this later, right now we have a serious predicament," Acacius whispers and looks around the garden.

"What?"

"Alpri is under attack," Acacius growls. Right as his words vanish beneath the booming thunder, lightning spikes down, illuminating the garden, I see a beast, leaping from a rose bush and into the air. It's snarling maw wide and bared at Lunan. The blade I stole is slicing through the air and slams into the Dreag's throat before the lightning vanishes. It clatters against the stones and Lunan gawks at me and looks from Acacius to me.

I don't have time to shrug before three giant tree monsters are appearing from the hedges. We thought Alpri would be safe, but little did we know that we weren't safe at all. We walked into the center of a war zone.

Chapter Twenty-Six

~Ariadae~

We left Janari and sprinted all the way to Febrei. Thankfully my mother's Forsaken legion hadn't attacked another kingdom from our knowledge and although I am always panicked when traveling, I'm relieved to have seen Febrei and Marzia intact. The Febrarian king didn't believe me when I told him of what happened to Janari and the oncoming onslaught of murderous beasts. When Jax and Kane had tried to reason with him a form of agreement over an alliance and tying our armies together, the king hadn't answered. He told us to leave his kingdom before he showed us a real monster.

Marzia was slightly different. The Marizian emperor didn't reject or agree to our contract and alliance. He had said that his father's grandfather was alive for the last signs of the immortal and mortal war. And for the past two centuries his family believed of a war coming from Elkwood. He fears the Fae and their wrath. With the odds seemingly in my favor he said that he will be considering the terms of our alliance and isn't ready to tie a new allegiance until he handled the current battle with his adjacent kingdom, Mala. We didn't have any more time to waste, so we accepted his "maybe" and headed to Alpri.

We arrive before the heavy storm outside that has only just broke from the clouds above. The High Priestess of Alpri sits at her throne of golden swords. The towering chair might as well be a small structure, but again humans love their symbolism of power. I tried to ignore the purple flags, and carpets and the gold accents because it reminded me too much of the Summer Kingdom. The colors on the Summer Kingdom flag are violet and sun yellow. I draw my focus to the mortal woman before me and her ridiculous dress of chainmail.

"Who do I have to thank for an immortal arrival in my kingdom?" Her voice is rich and welcoming, but behind her pretty face and lack of revealing clothes I bet she is a snake in a basket, waiting for the lid to be lifted. "Alpri is a home of many from all around the world, but not for many centuries has it seen an immortal."

Lightning flashes outside the giant windows positioned on both sides of the throne room. I smile at the High Priestess trying to show off my slightly elongated canines. "I've come with a warning."

She chuckles to herself and looks to me, her eyes saying to continue.

"There is a kingdom in Elkwood Forest, ruled by a tyrant Fae named, Evaflora," I continue. Kane and Jax stand just a step away on either side of me and Zube is wandering around the chamber, gawking at the immaculate works of art. "She wants to enslave all mortals on Abella and she has an army of monsters to follow through with her desires. I wish to stop her before she acquires what she wants." I don't tell her anything more. The High Priestess doesn't need to know of my relation with Evaflora.

The High Priestess stares at me, her eyes glossed over. Her headdress of curling metal reflects the chandeliers above like a mirror. She chews on her tongue as if pondering my words and thinking of what to say. I'm suddenly aware that, to my surprise, besides my friends and her, the room is empty of guards or sentinels.

"What other kingdoms know of this?" She spits like she tasted a vile drink. Her voice echoes through the chamber and I try not to shrink away. Why do I fear her? She is nothing but a powerless human. I have true power. I think of the Void, my telekinesis, and the new power crawling within me, yearning to come out. I still haven't tried to use my Winter Kingdom High Lady abilities.

"Febrei and Marzia," I say. I look to Kane who steps forward trying to take her attention and maybe convince this close-mind human.

"I am the High Lord to the Winter Kingdom, another Fae kingdom in Elkwood and we have allied with Equadoria," Kane explains to the High Priestess. She smiles at him and lets her eyes travel down his body. I uncontrollably snarl at the queen. She shifts her eyes to me; a dark glare of hatred glosses them. Jax even stiffens behind me and I almost heave a sigh for letting my emotions slip. I have been working so hard at hating Kane that it's becoming hard to continue, but I just remember his lie and manipulation and then I am fine.

"How dare you growl at me," She seethes as she rises from her throne and looks down at me. I step forward and stare right back.

"Don't threaten a coiled snake," I tell the High Priestess and she steps off her dais and approaches Kane. Zube stares out the window as another bolt of lightning flashes. Even after it passes I see large bolts of electricity arc along the ground as if the lightning had struck metal. Zube glances from me to the window. Thunder shakes the castle and the High Priestess smiles as she studies Kane, and then Jax.

"You have some very strong henchman," She smiles.

"They're not henchmen."

"Than what are they?"

"My friends," I bite my tongue, keeping myself from spitting a string of curses as she slides a hand across Jax's chest. He glances from me to the High Priestess, and I barely stop the growl that wants to come out of me. "I don't treat my friends as property, unlike you."

The Queen just waves her hand in a circle tossing my explanation away like a spoiled fruit. She saunters back up her dais and sighs onto her throne. With a bored look on her face she glances between me, my mate, and my greatest ally.

"I want them."

Jax bursts into laughter, genuine laughter for once in his immortal life. Surprise makes me look at him and Kane, who chuckles as well. "You want friends?" Jax chokes through cackles and a grin splits my features.

"*No!*" The High Priestess howls. We instantly go silent. "I want the two immortals as a trade for my army."

A laugh, louder than Jax's, passes my lips. Then I notice her serious features. "Never," I say with even words so she gets my point. I would never trade my mate and Jax for a simple alliance with a mortal kingdom.

"Then don't expect me to give you my army," the High Priestess plays with an invisible lint on her metal dress. I glare at the human queen and she refuses to look at me.

"But you don't understand," Jax begins to mutter, but then Zube looks back to us, panic in his eyes.

"Guys," Zube mutters. "You need to see this."

"I do understand!" The queen booms and I look to the window. Lightning sparkles from outside and I also see the warm glow of fire. A large ball of fire flies at the window and Zube rolls out of the way as the fire implodes the glass. Rain slants sideways into the second story room and the High Priestess is immediately off her dais and running for the throne room doors. I run to Zube and pull him onto his feet. Before I can look outside the window, two sentinels who were guarding the door, bust in and look for the High Priestess.

"Alpri is under attack," One of the men shouts with a quivering voice, his fear filling my nose. I don't have to try hard to guess what may be attacking, but maybe like Marzia, Alpri has trouble with another Mortal Kingdom.

"By whom?" The queen asks. The two sentinels look at each other, then back to their leader.

"Monsters," answers the other man. The High Priestess looks at me and I run past them all. Kane, Jax, and Zube follow me through the entry hall and outside into the penetrating rain that beats down like heavy pebbles against our skin. I hiss at the heat the large droplets leave and I wander around the side of the castle. As I round the corner, I see the growling and snarling horde of Forsaken. They all are running towards the gardens, and I follow. Above the tall hedges I see a purple aura from the lightning and flames light mixing together. Their origin is unknown to me, but I know what I need to do, and I ignore Kane and Jax's shouts of disapproval as I follow the Forsaken into the maze garden. I turn down path after path and eventually find myself turned around, lost within the maze. I try a different path each time, only to find a similar walkway to a turn I passed. I make a right and I see a long path that breaks off, but straight ahead is the center. A Dreag falls before me, it climbed over the hedges. It snarls but I ignore the strange facial structure of the abomination. It isn't muscled like the one in my Proving, but I feel the beast is dangerous all the same. I feel its ribs with telekinetic fingers and shatter every damned bone in the creature's body until nothing is left but a pile of skin and blood on the gravel of the garden.

The sky lights up and I run toward the center of the maze. A multi-level ring descends to a stone well, overflowing with water at the center. The large circle is filling with water and I stomp through the pool. I don't care for wet shoes, but because of this pounding rain I'm soaked through and through whether I stand in the small lake or not.

I look down the different paths that break away from the center, all of them different paths that lead to the middle of the maze. Somewhere within these gardens is whatever it is the Umbra wants me to find. I don't know how I know, but it's a roiling feeling in my gut, like this was meant to happen.

"Ariadae!" Someone yells from behind me and I look towards the direction from where I came to see Jax, Kane, and Zube all running towards me. I just stare at them until my hair stands on end. A prickling feeling crawls up my spine and I realize my Fae instincts are roaring. I turn around and see about thirty Forsaken beasts coming towards me from the path ahead. My hands erupt with Void flames that illuminate the impenetrable darkness with purple hues and I toss up shields of flame that melt the arrows flying from the Troglodyte quivers. An Arbor roars and Kane starts firing large, dagger size, ice shards at the beasts that are huddled in the path. Jax blasts a wall of wind at the creatures, throwing them off balance and keeping them from coming into the center. I cast telekinetic shields around my group and start sending whips of purple flame down upon the Forsaken. The Arbors get swallowed by my hot flame and the Dreag wail as they die.

"Guys," Zube shouts from behind us. "A little help please!"

I glance at him and notice all he has is a sword against a Troglodyte warrior. When I look in front of him I see another horde of Forsaken beasts coming down a different path. I run towards Zube and let my void consume the Troglodyte he was fighting. He nods his thanks to me and I begin sending walls of flame at the scrambling abominations. This time instead of normal Forsaken, I see armored Troglodytes, muscled Dreag and Wendigos, Tall, long limbed Nymphs, and even Arbors made of marrow, not bark. Evaflora's army is changing and mine hasn't even been completed. Maybe this will show the High Priestess of Alpri that messing with the Fae is not something you want to do, and getting into a war with Evaflora will be way worse than becoming allies with Equadoria. I feel my body trembling as I break bones, snap necks, burn bone and skin alike. The Forsaken die, but more come, they arrive quicker and quicker and we can't kill them fast enough. Another path gets blocked with another dawning horde. Soon we can't keep the monsters contained to the paths. They leap from hedges and claw at my friends. We all begin to become a singular unit working together to keep one another alive against this onslaught of Forsaken that somehow nobody saw coming. I would ask Prometheus for help, but the damned gods have seemed to curse my troupe with the worst luck in Abella history.

Soon the tall walls of ivy surrounding the center are burning bright golden flames like the ones I saw in the throne room, that send ashes into the storm cloud above. I ignore the gruesome scene of black blood flying everywhere, my friends and my mate focused in battle. I keep an eye on Kane and observe the perfect killing machine he truly is. Ice spikes rise from the pool of water, penetrating a body and vanish before coming back and giving another killing blow to a different beast. Zube is in his Fae body and using the Alprian sword to his advantage. The scim is firm in his white knuckled hand as the steel slices through skin and bone, showering him in blood. I cut down two Wood Nymphs; their new tall limbs make them even scarier; as if their hunger for human teeth wasn't horrifying enough. I glance at Jax who uses his wind-thanks to his mother Lhys- to send large flowing gusts into the Forsaken's nostrils and mouths causing them to explode from the inside out. Some just fall mid leap and I don't want to know what he is doing to them with his strong powerful wind.

I focus back into the battle and continue to kill Forsaken. Soon all I see is rage, blood, battle, fire, and death. I hear a constant ringing and before I know it the Forsaken numbers are dwindling. My hope rises and I start to see an end to this battle.

I scan the battle field; my partners have vacated the scene. About fifty Forsaken have turned their attention onto me. I let the Void whisper to me as my splayed palms erupt in flames. A hand grabs my arm yanking me clean out of the center of the circle. I stare into sea-green eyes and I fall into his form. Tears stain my cheeks. They haven't left me. I look back at the approaching legion and gasp as lightning strikes down from the storm cloud above and claps against the puddle before sparkling atop the water. It crawls into each beast standing in the foot-deep pool of water that formed from the well and the rain. Each monster, shaking and writhing, splashes into the obsidian pool and thrashes around turning the dark water into an ocean with waves that lap over the steps onto the stones and gravel.

The fires burning the hedges were from the golden glow I saw while inside the castle. The lightning is from the Fae Druid of the Storm, the girl with the white hair beside me. The flames are from the Fae Druid of the Solar, Lunan who is next to the girl. And I am the Fae Druid of the Void. We are together; Lunan offers me a hand and pulls me to my feet. I grip his tall form in a hug. He's my brother. He told me how to save my father. He was one of my few allies in the Summer Kingdom during the summer. I look over his shoulder to the female with snow white hair. I saw her for the first time in Elkwood when an Umbra took on the form of her slim body. *Find the girl who sparkles like lightning and the male who burns like a thousand suns.*

I have found them, Prometheus. And for once in the start of my immortal life, I see the most beautiful thing ever.

I see the possibility of us winning this war.

~The End~

Acknowledgments

Writing book two has been a whirlwind of emotions. I can't describe the feeling of when my friends read my book and get passionate about the characters or world! It's like a blooming of warmth in my stomach that is so euphoric I can't help, but get all giddy. So thank you to those of you who have taken the time to read the book.

Thank you, Heather Falotico. You have given me more and more opportunities and all of this happened because of you! As much as you want to be proud of me, be proud of yourself and thank you for this. Thank you for helping me find my path in life and continuing with me on this journey that I know I will bring you on until the very end!

I also need to thank Danielle, James. You two have listened to me for hours and hours reading what I wrote from the horrible first draft. Even when I am the most annoying person on the earth you two stick around and show me your love. You two mean the world to me and your involvement in this book is the reason why it's dedicated to you two. I love you guys <3

And I need to acknowledge my friends and extended family! All of your support through this journey has been heartwarming and if it weren't for ya'll I wouldn't be so excited to share these stories with you, so thank you.

To my grandparents, (all of you) you guys have always been around, always loved and cared for me and the acceptance I receive along with that means more than the world. There's nothing better than giving your grandparents something to brag about to the neighbors! I love you all so dearly.

Mom, Dad, and Sam, ya'll see me every day and hear the ridiculous stories in my head through and through. I'm sorry for the bother, but I just love you guys and your support is truly helping me more than you know. I love you, and thank you.

Thank you to my readers, and my fans that have started following along my journey. Shout out to the girl who came excitedly squealing up to me at the movie theater! You scared me half to death, but it has to be one of the best fan experiences ever! I love everyone who I have seen at different schools and locations in New Jersey, who listen to my ramblings for whole class periods. You guys are giving me the dream I never knew I wanted. Thank you.

About The Author

Photo by Patty McKenna

Zachary James is a high school student who has turned his hatred into a passion. His first novel, *The Rise Of Titanium*, is the first of many in the future. His best friend is his cat named Kitty who gives him love and affection, his human friends and family are good supporters too. If you want to stay up to date on any of the bookish details from Zachary James follow him on the provided social media below.

Instagram: *@ZacharyJamesOfficial*

Twitter: *@_ZacharyJames_*

Facebook: *@Zachary James*

Youtube: *Zachary James*

Website: *https://zacharyjamesnovels.wixsite.com/novels*

The finale to the award nominated debut

series is coming…

A war waged between diamond, titanium, and blood

Three queens fighting for the power of all

The final battle that will bring down worlds

ARE YOU READY FOR THE FINAL *KINGDOM*
OF DIAMOND ANTLERS NOVEL?

Lightning Source UK Ltd.
Milton Keynes UK
UKHW040619011118
331575UK00001B/284/P

9 780692 187937